A HOUSE OF BELLS

J. T. CROFT

ELMFIRE PRESS

First published by Elmfire Press 2021

Copyright ©2021 by J. T. Croft

First edition

ISBN 978-1-8381089-3-9

Cover design by Fay Lane:

www.faylane.com

J. T. Croft asserts the moral right to be identified as the author of this work.

Elmfire Press

Unit 35590,

PO Box 15113,

Birmingham, B2 2NJ

United Kingdom

www.jtcroft.com

To the memory of Graham Thomas, who laid down to sleep as I laid down my pen.

31st December 2020

PREFACE

A House of Bells deals with silence, the area of sensitivity surrounding deafness, and the physical and mental impairments to speech. These are emotive subjects and the language used to describe the Deaf community and those unable or unwilling to speak has evolved. I have used the terms, such as they were, given the time period, in a way that reflects the use and prejudices of the time, and I wanted to address and give my reasons for the use of outdated and possibly offensive language so that readers understand why it has been used and my intentions behind it.

I am grateful to the British Deaf Association for their input and guidance on the history, terminology and sensitivities surrounding deafness, and the information on techniques used historically by 'oralist' teachers during the time that the novel is set (1918). The heroine shows awareness of and sensitivity about the significance of the terms people use to describe 'impairment', often challenging the stereotypes that existed (and still exist).

I have used and described British Sign Language (BSL) for hand signs and fingerspelling, having superimposed modern words and/or signs where historical ones do not exist, or could not be found.

There are non-gratuitous references to, and descriptions of, self-harm within the book and I hope that I have handled the sensitivity of the protagonist's predicament and anxieties in a sympathetic and caring manner; that was certainly my intention.

J. T. Croft
February 2021

ACKNOWLEDGMENTS

For all those who live in silence, and in sound.

To my Advance Reader Team, *The Muses*:

Richard Brulotte
Tracey Bryant
Lana Kamennof-Sine
Christine Ruiz Noriega-Hollnbuchner

CONTENTS

The fall had shattered the woman's neck and fractured bones right down to her ankles.

James completed his post-mortem examination on the covered billiard table and reset the broken body's dislocations.

She deserves better than this, he thought as he closed the rip in her sombre gown from which the splintered leg bone had violently erupted.

'I appreciate your help, Dr Croswell,' said the police inspector, yawning. He mopped his brow and glanced around at the stuffed animal trophies in the richly furnished room of Hemingworth Hall. Their black and lifeless eyes stared down at the makeshift mortuary. 'A dreadful business, to be sure.'

James barely registered the attempt at conversation. His mouth was dry, and he was numb from being woken three hours earlier; the final midnight call before the storm ripped down the telegraph lines to the house. The doctor accepted his responsibility as the closest and most qualified medical professional available at short notice. Still, he fought to remain detached from any emotional association with the governess lying on the green billiard cloth. No training or life experience could fully prepare him for the violent and sudden loss of a close confidant, and James struggled to separate the joyful spirit of Jane Urquhart from the lifeless, broken body before him. He gained comfort from the cold, congealed sweat on her unmarked face—she had landed feet first, sparing him the dreadful encounter with a heavily fractured skull.

Death had come quickly and mercifully, but not before a short period of agony in the arms of her traumatised young ward. James had administered the sedative to mollify the young girl, and the opiate would soon be rocking the horrific memory to sleep.

It was rare to work on violent deaths and injuries so severe, however accidental, so far from the city. The war had been a different matter, and James's role as a senior medic had prepared him for more than a life's instruction in setting bone, removing shrapnel or amputating limbs from the wrappings of their muddied military khaki. His muscle memory returned quickly to deal with the governess's fall—a small comfort under the circumstances.

'The storm is making it difficult to reach the coroner in Warwick,' said the inspector, shifting from foot to foot and scanning the surroundings of the stately room. 'I'm aware you knew the lady?'

James handed his completed notebook to the inspector.

'We played chess,' he said. 'She was an excellent teacher.'

'She taught you how to play?' said the inspector, nodding with professional approval as he flicked through the detailed report.

'She taught me how to lose with dignity.'

'What of the staining on the forefinger and thumb?' asked the inspector, pointing his cartridge pen to the lifeless right hand.

'It's in my report,' said James, pulling across a sheet to cover the body. 'It could be ink, soot from a pinched candlewick or bruising from the shock to the circulatory system at the ends of the fingers; it's not uncommon. I've scraped a sample onto a slide, and you can send it to the laboratory. I'll keep the coroner informed.'

James followed the glance of the inspector to the emerald glass bottle on a nearby tray.

'When the housemaid discovered the laudanum in her room,' said the inspector, 'you seemed surprised she was an addict?'

James turned and washed his hands in the makeshift basin, hastily prepared within the closed room. He paused, wiping them on a threadbare towel.

'I've given you a statement, along with everyone else in the house—'

'Not quite everybody.' The inspector pulled out his notebook and scanned a list of names. 'I still have to question the manservant, Mr Bishop.'

'I wish you luck with that,' said James, buttoning his rolled-down sleeves. 'The man's mute, but Captain Ferris and I can attest to his character; he's the reason Charles came back alive from Flanders at all, despite his injuries.'

The loose casement windows rattled with a sudden gust of air, and the lights dimmed, buzzing as the antiquated electrics fought to regain control from the October storm.

'If you take my advice,' he continued, 'I wouldn't call him a manservant, not to his face at any rate. He's much more than that.'

'Mr Bishop guards the valuables in the tower, does he not?' pressed the inspector.

James hesitated, unwilling to embellish the ridiculous notion that great stores of Reformation silver, the legendary wealth of the family, lay hidden and unused in the decrepit manor house tower. 'Mr Bishop is diligent in all his duties,' he said, 'but guarding access to fabled treasure is not one of them.'

'I'm not insinuating anything, Dr Croswell. It's well known he has been a long-standing support to Captain Ferris since his return from the war.' The inspector bit on the end of his pen. 'Strange that so delicate a woman as Miss Urquhart could possess the strength to pull herself up and climb so high, don't you think?'

'Miss Urquhart was delicate only in body, Inspector, and the mind is capable of extraordinary things, when under periods of mental stress.'

The inspector held up a finger to strengthen his point. 'Perhaps fables of Catholic silver encouraged closer inspection of the tower? Belief is a powerful motivator.'

'I will not answer any more questions on fairy tales,' said James, shaking his head.

The inspector pursed his lips and tapped his pen against his cheek.

'Given her delicate mental state,' he said, 'and being under the influence of a powerful opiate—could this, in your medical opinion, be a motive for suicide? The housekeeper attests to seeing Miss Urquhart climbing on the outside of the spiral staircase before the railing gave way, and she fell to her death.'

James frowned, disgusted by the shameful assertion.

'Jane Urquhart loved life, and she was fond of Rose. What drove her to do those things is unknown, and possibly unknowable. I am not a psychoanalyst, but her death from that height results from the giving way of the dilapidated railings, two-thirds of the way up. You've seen how the house is falling apart?'

A gust of wind slammed into the house and forced its way up to the eaves of the roof, lifting and dislodging several slates. They smashed onto the cracked paving outside in the black autumn night.

The inspector shrugged. 'Returning to the laudanum—'

James closed his case and put on his coat. The mantelpiece clock chimed four times, barely audible over the sound of the howling gale.

'It's late, Inspector, and I have a full surgery ahead of me in four hours. I prescribe the tincture as a pain relief for Miss Ferris alongside other medicines for her deteriorating condition.' He met the curious gaze of the police officer. 'I do not prescribe it for recreational use.' He pulled at the bell rope, setting off a distant and muffled tinkling. The sound of rapidly approaching feet on stone came from the other side, hurrying to unlock the casement doors.

'I can only tell you what happened to the body at the time of her death and how she died,' added James. 'You and your men moved her to the billiard room before I arrived, but the injuries she sustained are consistent with a fall of some thirty feet onto a tiled floor. What her motives were and why she climbed to such a dangerous height are out of my jurisdiction.'

James turned to the prostrate form of the governess. 'And, out of respect, I do not wish to speculate on the motive or cause of her sudden and unbalanced mental state; that is your job to deduce. Mine is to mourn.'

The doors unlocked and swung outwards, revealing the fearful face of the housemaid in the main hall. 'The master has asked to see you before you leave, Dr Croswell,' she said.

James nodded and offered the police officer the door. The inspector collected his hat from the horns of a nearby wall-mounted stag.

'Can you tell Captain Ferris that I will return with the undertaker this afternoon?' said the inspector. He turned, glancing at the blanched and terrified face of the house servant.

'I'm not a man prone to fancy, Dr Croswell, but given the governess's alleged wild ramblings before her demise, not to mention Hemingworth's reputation for being an unquiet house—'

James pivoted. 'Neither am I, Inspector. A meeting with ghosts or ghouls did not cause Miss Urquhart's death.' He raised his arm to usher the police officer from the room and signal the conversation was at an end.

'The force of gravity, intersecting with the surface of the earth, killed my friend lying there.'

'Isn't it a bit early for that, Charles?' asked James disapprovingly as his friend fumbled with the stopper to the whisky. The candle- and firelight fractured by the crystal decanter sent fragments of amber sparking across the drawing-room panelling.

'It's late,' said Charles Ferris, shakily raising the tumbler to his lips. 'I haven't been to bed yet.'

'You haven't slept properly for weeks. Have you been taking the—'

'I haven't slept since Sophia died and this nonsense started, so don't bother to lecture me about it, James.' Charles downed the whisky and misjudged the side table as he replaced the glass. The crystal tumbler slipped to the floor, smashing into a myriad of glistening pieces.

James strode towards his friend in the wheelchair, knelt in front of him, and stared into his dead eyes.

'That was blindness before you lecture me, *Dr Croswell*. I've not had nearly enough yet.' He yelled out for the house-keeper before glancing over with opaque eyes.

'We've known each other since Cambridge, *Captain Ferris*, and I will for the sake of our friendship lecture you however I damn well please.'

Charles snorted. 'That's some bedside manner you've developed out here in the wilds.'

'It's called tough love, Charles, though I prefer to call it honesty.' James kicked the lifeless boot of his best friend.

'You'll never know how much I wish I could feel that. I barely feel anything anymore.' Charles twisted the chair towards the fire and held out his hand.

James threw on a log of seasoned oak; sparks scattered up the chimney. The flue sucked the glowing fragments rapidly out into the turbulent air outside. 'What will you do with Rose, now that Jane—'

'She was bloody good, you know?' said Charles thoughtfully. 'Jane was making real progress; I almost thought I heard Rose murmuring in her sleep two nights ago.'

He looked up towards James. 'I'm not sending her away to some asylum, or whatever you call them these days. She's staying here with me until I'm sure that what haunts this damn place is no longer a threat. Who's saying it wouldn't follow her, anyway?'

'You need another governess then—'

'I need a miracle, James.'

'—one skilled in communicating with the deaf and dumb,' continued the doctor, ignoring the interruption.

Charles stiffened and gripped the end of his chair tightly. 'She's neither.' He relaxed his hands. 'I used to be annoyed by the constant running around the house by them; what I wouldn't give for an hour like that now, even ten minutes ...'

'I'll put my feelers out,' said James. 'For someone suitably qualified. There may be some at the Cambria Institute—'

Charles reversed back into the corner of the room, knocking into the writing desk. He reached behind him and fumbled for a letter. 'No need. I've already made arrangements with an agent in Mayfair; someone that has already offered me guidance on spiritual matters—defence in particular.'

'Defence?' said James, uncomfortable with his friend's recent interest in matters that lay outside of science and reason.

'Come,' said Charles, 'I'll show you before I lock the damn chamber for good.'

Charles wheeled across to the door as the housekeeper arrived. 'Mrs Stanton, will you be so good as to arrange the clearance of the glass near the hearth,' he said. 'My friend here has had a terrible evening, as have we all, and has dropped one of the 1878 set.'

Mrs Stanton pressed her lips together as James silently protested with a look of innocence. He gave the woman a short shake of his head; it wasn't as if Charles was likely to see the exchange, not in the dim light. The sharp features of the housekeeper cast shadows across her pockmarked face as she realised the ruse. She placed a hand gently on her employer's shoulder; Charles flinched.

'And where is Bishop? I need the damn lights on,' he said, wheeling out into the main hall. 'How am I supposed to see anything at all with these blasted eyes without light!'

The doctor and housekeeper followed swiftly.

'Mr Bishop is with Billy, sir,' said Mrs Stanton. 'He's finishing the preparations you requested, in the tower wing.'

'I'll see to him myself,' barked Charles. 'Check on Rose. Make sure she is where she is supposed to be and not wandering the house again at ungodly hours.'

James passed the housekeeper, who was still in the process of a short curtsy. It was a habit long learned, but now not necessary or noticed except during his closest friend's regular visits.

'From now on,' said Charles, heading to the partly glazed double doors at the end of the corridor to the tower rooms, 'no one goes up there, and nothing gets out.'

James caught up and glanced through the small stained-glass panels to see movement and candlelight beyond. Charles leaned forwards from his chair and banged on the door with the side of his fist. The tower boomed with the echo and James looked behind at the house staff's timid faces, leaning out from other doorways. The doors opened, and a man of great size all but blotted out the dimly lit room beyond.

'Is it done?' said Charles, entering the chamber. 'Is all prepared, Bishop?'

The giant mute nodded, clapped once in his affirmation, and pointed behind him.

James stood in the lower chamber of the tower, once so familiar to him—the bell staircase of Hemingworth Hall. He recalled his childhood, racing up and down the two hundred steps until Charles's father would come out of the study and sue for peace. The distant ceiling above always gave him a sense of vertigo, and he shivered with the memory of trying to outdo his closest rival in the deadly spiral slide down the handrail; the same that had given way hours before.

The staircase was now monstrously transformed. Candlelit lamps and wall sconces illuminated the circular walls of the four-storey tower. The self-supporting stone treads, keyed in one on top of another, were a marvel of post-Reformation period architecture. They were bounded on one side by dark oak panelling, and on the other by an ornate wrought-iron filigree railing with a polished wooden handrail. James gazed in disbelief at the grand entrance to the bell staircase; the hall's crowning glory was now webbed with great silver strands of taut silk thread and rope. Tarnished steel bells, removed from their delicate hangings within the railings, glistened and swung at points along the lines, ringing as Bishop and the teenage boy assisting him attached the final strands around the base of the steps and across the central void. Sitting centrally and suspended like a great spider within the midst of the web hung a wheel-like oil lamp chandelier. It burned brightly above the central opening, casting its light and shadows to the barricaded and webbed doorways that led off to adjoining floors, and to the embossed ceiling rose eighty feet above.

'Good God, man,' said James. 'What have you done?'

Charles halted beneath the centre of the chamber and spun round, tilting back his head to peer blindly into the darkness.

'What I should have done a long time ago,' he said, beckoning to his sole remaining friend. 'Come and see it one last time before I lock the damn thing for good—let this be an end to it.'

James gingerly moved to meet him, greeted by the sounds of hundreds of minutely swinging bells. The young servant perched on a ladder and tied several remaining bells to recently installed finger-width ropes. Bishop hauled and tensioned them across the void to great iron rings on the outer staircase wall. The teenager shook, setting off the bells on the strand, and glanced up nervously at the door to the tower room high above, webbed in like manner. The giant grunted a gruff-throated bark, and the apprentice returned to fumble with the bells once more.

James reached out and tugged at the soft grey silken rope, setting off several of the bells.

'I've taken them all off, every bloody one of them,' said Charles. 'Bishop and Billy are spanning the void so nothing can climb the outsides of the staircase, from anywhere.' He pointed to the opening to the tower, and then to the room above. 'The defences are complete now.'

'Are you mad?' said James, glancing down at a large chunk

of fallen masonry embedded with a section of railing. The cracked black-and-white tiles were testament to its fall from grace high above, alongside the falling body of Jane Urquhart. A mop and bucket lay nearby, but thankfully, at that moment, the light was too dim to shine upon its bloodied contents. James sat on his haunches and looked into his friend's soulless eyes. 'Is this necessary?'

Charles stared back. 'Nothing goes in or out of that room while I still have breath in these mustard-gas-ridden lungs. If only I had listened to her advice earlier.'

'Whose advice?'

'Emeline Foster,' said Charles, sheepishly. 'The agent I spoke of.'

'The medium of Mayfair!' said James. 'Have you lost your mind? Her reputation—'

'What about my reputation? A broken man in a broken house!' said Charles, raising his voice. The echo resounded upwards, repeating itself for several moments. Charles bowed his head and whispered, 'Promise me, you will speak of this to no one?'

James looked back through the open doors at the distant faces, disappearing and peering beyond the main hall's rooms. Who could keep a secret like this safe, when the whole house knew? He patted Charles on the shoulder in affirmation.

'What did the inspector and his men make of it?' he asked.

Charles leaned over and whispered again. 'I told him I was paranoid about intruders and that there were personal items of my wife's I did not want spoiled or stolen. He is aware of the silly stories about the silver, but also about what happened to Sophia, by rumour if not by professional insight.' He straightened and called out, 'Is it done yet, Bishop? I want another drink.'

Bishop tied the final knot and clapped his enormous

palms together, sending a deafening echo into the darkness above. Billy retreated down the ladder and hurried past the mop bucket to stand beside him.

'Good,' said Charles, placing his hands on the wheels of the chair. 'We'll have no more unannounced visitations from the living or the dead.'

James took a long last glance up at the spiralling staircase, noting the sparkling metal fractures in the opening where the railings had snapped. The stone treads on the outside of the handrail afforded little purchase, even for a foot so small as Jane Urquhart's.

'Whatever possessed her to go up there?' he whispered, following Charles back to the main hall.

'What possessed her indeed,' said Charles, wheeling out of the chamber. 'Lock it, Bishop, and make sure no one goes in there again.'

Bishop waited until the master of the house and the doctor disappeared from view. He gestured to the young man, putting an enormous finger to his mouth.

'I won't say a word about what I saw, Mr Bishop, honest,' said Billy, eager to be out of the tower. Bishop held him long in his gaze and released him, watching as the young man hurried from the room.

Alone in the chamber, Bishop turned to the wall where long chains hung, wrapped in fine silk, the smaller of which lowered the central glass oil lamp from its nest within the chandelier. He let out the rattling links and tied the chain before extinguishing the burning wick with his rough, bare fingers, leaving only the wall-mounted candle sconces and the solitary undamaged candelabra alight. A gust of wind from the hall rushed into the chamber and up into the black void.

The candles flickered and recovered. Bishop looked up, as though waiting for a response. He collected the candelabra from the dresser and tip-toed alongside the panelling, listening intently. Pivoting to his right, Bishop spread his great hand to his heart and then outwards to the panel without a glance.

The girl beyond responded with a corresponding motion, watching through the narrowest of slits. She maintained her hand on the inside of the hidden passage as the retreating candlelight from the manservant highlighted the recent nail marks cut into her wrists. She licked at the wounds, hearing the double doors lock shut, setting off the tinkling of the bells on the impenetrable staircase.

The disturbed air rose again through the tower, flickering the candles on the wall. The final sconce next to the upper-most chamber flared intensely and went out as the air swirled around it. The swirl rebounded and coiled back down the outside wall like water disappearing down a swirling drain, putting out all the candles and plunging the tower chamber and bell staircase into darkness.

The bells fell silent, and all became still, except for the shaking of the little girl, hiding within the panel-fronted priest hole, secret and safe in the silence of the slumbering staircase.

CHAPTER 1

G race Meadows shivered in the chilly, dark room. Darkness brought many things.

She knew he would be there; she could feel him. All she had to do was look out from her sparse and lonely room, and he would be there. Unclear at first, but present none the less. One thing could banish him, at least for tonight. She desperately needed sleep but had promised not to hurt herself again. The urge to do so was overwhelming, and she breathed deeply, putting into practice the calming exercises learned from a recent paper on controlling harmful compulsions.

The meditations didn't work, but nor were they meant to for such trauma.

Grace fought against the desire and raged with all her will against the inevitable. She turned her wrists, pale and scarred from a year of turmoil. If she could do this one more time, just enough to banish the guilt, then she would begin again tomorrow when the anxiety and fear had subsided. This would be the last time.

In matt contrast to her forearms' unblemished young

skin, the old burn marks on her wrists reflected in the wan moonlight. The night brought fear, but it also caused the need for fire. Even a small one in the meagre hearth, able to be put out quickly, would set off her panic and sleeplessness for the rest of the night. Better to do it quickly, and with a single flame; the fire would hurt—yes, but only for a moment, then the guilt and compulsion would return to its grave, along with the child outside.

She splayed her tiny hands on the desk, and bit her lip as the battle for control began its endless cycle again.

Fight it, Grace. Fight it! They'll find out, and you'll be gone.

No! Give in, Grace. No one will know, no one must ever know. We'll be safe if we hide our wrists tomorrow.

Grace closed her eyes and breathed deeply with one last effort, barely noticing her left hand reaching for the matches in the desk drawer. She opened her eyes and stared out of the window at the moonlit walled garden. Her other hand paused at the stub of a candle, sitting in its tarnished holder, and she scanned the empty, dew-laden quarters of the lawn. The cruciform paths to the central plinth were silent and still. She exhaled deeply with relief, frosting the inside of the glass. The outstretched hand around the handle struggled to retreat to her side as the blurred image of the central sundial became clearer. Something small was moving around it, silently, as though in joyful play. The wet breath on the glass cleared and the moon-shadowed silhouette of the boy halted and turned solemnly to look up at the window.

The battle was over; she had lost this time.

She threw open the drawer and grabbed at the matches, scattering them across the floor. The candle holder slipped from her grasp and tumbled towards them, as though willingly assisting in the self-harm that was to come. The thud of the pewter resonated on the floorboards, and she heard movement outside in the servants' passage. Grace fell to the floor and froze, peering beneath the door at the light peeping from the corridor beyond. A shadow disturbed the light, and she could make out the black leather of the housekeeper's shoes. They halted at the door for a moment, as if listening, before moving away to open a nearby cupboard door.

Grace collected the candle and hunted across the floor for the striking-box. The first match snapped in two with the urgency, but the second struck and blazed brightly, stinging her dark-adapted eyes and revealing the oak beams and cobwebs on the ceiling. She hesitated, searching for the inner strength to snuff out the painful light and all that it represented. Her will dissolved, and she lowered the lit match.

The candle wick crackled with glee, ready to accept her momentary sacrifice. Grace closed her eyes and rotated her right wrist high above the source of heat.

Just a little; just enough to banish it all, she thought.

Grace lowered her wrist, grimacing from prickly heat.

Just a little further, relief is coming ...

The sounds of a child running outside on the upper staircase receded as Grace made a fist and forced her wrist closer to the flame.

The pain came sharply, and she bit her lip, fighting against instinct, as the all-consuming physical pain wiped away the fatigue and memory behind it. The smell of burning flesh screamed for her to let go, but she clung on momentarily, to make sure, before losing control and crying out in agony. She rolled back, clutching at the charred and damaged wrist.

The sound of rapidly approaching feet heralded the sudden opening of the door to her bedroom and Grace struggled to get up, blinded by the light from beyond. The housekeeper stood, framed in the doorway, and ran in, snuffing out the candle that had spilt its wax onto the floor.

'You stupid girl,' she shouted, as she pulled Grace to her feet by the burning wrist. 'You promised!'

Grace yelped with new pain and spluttered senseless excuses.

'The window ... is he ... there?' she said, panting. 'Garden ... near the sundial—'

The housekeeper dragged Grace to the window and looked out.

'There's no one there, Grace. It's all in your head.'

The housekeeper shivered and glanced down at the cold ashes in the hearth. A bundle of kindling and a small but full scuttle of coal lay beside it, covered in days of dust. She released her grip and softened her face now that the shock was passing. Hurried feet ran up the creaking staircase, accompanied by the joyous and mischievous laughter of a small boy.

'Those are wood ashes, Grace. Where did you get them from this time—the gardener?' She held out the blistered wrist to the edge of the light from the corridor.

'Please, Mrs Tatton, I didn't mean to—'

'The mistress will have to hear of this; I can't shield you again, no matter how much I think of you,' said the housekeeper, eyes brimming with tears. 'He was just learning to speak because of you.'

Cries from below indicated a chase of some sort and a light patter of feet raced up the final few treads to the corridor; the boy was laughing but obviously out of breath.

Grace turned away, shamed by her weakness and broken promise to the woman who protected the household.

'Get dressed, and I'll fetch the ointment and bandages.' The housekeeper stopped in the doorway as the young boy emerged from the stairwell and ran along the corridor, desperate to reach his beloved playmate and governess.

'You must leave, you know that?' she said as she turned,

colliding with the exuberant child. The boy stopped, panting, confused by the sentiment that Grace could even contemplate leaving him, returning him to a world of silence.

'Master Oliver,' exclaimed Mrs Tatton, 'return to your room, it is past nine o'clock, and your games must cease.'

The boy peered around the bulk of the housekeeper, struggling out of reach of her groping arms. Grace stared back, humiliated, bedraggled and shaking in her nightdress. She made the signs with her hands for him to return to bed. He responded with confused questions, and his hands whirled, escaping the clutches of Mrs Tatton. He caught sight of Grace's wrist and the spent candle and matches on the floor.

'G ... Grace?' he mouthed, forming the words and desperate to understand.

Several out-of-breath servants came down the corridor searching for the heir and miscreant of the household. They apologised for the noise and followed the gaze of the young boy into the room beyond.

'I'm sorry, sorry to you all,' said Grace, clutching at her wrist.

The sting of salty tears on her burned skin shook her into the realisation of what she had done. They would all know soon enough.

She looked into her ward's crying face—the sweet and silent child, so eager now to learn and speak.

'I'm sorry,' she mouthed while signing and stepping back into the shadow. 'Forgive me. Do as Mrs Tatton says and go back to bed.'

'Mrs Tatton assured me you had your compulsions under control,' said the elegantly dressed lady of the house, staring at

Grace's bandaged wrist. The drawing room was in stark contrast to the bedroom. Light and warmth filled the room, banishing all shadow and thought of darkness. A great blaze burned brightly in the marble fireplace. Grace stood, warily watching the fire, exhausted by the summons. A loud pop of exploding sap from a freshly placed log caused her to start. The sudden jolt dislodged her hasty attempt at setting her golden hair, and she poked a free strand into its loose and temporary plait.

'Forgive me, Lady Soames,' said Grace, head hung low. 'It was a moment of weakness.'

The seated woman glanced up, reaching across for a cigarette and lighter. She sprung open the slim silver case and sparked a small flame, her eyes glued to the governess. She lit the end of the cigarette and drew deeply, causing the tobacco to flare. Her manicured and painted nails reflected with the closeness of the glowing ember.

'I've employed no one with half as much patience, dedication or strength as you have shown with Oliver over the past three months,' she said, exhaling a cloud of menthol smoke. 'But I think we both know how this meeting is going to end.'

Grace swayed momentarily with the final confirmation. Until then, hope had remained that she could stay.

'If it's about the—' Grace raised her bandaged wrist. 'Then I can avoid having candles in my room?'

'It's not solely about that,' said Lady Soames, reaching for a letter on a nearby cushion. 'You've gone without heat, light and sleep for twice as long as you will admit to me, and Mrs Tatton.' Grace studied the attractive middle-aged woman for signs of doubt, finding only genuine distress.

'I know she is a soft touch, as am I, and has been shielding you from my attention. Oliver adores you, and you are making excellent progress with his speech, but I have to think of the household. The child looks to you for guidance and teaching, but he is picking up strange habits and an aversion to fire which is unnatural. I also have not received references from your previous employer, and three months have elapsed.

'Rumour and gossip in this house lead me to conclude there is something you aren't telling me about your previous position, despite your otherwise good but overly protective nature.'

Grace interjected, but Lady Soames raised a hand and continued. 'Your peculiar behaviour has not gone unnoticed by the rest of the household and my son. You agreed to defend and look after Oliver, while getting him to speak despite his deafness and reluctance. What he saw tonight on the servants' landing will haunt him for a long time.'

Grace stiffened at the word 'haunt' and wondered if its use was intentional.

'You are aware of the trust you have now broken?' said Lady Soames, studying the letter in her shaking hand. She took a long draw on the cigarette as if preparing for a difficult and testing few moments.

Grace nodded and drew from the depth of her considerable emotional well. 'I can never thank you enough for the time I have spent with your son, and the benefit it has been in coming to terms with my struggles.'

Lady Soames turned away as though hearing through one ear would make the pleading less painful to hear.

'I solemnly swear that if you give me the opportunity, I will make amends. I promised you a song from Oliver before Christmas,' said Grace, ignoring protocol and rushing to kneel at her employer's side. 'Let me make good on that promise and my own.' She held up her wrist and placed her other hand upon it, as though taking an oath.

Lady Soames put down the cigarette and turned away in

distress. She gripped the letter. 'A song by Christmas,' she whispered. 'You can do this?'

'He already has the first two lines. I was keeping it back from you,' said Grace, sensing an opportunity to remain in service. 'And he has to use less of the signs, just as you and Lord Soames wanted.'

Lady Soames stared at the letter.

'Your solemn oath that this episode will be the last? Swear it on your soul, and the life of my child,' she said, motioning for Grace to rise and return to stand by the vase of fading autumn dahlias. 'I know about Pennington Grange, and the likely reason your previous employers will not provide satisfactory references, despite no conclusive evidence that you or anyone else could have done anything differently.'

Grace felt faint with the mention of her previous situation and steadied herself on the octagonal table holding the vase.

Lady Soames held the letter aloft and reclaimed her cigarette. 'Swear it, Miss Meadows.'

'I swear,' said Grace, relief coursing through her veins. One employer without references was disastrous; a second would be ruinous. She glanced at the intricate parquet floor, planning how to frame her immense gratitude.

Lady Soames leaned over to place a finished supper plate on her lap and lit the letter's end with her cigarette. The paper took light as she continued.

'You will present yourself and your wrists to me each morning to prove the truth of the matter.'

Grace glanced up and nodded. The gratitude died on her lips as she saw her employer wrestling with the lit paper before tossing it onto the silver tray below. Lady Soames gripped the metal's edge and lifted it, ablaze, to the side table. Grace grabbed the vase and launched towards her, terrified with the sudden appearance of the uncontrolled flame. Lady Soames shrieked at the sudden action and dropped the tray onto the chaise longue, spilling the smouldering fragments.

Grace pushed her employer away with such force that Lady Soames collapsed against the opposite wall. She doused the remains of the burning letter. The fear of fire was suddenly all around her: electric lights burning everywhere, the smoulder on the chair below, the oil lamp on the far dresser, and the open fire roaring to her side.

Nothing else mattered. It all had to be extinguished to make sure the past didn't repeat itself. Grace heard a repeated call for aid from Lady Soames as she threw the remaining water into the fireplace, causing a steaming hiss and splutter. A great cloud of wood smoke heralded Mrs Tatton and the first footman.

'It's all right, Grace,' said the man, removing the heavy crystal vase from her grip. 'It's over now; the fire's out.'

Mrs Tatton helped Lady Soames to her feet. Grace saw the look of abject confusion on both the servants' faces as her employer smoothed down her gown and regained her composure.

'Out,' she said to the housekeeper and footman. 'Get out, I say!'

The pair fled from the room, and Grace recovered her wits.

'I expect you to be gone by noon tomorrow,' said Lady Soames, her voice quavering, 'before Lord Soames and my father arrive. For the safety of my son and the household, not to mention my own, I have to let you go.'

Grace put her face into her hands and nodded.

'You cannot remain here while you are plagued by what happened at Pennington.'

She reached for a cigarette. 'As a final courtesy, I will keep this from my husband; I share the blame for employing you without a reference. It is my fault I hired you, not yours. You must seek help, Grace.'

Grace wiped her eyes. 'Can I rely upon a reference, just for the three months? I have nowhere to go, and situations will be hard this close to Christmas. Can I at least see Oliver?'

'What you ask for is not possible. You are a danger to yourself, and I cannot, in good conscience among my peers, recommend staff with a history, no matter how gifted they are. If you attempt to contact my son or come within a mile of the house, my husband will learn you tried to assault me, and you will answer to him and his officials.' Lady Soames, seemingly struck by the severity of her conviction, softened as she drew on the cigarette for support.

'I will telephone ahead and arrange for you to see Mrs Bridges at the almshouses,' she said. 'Those that did not join the Glorious Dead are always looking for nurses to help them face an inglorious future.'

Grace blanched at the prospect. 'I trained for four years as an oralist to help deaf and mute children communicate; I don't think I could manage—'

'Then you have until my family arrives to leave the estate with your belongings, and this—' Lady Soames moved to the dresser and opened a drawer. She returned, holding a small and richly embroidered purse.

'Without you, Oliver would still be grunting like an animal,' she said, fighting back her emotions. 'I would never have heard my son call me "mother". I owe you at least this much.' She threw the jingling purse onto the table.

Grace straightened and rose above her shame. She was no longer an employable governess and would no longer pursue a passion for bringing voices to the silent. It would take time to sink in—time she no longer had. Grace thought of Oliver, and the final image he would recall. Would he be able to put it into words? Would they tell him that his beloved governess was bad, mad, or somehow it was his fault for being up late?

She glanced at the purse; it was beautiful. A gesture made in good faith, but the thought of charity, no matter how well-intentioned, wounded her pride. She looked at Lady Soames, back turned, gazing into the fire. The long-ignored cigarette poked above her left shoulder and shed its long-ignored ash onto the hearth.

Grace left the room to the sound of hurrying servants outside, eager to avoid the accusation of eavesdropping. She did not look back to see the woman standing close to the fire, whose tears dried on her cheek as rapidly as they shed.

———

Grace sat on the floor, her arms wrapped around her knees. She buried her head into the bandaged wrists, shivering without thought of light or warmth. The matches and candle were gone, but it didn't matter. Tonight, she welcomed the torture: a penance for her weakness. The anxiety remained at a level not experienced since Pennington and would not subside, even when she tried to dig her bitten fingernails into the bandaged wrist.

There would be no sleep, not with thoughts of the incident below, the silent march to the third floor with Mrs Tatton, the final look of disappointment on the housekeeper's face as Grace closed the door and sat down on the bed, the prospect of nursing the wounded remnants of humanity in the almshouses, and the effort of a day's hard walking in the autumn gale to get there.

There would be no sleep now that the shadow in the corner was here, close at hand. Not until dawn, not until she was too weary to care about anything anymore. It shifted at the edge of the silver moonlight cutting across the floorboards. Grace glanced over through tired eyes, as the child's hands shot out into the dust-mote stream of light and made a sign.

In front of the shade's unseen body, with palms facing each other, the fingers wiggled while the little hands moved up and down alternately.

'Fire,' whispered Grace, recognising the sign and returning to hide her head in her knees. 'Good boy, Arthur. Good boy.'

CHAPTER 2

Daybreak crept into the room, grey and joyless. Grace opened her eyes from a short nap as the seriousness of her predicament came rushing back to her consciousness.

The corner of the room was empty, except for the washbasin and stand. Grace got up, stiffly, and shuffled to the window. Her breath steamed in the chill air as she rubbed away the rime frost from a section of the glass. She looked out at the silvered lawn and through the fog to the end of the walled garden. The skeletal armillary sphere, a sundial for the stars, dripped its dew-laden jewels from the countless spider webs that netted among the dark bands of iron. Grace did not expect to see footprints in the frost, and there were none.

She inched over to the corner of the room and poured the ice-cold water into the chipped porcelain basin. After a few droplets splashed upon her face, she removed the bandage and stared at the stinging source of relief and misery. She plunged the sore flesh beneath the water and curled her toes, fighting back the contrast in pain. Hot and cold sensations melded into one and then subsided as the water washed away the ointment and the thoughts of the night before.

Grace glanced up into the tarnished mirror. The face looked older than twenty-three years would suggest, and who now would look at the once joyful face so worn in an almshouse? She had heard of the place from the other servants. A maid's husband lay in one ward, shell-shocked and immobile, reliving the war endlessly in his locked mind. Grace clasped the small silver locket at her neck and envied the woman in that respect; at least the maid knew where her beloved lay.

She dressed quickly and packed her clothes and belongings: mostly tools, games and books to help build the trust and communication process with deaf and silent children. A hairbrush and a pack of playing cards crowned the items before she pulled down the lid of the battered trunk. She lifted the chest. It was light enough to carry for several hours, and there would be several stops on the fifteen miles to Bourne, far over the Great North Road. She glanced up at her most-prized possession from the last three months—a crude but colourful painting of the two of them, painted by Oliver, created on the same day that the breakthrough had happened when a few precious words had broken a lifetime of silence. *Mary had a little lamb, October 1918* was sketched in Grace's handwriting at the top, repeating in written form the phrase first uttered that joyous morning. That afternoon had been glorious, with rewards and treats showered upon the intelligent young ward. The real work began after that: building Oliver's confidence, hour after hour in front of the mirror to form the right shapes with his mouth for the words to be understood. There were setbacks, of course, and a reversion to hand signals regularly occurred as the old ways sought to reinforce their dominance over the new, but Grace allowed it, alongside the oral work; any communication was better than silence.

She took the painting down from above the bed and carefully folded it before putting it into her shoulder purse.

Opening the door revealed a small tray of bread, milk and packed provisions. Grace stooped to take a few bites from the bread, beneath which was a strip of paper revealing the handwriting of the housekeeper:

The past teaches us how to be present and go forward with our lives.

Grace smiled with the bittersweet memory and lifted the milk to her lips. Mrs Tatton had received the news of her son's death shortly after the governess's arrival. Days of compassion and consolation followed, difficult in a formal household, but Grace had been there, holding her hand and whispering words of comfort. The phrase on the paper had resonated with the housekeeper and had now returned as a parting gift.

Grace clicked open her trunk and put the rations inside, listening for signs of life. The servants would be in the kitchen by now, breaking their fast and readying for Lady Soames' husband and father, the old duke. A bell sounded from the floor below, calling for service to Lady Soames' chamber, and Grace got to her feet, turned to say a silent farewell to the spartan room, and padded down the stairs to the lower floor.

She reached the open door of the drawing room and peered inside. A newly laid fire burned in the swept grate, but otherwise, the space was empty. Grace knocked as a courtesy and slipped inside, heading for the purse that still lay on the table. She fought the anxiety arising from the fire, and the memories of the previous night, before glancing down at the embroidered purse and the lifeline it contained. It was not until that moment that Grace decided what to do, but now it seemed clear. After unfolding the painting from her pocket, she lifted the purse and laid the colourful image down in its place. No amount could ever be worth the picture, but she weighed the pouch in her hand against what she was about to leave behind.

She left the room and determined to go by the front door and main drive, but the thought of not saying farewell and some basic explanation to Oliver was overwhelming. A grandfather clock sounded for seven o'clock; he would be having his breakfast soon in the ground-floor nursery, the room with a large bay window that overlooked the long lawn and lake beyond. The parting would be grievous, but Grace knew she would regret not saying goodbye, almost as soon as she passed through the estate gates.

She opened the main entrance door and tip-toed down the stone steps to the gravel path that led to the side of the house. The fog hugged the ground and muffled her approach as she darted in and out of the yew hedge buttresses. Oliver was already there, stubbornly refusing to eat, despite the protestations and encouragement of the housemaid unused to childcare and obstinacy.

Grace smiled. 'Welcome to my world.'

The housemaid threw up her hands and made some pointless and arbitrary threat against arguably the most powerful and important human being in the house. He looked out defiantly as the door closed and then gazed mournfully at a landscape and sky that signalled an entire day inside. Grace took her chance and approached the thick glass of the sash windows. Oliver's expression turned to one of surprise and genuine glee. He banged on the window in excitement, then saw the trunk at Grace's side as she placed it on the path.

'W... why?' he began before Grace put a finger to her lips.

'Use your hands; I can't hear you,' she mouthed. 'I only have a moment ...'

Oliver leapt into signing, and Grace responded in silence using matching hand signals.

'*Why are you leaving? Is it because I didn't go to bed last night? Are they sending you away because I am bad?*'

'No,' signed Grace, '*I made a mistake and broke a promise to Ma-ma.*'

'*They told me you hurt yourself because you were sad. Why are you sad, is it me?*'

'I'm not sad with you,' said Grace out loud, placing her hands on the glass. 'I'm sad because of something that happened to someone I loved very much, and I do bad things to punish myself.'

Oliver looked down at her exposed wrist emerging from her worn cuff. He scrunched his face and touched the burn delicately through the glass, as though fearing to cause further pain.

'*Does it hurt?*' he signed, slowly and mournfully.

'Not as much as the reason I do bad things,' said Grace.

Oliver turned. '*Someone's coming; it's Ma-ma. I didn't eat my egg.*'

'I have little time,' said Grace. 'I want you to grow up and be a big strong boy that sings, and reads *Robinson Crusoe* out loud; will you promise me you'll do that? Will you promise me you'll sing what I taught you?'

The door opened, and in strode Lady Soames. She was expecting to find a stubborn child in front of a cold and untouched egg, not the parting of two friends at the bay window. 'Oliver!' she said, hitching up her dress and striding towards her son.

The child turned and slammed his hands against the glass, forcing them against those on the other side. Grace saw the boy begin to cry, and Lady Soames looking down in anguish as she attempted to drag her son from the glass. 'Get away, Grace. Get out!'

'*I'll never speak again*,' signed Oliver, silently shouting with enlarged gestures.

Grace stepped back. 'No! Sing for me, sing as loud as you can, now and forever. I won't forget you.' Grace dragged her trunk as she struggled down the path and out of his life.

She feared some repercussion for her indiscretion and raced down the long gravel drive, tears streaking down the side of her face. She would run until every painful thought and emotion surrendered to the exertion; her lungs would burn today in punishment and penance for her weakness.

A chauffeur-driven Rolls-Royce carrying two men sped past, and she leapt over onto the verge, watching as the older of the two men frowned from the right window in recognition. There was a halt before he wound down the window and poked his head from the vehicle. 'Miss Meadows, is it?' he said. 'Are you all right?'

Grace turned to the old duke's kindly face and curtsied from habit before shaking her head and hurrying towards the gates.

She heard the call of the younger Lord Soames to drive on before the car continued its crackling journey down the gravel drive to the house.

Grace tired, but she was determined to make it to the distant gates before slowing down. No one had the authority to upset her or question her after that.

Four hundred yards later, she heard a cry from behind, followed by the running of a young boy desperate to follow her. She stopped and looked round to see Oliver being shoved by his father back to the house. The old duke was still getting out of the car in bewilderment and listening to the explanations of his daughter, Lady Soames.

Oliver escaped back to the steps and turned. He broke into a long-rehearsed song, the most beautiful and unexpected thing Grace had ever heard, as she rounded the gate pillar and listened. The words of Longfellow's poem long ago set to music rang out sweetly from the child's desperate promise that he would honour Grace's final wish.

'I heard the bells on Christmas Day, their old, familiar carols play!'

The clear line rang out against the raucous croaks of the unsettled rooks in the barren trees above, and Grace spun round, looking through the drifting fog that hid the front of the hall. The carol's opening line repeated a third time before Oliver was bundled back into the hall and the distant door slammed shut.

Grace stared proudly down the drive and was about to turn when something emerged to stand at the edge of the fog —the silhouette of a small boy. 'Oliver?' she called, knowing that it was not so.

The child raised his forearm until it reached the horizontal. The elbow pivoted as the hand tightened into a fist.

'No,' said Grace. 'Please don't take this moment from me.'

The child punched out his elbow and repeated the action several times.

'Train ... Locomotive?' said Grace. 'I don't understand?'

The boy repeated the sign and stepped back into the fog.

A passing horse and cart on the lane broke the silence. Grace turned to see if the horses were coming to the hall, but they passed by, snorting their hot breath into the air, spooked by the vision halfway down the drive.

When Grace looked back, the child was gone.

'So what do we do now?' asked Lord Henry Soames, taking the china teacup from his wife.

Lady Soames returned to the table and poured her father a cup, declining to answer straight away. She glanced up at him for reassurance.

'Put an advert in *The Lady*, I guess,' said the old duke, plucking at his grey moustache. 'My daughter has every right, Henry, to do as she feels right for my grandson and the smooth running of the house.' He took the tea and walked over to the long table of the drawing room. 'I'm going to miss that one though,' he said, glancing down at the purse and drawing on the table.

'What's this?' he said.

Lady Soames lit a cigarette and sat down. 'It's a drawing. Oliver must have painted it the day he first learned to speak.'

'And this?' said the old duke, lifting the purse. 'Wasn't this your mother's?'

Lady Soames nodded. 'I never used it, Father, and Grace —' Lady Soames corrected her informality '—Miss Meadows seemed to take a special liking to it.'

'She left her purse?' said her husband, unfolding the morning newspaper. 'How very careless.'

'Not exactly,' she continued. 'I offered it to her as a parting gift, but—'

'But she left you something of her own,' said the duke, lifting it for her to see. 'Where is she going now?'

'I offered to telephone the almshouses—'

'Not the asylum?' said the duke sharply. 'At least send the girl away with some hope of a decent future, Constance.'

'You're just sad you won't have someone to beat at cards; you know she let you win most of the time,' said Henry, from behind the obituaries page.

Lady Soames smacked her husband's feet from the coffee table. 'I can't give her a reference, Father. Did you hear about Pennington Grange?'

The duke sat down, studying the crude but charming painting, recalling the day his daughter had telephoned, and he had heard his only grandson speak the words that lay along the top. 'The place that burned down earlier this year, Forsythe's place? Didn't he lose a son?'

Lady Soames glanced nervously at the newspaper, shielding her husband. 'She was the governess there when it happened.'

Henry Soames laid down the paper and frowned. 'You took on someone responsible for a child that burned to death? Why didn't you tell me?'

'I didn't know at the time,' she said, holding out her hands to ward off further condemnation. 'Her references never arrived, and I overheard the servants discussing where she had been before; it turns out Forsythe dismissed her shortly after.'

'You can't instruct a dead child, Constance,' said her husband. 'I'd say we got off lightly.'

The old duke leaned forwards. 'If you want to learn anything, listen to downstairs in any household,' he said. 'She'd be in Holloway prison, or worse, if she had been responsible for the sorry affair.'

He sipped at his tea. 'You said she tried to put out that bit of flame last night—frightened her, you said?'

Lady Soames nodded. 'She had issues with fire, and I thought she was going to kill me with that vase. She had other oddities which I don't want to go into.'

'But she ran towards the danger, not away?' said the duke, pressing the issue.

'Yes, if you put it like that. Tatton and Simpkins ran in and caught the end of it. I can't reverse my decision considering that, not even for Oliver's sake,' she glanced at her father, 'or your notorious sense of compassion.'

Henry Soames returned to his paper. 'Well, we return to my original question. It's going to be tough finding a replacement this close to Christmas, and there are only two terms before he starts at Eton Prep.'

The old duke rose, collected the purse and painting, and called for the footman. 'Get me my coat, Constance.'

'Where are you going, now?' said Henry. 'You can't get her back without upsetting the whole house and my wife. What's done is done, old man. Chivalry is a thing of the past, as is that governess. Let's move on and have the weekend start on a fresh note.'

The footman arrived bearing an umbrella and hat.

'Ready my driver, Simpkins,' said the duke. 'We are going to return these items to a damsel in distress.' He clutched at his breast pocket, feeling for his calling-card case. 'And to add something of my own.'

CHAPTER 3

Grace changed her grip once more as the trunk became too heavy for her tired left hand to bear. It was happening more regularly now, three miles along the muddy lane from the hall. The old wax coat and hood were heavy and dragged behind her small frame like a mud-smeared wedding train, but at least she wasn't carrying them now. She wiped away the incessant drizzle from her numb cheeks and heard the approach of a vehicle. The last lorry had not stopped, nor had the draught horse and cart, but she turned in the hope of a few miles saved by a charitable driver.

The Rolls-Royce appeared around the corner, and Grace panicked with the thought of officials coming to arrest her for the misdemeanour two hours earlier; she had sworn to avoid contact with Oliver Soames. Considering the child's frantic efforts to reach her, it seemed likely.

But why send a Rolls-Royce?

The elegant silver car slowed to a halt in a layby not far behind her, and the chauffeur opened the driver's door and looked out miserably at the wind-blown squall.

'Miss Meadows,' he shouted. 'Do you have a moment? The duke would like to converse with you in private.'

Grace considered the alternative. She could hardly escape, but the thought of encountering Lady Soames' father did not appeal, even if he were coming to overrule his daughter.

The chauffeur got out of the car, awkwardly trying, without success, to avoid the mud and puddles from spoiling his patent-leather boots. Putting up an umbrella, he circumnavigated the vehicle and stood ready at the rear door.

'Miss Meadows? The duke is waiting.'

Grace slipped in the ruts of muddied sludge towards the gleaming vehicle and the shivering driver.

He opened the door, and the old duke smiled back.

'Won't you come in, Miss Meadows? You look quite wet.'

Grace dropped her trunk in surprise and curtsied.

'Forgive me, Your Grace, but I am wetter and muddier than I look and cannot in good conscience agree to your request.' She glanced around at the white leather interior and down at her sodden boots, caked with clay.

'Nonsense,' said the duke. 'Chivalry is not dead, despite the insistence among certain members of my family that it belongs firmly with me in the past.' He beckoned for her to enter, and she hesitated.

'If you do not come in, Grace, I will be forced to come out.' He pulled the tartan rug from his lap and laid it in the footwell in comic imitation of inviting a queen across a muddied puddle.

'There,' he said. 'What was once good enough for Raleigh, is now good enough for me. Now we will not incur the wrath of the driver.'

Grace held out her hand and was guided into the small space to sit alongside the nobleman. He swivelled to study her face.

Grace broke protocol and spoke first. 'I apologise for

upsetting your grandson and Lady Soames. It was very selfish of me, and I regret it.' She folded her thumbs into her fingers, desperate to get some warmth into her numb hands.

'I don't,' said the duke, taking out his pocket watch and checking the time. 'He hasn't stopped singing for the past two hours.'

Grace frowned at the kindly old man before she smiled at the thought. 'He kept his promise, then?'

The duke returned the smile. 'As did you.' He wiped at the condensation steaming up the side window and chuckled. 'How ever do you make it stop?'

Grace giggled and relaxed her hands onto her damp knees. It felt good to laugh, just for a moment. She glanced around at the exquisite surroundings. Here she was, laughing in a Rolls-Royce with the kindest member of the gentry she had met since leaving the institute and entering the formal world of private service.

'I believe you left something behind,' said the duke, opening a compartment and removing the painting and purse. 'The point was well made,' he said from beneath his bristling grey eyebrows, 'and well-taken.'

He extended the items. 'Take it as a gift from me, not as a final payment from my daughter.'

Grace received them gratefully, noting that she was not being recalled, despite the old man's authority. The household was strictly the domain of Lady Soames, and not even he would break that commandment.

'I see that you are in some distress or dilemma,' he said. 'I have no wish to pry into your personal affairs or bring up anything you wish to keep to yourself, but I would only say that I do not believe you could ever harm a child. The progress you have made with Oliver is borderline miraculous —do not become a nursemaid, Miss Meadows.'

'My options are rather limited at the moment, but I will consider your advice, Your Grace.'

'You have a family? A fiancé, perhaps?'

'Yes, on the north-west coast,' she said, glancing into his bright eyes. 'Nursing will be preferable to a life in the herring factories.' She placed a hand on the locket around her neck, and the old man's eyes noted the faint touch.

'I was engaged to a soldier—'

The duke sighed and placed a hand on her shoulder. The breaking of protocol made them even.

'Someone once told me that death ends a life, not a relationship,' he said, rotating a golden wedding ring on his bony finger. 'As I approach my twentieth year alone on this imperfect globe, I believe it, but am not bound by it.'

Grace nodded, gingerly placing her hand on top of his.

'My point is, Miss Meadows, that not coming to terms with our past only prevents us from taking action for a better future. Sometimes, the best way out is forward and through.'

Grace pondered the words. 'Sometimes it's easier said than done.'

'Yes,' said the duke, smiling as he squeezed her cold hand. 'Like getting silent children to speak; yet somehow you managed that.'

He clicked open a slim case from his breast pocket and flicked through several notelets until he reached a worn calling card. Grace watched as he rubbed at it, recalling some memory of happier times. 'I've carried you with me long enough,' he whispered, handing over the soft water-stained card containing names and an address.

'Take this,' he said. 'Find the woman on it if she still lives and tell her I sent you.'

Grace received the calling card and glanced at the faded gold lettering. The duke pointed at the second name:

Lady Foster
Miss Emeline Foster
6 Cadogan Sq, London.

'Who is she?' asked Grace, noting the convention of placing the unmarried daughter below that of her mother.

'An incredible woman. She was an agent, of sorts; or she was the last time I heard her name mentioned. It was several years ago, however,' he said. 'She had unusual methods of helping people and being influential in placing domestic staff within exclusive and discerning households.'

'You think she could help me find a situation, with my—'

'Experience?'

'I was going to say history or perhaps reputation,' said Grace, blushing with embarrassment.

The duke courteously deflected the conversation.

'She was eighteen years old when I last saw her; closer to fifty now, I suspect. She may remember me, or perhaps not.'

He showed her an ornate silver-handled umbrella. 'She gave me this a very long time ago.' He smiled. 'And now I give it to you.' He passed over the umbrella, forcing it into Grace's closed hand. 'Tell her I send someone worthier than a young fool; I feel it hypocritical to lecture you on the past without first resolving my own.' He twisted the card in her hand to reveal a blank reverse with a single word in a woman's handwriting:

Tomorrow

'What does that signify?' she asked.

He shifted uncomfortably on the leather seat.

'Regret mostly.'

'I don't understand,' said Grace.

'She will.' He sat back and looked out of the misted window. 'Emeline's a wild one, but don't be afraid of her.

Speak plainly, and she'll help you, I'm certain of it. You are very much alike—in mind if not in body.'

'No, I mean I don't understand why you are doing this for me,' said Grace, admiring the black polished wood and silver inlay of the umbrella. A collar of silver stamped with an emblazoned star ringed the top of the curved handle.

'For my grandson, my daughter, and to hopefully put right an old wrong with your help.' He lifted the umbrella tip and tapped at the window, gaining the attention of the sodden chauffeur.

'Goodbye, Miss Meadows. I hope we shall meet again. Promise me you'll make another child sing again?'

The door opened, and a wagon appeared in the lane behind, beeping a horn.

'Driver,' he said, as the man peered into the rear. 'Please escort Miss Meadows to the vehicle behind and ensure the man will take her to the crossroads beyond Stainby.' He reached into his wallet and passed the man a silver half-crown.

'Thank you,' said Grace as she got out of the warm car and into the cool, damp air. The driver marched over and after a few moments signalled that the driver had accepted the deal.

Grace picked up her trunk and made a move to go.

'One last thing, Miss Meadows,' said the duke, mischievously. 'Did you always let me win at cards?'

She smiled and curtsied. 'Only when I wasn't bluffing, Your Grace.' She closed the door with a gentle bow of her head before the old man had time to reply. Grace knew he would find the paper strip she had left behind:

The past teaches us how to be present and go forward with our lives.

The truck rumbled through the village of Buckminster. The rain eased to be replaced by a settling mist in the Lincolnshire countryside's hollows and scattered hamlets. The single-toothed leather-faced haulier was not one for conversation, and for once, Grace had no desire to encourage communication.

Grace knew little of the area, and every turn brought views of much the same. Tall hedgerows, autumn bonfires and the occasional farm labourer dragging a cart, long clay pipes perched precariously in their mouths.

After a long descent into the foggy bottom of a tributary valley, the road rose, and Grace caught the silver disc of the sun, wan and weak, trying to break through.

'Stainby crossroads up ahead, missus,' grunted the driver, wiping his dribbling nose on the back of his sleeve. 'I'm bound for Witham. Bourne is straight on, and I can take you a mile or so further before I turn off if you like?'

Grace had spent the previous half-hour deciding. The truck came to a standstill, and the driver folded his arms over the steering wheel and glanced over.

'How far to Bourne?' she asked.

The driver scratched his head. 'About fifteen miles, but you'll pick up a lot more traffic coming off the Great Road; someone will gift you a lift, I'm sure.'

She looked beyond him, through the window, at the southern lane leading from the crossroads. The nearby sign-post was unreadable in the thickening fog. The outline of a child stood motionless at the edge of visibility. Grace took a sharp intake of breath.

'What's down there?' she said.

The driver frowned at her and turned to look down the empty lane.

'Trains,' he said. 'Trains to Grantham. It's Stainby station, about a mile down the lane.'

'Is it safe?' she asked.

The driver glanced back at her questioningly. 'You mean trains or Stainby?'

Grace looked out through the windscreen, and down at the faded calling card in her hand, recalling the duke's words.

The best way out is forward and through.

She turned back to the side window. The lane was empty.

'Do trains go to London from Grantham?'

'London!' cried the driver. 'Why the devil do you want to go there for? I thought you were bound for Bourne.'

Grace bit her lip with the decision, flung open the door and leapt to the ground. She collected her belongings from among the scrap metal that had shifted during the journey and wandered over to the dark signpost for Stainby station. She peered down the lane for signs of life as the driver stuck out his head from the window.

'You'll need a train to Grantham first; you can board a train to London from there. Good luck to you!'

Grace nodded, still fixated on the lane as the engine started, and the lorry drove onwards and out of hearing. Subconsciously, she raised her forearm to the horizontal, making a vertical fist and punching out into the air in front of her.

'Train ...' she whispered to herself.

The clicking of a pheasant broke her reverie, and she picked up her case and put up her umbrella. With one long look at the crossroads behind her, she turned her back on Bourne, nursing, and certainty. A bell from a church sounded in the distance as if signalling for her to start; Grace strode down the lane, knowing it would be a one-way trip to London to find the woman on the card. A one-way trip into an uncertain future—except, this time, she had a purpose.

She had a chance.

CHAPTER 4

Two days of wandering the better suburbs of London was taking its toll. Grace's money was gone, spent on the fare to the bustling city, lodgings in a safe district, and trams across the urban sprawl. She was desperate to meet with leads, hoping to find where the elusive Emeline Foster now lived, if indeed she lived at all.

It was not at 6 Cadogan Square.

The maid at the exclusive Kensington townhouse had broken the news that no such person lived at the address. Panic set in as the door closed and the awkwardness of asking wealthy passers-by for information skyrocketed her anxiety and fear of what might happen when the money ran out, and she was forced onto the streets. She looked down at the elegant umbrella, wondering if she might have to sell the precious item for a handful of copper.

Several enquiries from patrolling policemen indicated that a lady by that name had once lived and died in the vicinity, but not before reaching a great age. Where the daughter had moved to, or was now, was unknown. It was also possible that Emeline Foster no longer bore her maiden name.

Grace sat, dejected, on a park bench. The town clerk had promised to look into census reports, but with the increased workload from recording deaths from the war, it would likely be several weeks before anyone could mount a serious enquiry.

Grace's stomach rumbled with hunger, and she unwrapped the stale bread, the last of the parting gift from Mrs Tatton. The housekeeper would be enjoying buttered muffins right about now; afternoon tea in the nursery and maybe a game of charades with Oliver, in her capacity as the surrogate governess.

She picked at the bread, discarding a few crumbs of comfort to the flocking pigeons, cooing and strutting on the pavement. She didn't see the figure across the lake until she realised the other pedestrians were walking through and not around the child. Grace looked blankly across, detached, too exhausted to respond emotionally to any further panic from his presence. He would follow her wherever she went; she knew that now—a permanent reminder of her failure and grief.

'Trains ...' she whispered, thinking of the apparition on the drive, and her foolishness at the crossroads. Why hadn't she taken the road to Bourne and a safe, warm place of certainty and work? Unpleasant, yes, but better than what likely lay ahead for a young girl in a city desperate for new diversions.

The boy stared back and made an 'O' shape with his left forefinger and thumb. Grace frowned and got up, spilling the crusty bread onto the floor and dropping her umbrella. A mob of pigeons descended as she strode towards the side of the lake to see his hands more closely. The boy turned the pinched fingers and held them beneath his nose, moving the fingers back and forth as though smelling something invisible held delicately in front of his face.

Grace rushed to the water's edge, knowing the sign. She repeated it.

'Flower?' she said, enlarging and shouting the sign again in frustration. 'Why flower? I don't understand,' she called. The boy repeated the motion just as a nanny, pushing a pram, drove straight through the phantom.

'I say,' said someone behind her. 'Are you all right, miss?'

Grace turned to the policeman, mildly out of breath after the chase down the grass to the lake's edge. She looked back to the opposite shore to find the child gone.

'Actually, I'm not. You wouldn't know anyone by the name of Foster, would you? Emeline Foster by any chance?'

The policeman stuck out his lip. 'Sounds familiar—a relative, perhaps?'

'Not quite,' said Grace, showing off her bedraggled appearance. 'I'm hoping she may be able to help me. I'm new in London and rather at my wits' end trying to find her.'

'Well, I don't know an Emeline Foster, but I know where several Fosters might be at the moment.'

Grace felt her heart leap into her mouth, and she grabbed hold of the man's uniformed arms. 'Please, will you tell me where? It's urgent.'

The policeman removed her hands, nodding his intention to do so. 'I'm sorry if I misled you,' he said, 'but what I meant to say is I know where members of the family might be found now; lying in the ground, so to speak.'

Hope died as the realisation of the constable's meaning struck home. She glanced back at the water and the empty opposite shore in desperation.

'There are some mighty impressive graves over there in the cemetery, and I'm sure one or two of the newer ones on the left have Fosters in them; they are originally from Kensington, aren't they?'

Grace nodded and followed the policeman's finger to the

church tower peeping above the yellowing leaves of the beech trees that lined the park.

'Thank you,' she said, walking towards the sound of the bells. 'I'm all right now, honestly.'

'You nearly forgot your umbrella,' said the policeman as he handed it to her. 'Handsome thing, isn't it?'

After crossing the busy road, she followed the sinuous brick wall to the sprawling cemetery's iron gates. She passed a flower seller at the entrance and meandered her way through the busy thoroughfare that ran through and out onto the road leading to Waterloo station.

She made for an area of recently erected tombs and memorials. The coal-smoked grime had stained the older graves for far longer, and they grinned back haphazardly, like worn and lichen-covered teeth. Few had any remaining offerings, flowers or tokens from loved ones; long gone were those who had any remembrances of the doctors, lawyers, and bankers that lay beneath.

Lighter, cleaner stones and brighter flower-stacked memorials lay further ahead, and Grace wove in and out of the graves, searching for the right name. Unsure what she would do or find, she scanned the stones for signs of the Foster family name. She prayed as she hurried between the tombs, like a country hedge-witch on All Hallows' Eve, that Emeline's name would not be engraved upon one of them.

She caught her foot against a metal guard post to a weedy and overgrown plot and fell to the damp grass. She looked up to see bright blue asters, bunched against a large white stone at the head of a larger memorial. She crawled forwards, seeing the large initial letter, intricately carved into the pale granite:

Baron Sir George Anthony Algernon Foster

*Husband, father and Knight of the Realm who departed this life
March 17th 1896.*

A recent addition lay engraved beneath.

*And of his wife, Lady Abigail Mary Coleridge-Foster
Who laid down to rest June 23rd 1901 in the certainty of resurrection.
Also their beloved daughter, Florence Constance...*

Grace knelt at the stone, tracing the star-shaped emblem below the inscription, the same as that which adorned her umbrella. She had found the first name on the card, but not the second. Emeline Foster, wherever she was now, still lived. The fragrance of the asters came blissfully up from the crushed stems.

Fresh stems.

Grace pinched her forefinger to her thumb and wafted it beneath her nose, imitating the sign from the child in the park.

Flowers.

Grace shot up and ran back through the no man's land of stones and graves towards the flower seller.

The old woman sat, unperturbed by Grace's frantic searching through the little tin buckets until she found the blue asters.

'Please,' she said, collecting her breath and taking a bunch from the vase. 'Did anyone buy asters for the Fosters recently, today perhaps?'

The old woman rose, took them and tied them with a ribbon. 'Taking them or leaving them?' she asked.

'No, you misunderstand,' said Grace. 'I just wanted to know if anyone bought these flowers from you today.'

The old woman continued to wrap the flowers in a piece of tissue paper. 'Sixpence,' she said, holding out her hand. 'For both.'

'Both?'

'Flowers and my "deteriorating" memory,' said the old woman. 'We all have to make a livin', deary.'

Grace brought out the embroidered purse in her pocket. Three pennies and a farthing fell into the woman's hand; it was not enough. Grace looked imploringly into the flower seller's stoic and unmoved face.

'Plus the purse?' said Grace, seeing the greedy look in the woman's eyes.

The flower seller spat into her hands and grabbed at the embroidered purse. It was worth a hundred times the value, but Grace was desperate.

'You'll be wanting the daughter—the last remaining one?' said the flower seller.

'Yes,' said Grace impatiently. 'Do you know where she lives?'

'That ain't no secret,' said the old woman, thrusting the flowers into Grace's hands and pointing over the wall in a southerly direction. 'Wellington Avenue—it's the one with the bell yoke above the door; a queer place by all accounts.'

Grace ignored the opinion and breathed a sigh of relief, turning to go.

'I could tell you were looking for her,' said the flower seller, sitting down on her milking stool. 'You all look the same before you find her.'

'What do you mean?' said Grace, sure that a compliment was not forthcoming. 'What look?'

'Haunted,' said the woman, getting up to serve a customer.

Grace rushed through the gates and across the street. Several young men raised their hats, looking confused at the sight of a young woman veering through the crowd with an umbrella in one hand and scattering flower-heads on the pavement with another.

Three streets along the main thoroughfare, she halted and looked up at the sign. She turned and glanced down the row of elegant white townhouses. Running down the avenue, she glanced left and right, looking for a bell of any description. Passing several more railings and perched bicycles, she caught sight of the polished black door above which hung a tarnished brass bell set in a swinging yoke and attached to a fine chain.

Grace mounted the steps and peered at her breathless and unkempt reflection in the shining brass nameplate.

E. Foster
Strictly by Appointment Only

Etiquette frowned upon introductions outside of calling times, usually between three and five in the afternoon. Still, Grace smoothed her hair in the metallic reflection and removed the duke's card from her pocket, unsure whether to use the heavy knocker or the bell chain.

She reached out, still holding the flowers, and pulled the chain. The bell swung in its yoke, making an unpleasant hollow sound. After several moments a housekeeper appeared at a crack in the door, frowning down at the frocked hedge sparrow on the steps.

'Don't be ringing that,' said the woman, gruffly. 'Civilised folk use the door knocker.' She took another dismissive look. 'Trades' entrance is round the back.'

The door slammed shut, and Grace's prepared words died on her lips, along with her hope of gaining access to the house.

She put the card in her teeth, lifted the knocker and rapped it repeatedly on the gloss ebony paintwork.

The housekeeper returned sharply. 'What do you want? Mistress is with a client and won't be disturbed.'

Grace spat out the card.

'I'm here to see Lady Emeline Foster,' she said, picking up the card and handing it to the housekeeper.

'Crikey,' said the housekeeper, wiping the card down her lace shawl. 'Who'd you steal this off, a corpse?'

'It was given to me,' said Grace, 'as a token of esteem and chivalry.'

The housekeeper snorted.

'I have other references ...' said Grace, fumbling in her bag. She offered the flowers and papers to the housekeeper.

The housekeeper widened the door, and a sweet smell of incense escaped to the coal-smoked street. 'You here about the job?'

'Any job,' said Grace, trying her best to look employable. 'But I'm a governess by training.'

'Wait here,' said the housekeeper, closing the door. She re-emerged after several minutes. Grace's hopes of entry sank as she saw the housekeeper's lips purse into an appearance she knew all too well; a look reserved for hawkers, undesirables, and those not suitably socially acceptable to gain entry.

'Mistress won't be seeing you, not today, or on any other,' she said, glancing away and shutting the door slowly behind her.

CHAPTER 5

Grace played a final gambit and jabbed the end of the umbrella into the doorway, just as the door was about to shut. The polished oak juddered and rebounded as the housekeeper kicked at the silver capped tip, trying to dislodge the impertinence and the object at the same time. She tried in vain to close the door as Grace lunged and countered with the makeshift fencing sword.

'Get away,' said the housekeeper. 'I'll call the police!'

Grace jammed her foot into the narrow slit of the doorway as she removed the umbrella.

'Please, I beg you,' she said, showing the flustered housekeeper the umbrella handle. The woman glanced at the emblazoned star emblem on the cane and stopped forcing the door from the inside.

Grace knew she had one last chance to breach the housekeeper and gain access to the house.

'Give her this,' she said, 'and the message I was meant to deliver.'

'What message?'

'That one who now returns it is worthier than the one to whom she gave it, over thirty years ago,' said Grace.

'You are a saucy one, talking like that in earshot of your betters; very full of yourself, I'm sure,' said the housekeeper, snatching the umbrella. 'Who gave you such a message?'

'The Duke of Rutland,' said Grace, straightening and gaining confidence. 'He presented it to me, and the card, at our parting.'

The housekeeper's eyes widened. 'Thought he was dead,' she said, looking nervously inside. 'So did she.'

'Please,' said Grace. 'This is my last chance, and maybe theirs, to let go of the past and move on.' She looked into the softening and understanding face of the housekeeper, who nodded.

'I'll relay the message,' she said, '*if* you'll kindly remove your foot from the door.'

Grace stepped back as the door clicked shut and set the bell above gently swinging. She waited expectantly, like a dog waiting for a door to open and food to be thrown out. The idea of food set off her stomach once more and the thought of the hopeless, hungry hike back to her distant lodgings for a final night in a bed before the landlord evicted her in the morning.

The door remained shut, and she stared at the knocker and the bell, wondering whether to try once more. The housekeeper had her old references from the institute, however pointless they were now going to be. She glanced down at the frayed edges of her weather-beaten skirt and scuffed blistering boots and sat on the steps, head in hands.

Why had she given up on the almshouses? or even the herring-canning factory; at least she would have been safe. She glanced at the passers-by, beggar-like, who were oblivious to the misery playing out as they passed with a raise of their hat or cane. Several minutes passed, and she got to her sore feet, ready for the trek back across London to collect her trunk and make plans for the day to come.

At that moment, the housekeeper opened the door. Grace turned, ready to spring up the steps like an expectant hound. The woman raised an eyebrow and cocked her head, beckoning her in.

'Wipe your feet,' she said. 'I polished these tiles yesterday, and I don't want waifs and strays making my life any harder than it needs to be. Follow me; there's one already here for the position, so don't get your hopes up. Her Ladyship will call me when it is time for your turn.'

Grace followed the housekeeper into a dark and bohemian central lobby. Luxurious burgundy curtains clung to the ceiling and hung from tasselled pelmets against a backdrop of flocked silk wallpaper, while a richly furnished chaise lay along one wall, below the wooden back of a turned mirror.

'Wait here,' said the housekeeper, disappearing through the inner door, 'and touch nothing.'

Grace breathed in the intoxicating incense and marvelled at the rich furnishings of the house. Nervously, she tapped the umbrella tip on the patterned tiles. She stopped herself and glanced down, realising she stood within the centre of an emblazoned star, identical to the engraving on the family tomb and the crest on the umbrella in her hand. A gap in the floor to ceiling velvet along one side of the octagonal lobby showed a room beyond, and Grace crept forwards to peer through the slit.

A young woman of about Grace's age and complexion stood staring back from a dim, gas-lit parlour. The woman raised a finger to her lips and raised the other to beckon her through.

Grace jumped back and looked in the direction the housekeeper was likely to appear from at any moment. She drew aside one of the velvet curtains and stepped through to the now empty room.

It was a parlour in name only and richly furnished with oriental and mystical symbolism. A wide mahogany table lay beneath a blown-glass oil lamp casting its diffuse scarlet glow across the rest of the room. An African phallic carving stood erect at its centre next to a burning incense jar. Grace thought little of the threat of the smouldering myrrh as she turned to see the long room continue for over thirty feet. The far wall ended at a pair of enormous door curtains next to a stuffed upright tiger. The creature's eyes glittered with deathless reflection, permanently fixed by the skilled taxidermist in its last moment of fruitless attack.

Grace caught the passage of a retreating hand through the curtains to another room beyond. A forefinger twisted and beckoned Grace onwards before disappearing through to what lay beyond.

Just a quick peep out of curiosity and then a rapid return to the lobby, she thought, tip-toeing to stand before the dark plush drapes.

She parted the curtains to discover another set almost immediately beyond. The dense curtains covered both ends of a recessed casement door with just enough room to stand between them. Her heart pounded in her chest with the thought of being caught, but she slipped through, closing the material so securely behind that it plunged the tiny space into darkness.

Her eyes adjusted and pinpointed flickering candlelight squinting through the narrowest of partings in the opposing curtains. Grace put her face to the soft material and looked through, wide-eyed, at the two seated figures in the room beyond.

What she saw next would remain a pivotal moment for the rest of her life.

'Once for yes,' said a beautiful raven-haired woman in her late forties beneath tightly closed eyes and furrowed brow. Grace marvelled at the beguiling sensual silk of her floor-length dress, and the crystal-studded lace veil covering the upper part of her powdered face. The woman's head bent, unseeing, over her bare and extended arms gripped tightly around the plain brown woollen sleeves of a nervous-looking woman seated opposite. The tense, fidgeting person stared at the tendon-tight fingers clasped leech-like above her own calloused hands.

'Concentrate, Mrs Jellicoe!' commanded the veiled woman, deep and resonant, her eyes firmly shut.

Mrs Jellicoe locked her attention on a small brass bell, suspended by barely visible silken threads within a yoke of delicate ebony. Its smooth carrying handle, firmly nestled in the centre of the lace-draped octagonal side table, reflected the candlelight of the dimly lit salon.

Grace stared at the private seance taking place, and at the impressively feminine but dominant medium sharply exhaling with the effort of forming a connection with the spirit world. Her brightly painted blood-red lips twitched in harmony with a single bobbing candle fluttering on a nearby dresser in front of another turned mirror. It cast flickering shadows across a monstrously carved fireplace, giving movement to the writhing mythical beasts etched into its dark wood. Mrs Jellicoe trembled, fixated on the bell.

'Once for yes,' repeated the medium sternly.

Her eyes scanned the inside of her eyelids, as though in dream-fitted sleep. She exhaled with a spittle-ridden sigh, and her hands slipped down and into the client's curled and shaking fingers.

Someone, from beyond, had answered the call, and the bell twitched in its web-like cradle.

'H ... Henry?' whimpered Mrs Jellicoe.

'Hush!' hissed the medium. 'Do not speak. I promised a single question only—charity has its bounds, as does my strength.'

Grace stared through the darkness and shadows at the bell. It swung with minute jerks, as though something unseen was tugging on its connected silken threads.

The face of the medium contorted into further creases, dragging in age-worn lines not visible before. Sweat beaded upon her veiled brow and Grace saw her eyes tighten, pulling together the finely plucked eyebrows and shutting out this world to see better in the next. Unseen hands thrust themselves into the soft silk of the medium's abdomen, forcing the air from her lungs and buckling her backwards into the button-backed high chair. Grace could just make out the handprints on the silk as they released, leaving the medium able to draw a precious breath of air.

The seal between worlds shattered, and Grace covered her mouth to stifle the gasp of surprise. The medium was no fairground charlatan; Grace could feel the presence within the room.

Mrs Jellicoe whimpered as she was dragged violently forwards by the woman's vice-like grip.

'No!—please!' said Mrs Jellicoe, frightened and desperate to be released.

'Once for yes,' repeated the medium through pursed lips. 'Hurry! Henry Jellicoe, were you innocent of the crimes for which you were hanged?'

Mrs Jellicoe's gaze shifted to the staccato shudder of the medium's head, then back to the glittering bell, gently swinging in the candlelit centre of the table.

Grace saw something materialise from the shadow beyond the bell, unseen by the transfixed widow. A sudden tug on one of the silken support threads set the bell into a more aggressive motion, and the bell sounded. Grace covered her mouth to stifle a gasp as the form of a hand retreated to the shadows to join the distinct silhouette of the young woman she had followed into the parlour.

The widow sat rigid with the shock of being in the presence of what she believed to be her hanged husband. She stared, transfixed upon the bell now coming to rest. The answer was clear; Henry Jellicoe was a good man, a good husband, wrongly accused and arrested by being in the wrong place at the wrong time. She relaxed back into the hard leather armchair, pulling against the grip of the veiled woman opposite.

The medium resisted, drawing Mrs Jellicoe back into an upright position. It was not over.

Grace saw sharp and painted nails bite into the widow's exposed wrist, as the veiled woman struggled to hold on to the joining between worlds. Mrs Jellicoe flinched with the sting of the small cuts to her skin and glanced up in dread to see the awkward movements of the medium's head shaking from side to side as though foretelling the final truth.

The bell sounded for a second time.

The widow writhed and jerked her hands free to her face in horror, disentangling herself from the clutches of the medium and severing the connection. Scarlet, raking welts appeared on the poor woman's wrists from the woman opposite, who attempted to cling on to the world beyond. For a sudden, frightening moment the medium opened her heavily dilated eyes and stared beyond the bell cradle into the space beyond. The ghostly form of the young woman leaned forwards, desperate to make itself known to her searching eyes, but sadly seeing no recognition. The spirit turned and stared pitifully at the far curtains, raising a pointed finger directly towards the hidden trespasser. Grace swung round, setting off the outer curtains, ready to escape back to the parlour, the lobby and the outside. She fought with the thick drapes which did not yield or part, then turned round to the room to see the spirit look tenderly at the sweat-stained silk of the medium, still trying to discern with mortal eyes what Grace could see clearly from some distance.

The parting of the two women's hands signalled the end of the seance, and the medium convulsed back into her chair, back into the arms of the physical world. After a moment, she spoke.

'The housekeeper will show you out, Mrs Jellicoe,' she whispered, rubbing at her stomach and struggling to compose herself after the exertion. 'I have my answer as to your honesty and integrity, and you have yours.' She frowned and glanced across at the settling curtains as Grace leaned sideways out of view.

Grace heard the widow sobbing. 'Thank you. I ... I need time to ...'

'Yes,' said the medium. 'Time to process and move on. All will be well.'

Grace peeped back to see the widow dabbing her eyes and wrists with a handkerchief.

'Have I done enough, ma'am? Will you—?'

The medium raised her veil upon her dark and plaited hair. 'Yes, Mrs Jellicoe,' she said, picking up and shaking a servant's handbell. 'My client will learn about your good character in tomorrow's post. His representative will be in touch.'

'Thank you,' said Mrs Jellicoe. 'God bless you, Your Ladyship.'

Grace tingled with the sudden recognition of who the beguiling medium was—the second name on the card. Unmarried, and still bearing the family name, Emeline Foster had inherited her mother's title.

Lady Emeline Foster grimaced as she sat upright, clutching her ribs, and held out her hand to signal the end of the audience.

The widow rose, stealing a final glance at the stationary brass bauble within the web of silk, as the housekeeper opened the interior door with a worried look on her face. She placed a silver tray nervously on the table next to the spirit bell, careful not to set it swinging. Grace saw the familiar references upon the tray, crowned with the calling card.

'I'm sorry, ma'am,' began the housekeeper, surely ready to impart the knowledge that the next appointment was missing, presumably somewhere in the house.

Grace cursed herself as she fumbled for the opening to the parlour behind. Perhaps she could say she was desperate to use the downstairs facilities and had become lost in the process?

All that effort to get inside, only to be thrown out as a liar, thief or worse, she thought.

'Whatever it is, Edith,' said Lady Foster, 'it can wait. Show Mrs Jellicoe out.'

'Very good, ma'am,' said the housekeeper, likely desperate to search the upper rooms for the impudent miscreant loose in the house.

From behind the heavy door curtains to the adjoining room, Grace heard the retreat of the sobbing widow, and the brief bustle of the Mayfair thoroughfare as the polished front door was opened. A shaft of sunlight illuminated the seated medium. Her face turned towards the bell and space beyond, searching unsuccessfully for the fading spirit as she reached out her shaking hand into the beam of light.

'Flo ...'

The solid lock of the closing front door echoed through the Georgian townhouse, extinguishing the sunlight and plunging the room back into near darkness.

The medium retracted her hand and lifted her veil, shuffling upright as the housekeeper came in. She reached over to the floor, hidden from Grace's view, and retrieved the ebony and silver umbrella.

'Begging your pardon, ma'am,' said Edith, 'but shall I find your next appointment?'

'No, I will do so myself,' said Lady Foster, with a wry smile.

Lady Foster rose and shuffled to the Bavarian carved oak fireplace with a wince of pain, leaning on the umbrella for support. The creases dropped away from the silk gown and clung to her perfectly proportioned curves, as she glanced across at several fading photographs, barely visible in the candlelight. They reflected with sepia images of younger faces and past times. She held out her left hand behind her and crooked a finger towards Grace's hiding place.

'You can come out now, Grace Meadows,' said Lady Emeline Foster. 'Eavesdropping on the dead is very dangerous, not to mention undignified.'

CHAPTER 6

Grace ground her teeth in shame, pushing through the curtain and gently drawing them behind her. The housekeeper reddened in the face.

'I told you to stay put,' she said, 'in the lobby.'

'I've only been there for a moment,' said Grace, unconvincingly. 'The beautiful blonde-haired lady beckoned for me to follow her, through the parlour.'

Lady Foster turned and looked upon Grace's smudged and hungry appearance. She glanced at the housekeeper who looked back, uncomfortable.

'There is no one that fits that description in the house,' said Lady Foster. 'What did you hear, just now?'

'I only heard the widow get up and—'

'Only the living tell lies, Miss Meadows,' said Lady Foster, pointing for her to sit in the chair vacated by Mrs Jellicoe. 'You have been there long enough to learn the fate of the poor woman's husband and that the position you seek has now been filled.'

Grace sidled over to stand by the vacant chair, aware of the woman's powerful and curious gaze.

'Lying makes you ugly, and old before your time,' continued Lady Foster.

'But you did it, just now, for example—' said Grace, realising the faux pas all too late.

Lady Foster widened her eyes at the petulance. She stepped forwards into the sunbeam streaming in from the antechamber connecting the lobby, and made her way to the dresser. The candlelight glittered in the black inkwells of her dilated eyes as she snuffed out the flame.

'Leave us, Edith,' said Lady Foster. 'Cancel the rest of my appointments for today.'

The housekeeper nodded and stepped out of the room, closing only one door to allow the light to illuminate the salon. Grace heard the retreating footsteps echoing in the empty house.

'How dare you call me a liar in front of my staff!' roared Lady Foster.

Grace breathed deeply to control her fight-or-flight emotion as the voice of the duke came back to her:

Speak plainly, and she'll help you.

Grace stood her ground.

'She asked you a question, one that she didn't get a truthful answer to.'

'I offered a joining with a spirit, on charitable terms, to a poor woman whose reputation is in tatters through no fault of her own,' countered Lady Foster.

'Yes, but not with who she thought. I saw who you let through; the hand pulling on the threads was a young woman, not a hanged man.' Grace reached out and pointed to the bell on the table behind the irate lady of the house.

'Only a sensitive or innocent would know that,' she said, coming to stand uncomfortably close to Grace. The perfume, so close, was heady with spice and musk. 'You see things that others do not?'

Grace swallowed hard. 'Ever since a train of events that led me to you,' she said. 'Why do you risk such trials—are they not dangerous?' Grace glanced down at the woman's hand, holding her ribs.

'Yes, they are,' said Lady Foster. 'I do so to test the integrity and honesty of broken women. I do not introduce them to my clients based solely on their word alone. My talents help the unfortunate, Miss Meadows; that is what I do.' Grace noticed the pounding of the woman's heart against the silk as she spoke again.

'And now you come to me for help; sent from one I thought long dead.'

Grace glanced up into the beautiful and ageless face. Perfection lay there, except in the wrinkles around her neck, and the slight hint of crow's feet at the margins of her sharply painted eyes. Even Lady Foster could not truly conquer age.

'You haven't answered my question,' said Grace, meeting the steely gaze. 'Why the deception?'

'Being sensitive to spirits is more than just conjuring the dead, Miss Meadows; it's as much about comforting those left behind,' said Lady Foster, releasing Grace from her gaze and twisting like a snake into the button-backed armchair. 'Marjorie Jellicoe needs to move on with her life and rebuild a tattered reputation—so does her husband, Henry; or what's left of his miserable life at any rate.'

'He's not dead?' said Grace.

'No,' said Lady Foster, easing into a comfortable position. 'The man they buried was a destitute, a blasted and broken soldier, framed and hanged in his name for Henry's wicked crimes. You don't need spirits to discover that truth; gossip is rife in the markets if you know where to listen.'

'Where is Henry Jellicoe now, then?'

Lady Foster extended a finger and plucked at the bell thread, setting it swinging gently. 'Practising his grave-robbing, arson and foul chemistry elsewhere most likely—I have no idea, and I don't care. He'll soon be running from the vengeful spirit of the man he framed for murder; the same man he exchanged clothes with before plying him with free liquor, if the rumour is to be believed. The only good news is that I sense Henry Jellicoe is close to passing over through some sudden act of desperate violence.'

She turned to Grace and kicked out the chair opposite, motioning for her to sit.

'You are correct,' she said. 'I lied, but I sweetened it. Her husband took everything, and Marjorie Jellicoe is close to ruin, through no fault of her own. I helped her, and what good would it be to inform her that her nefarious scoundrel of a husband caused the deaths of not one man, but two?'

Grace sat down and looked through the silken threads of the spirit bell. The intricate glistening lines, beautifully arranged with the brass bauble, spider-like, at its centre.

'What webs you weave ...' she began. 'Will you be able to find her a situation?'

'Yes, the very same you lied to gain entrance for,' said Lady Foster. 'I know she is innocent of anything her husband was involved with, and my word will be enough for an intro-duction. His face is ingrained in my memory; she still has feelings for the blaggard.' Grace watched as the woman looked distantly through the bell threads.

'You can't see the blonde-haired lady, can you?' said Grace.

'No,' said Lady Foster. 'Or any spirit, not now my inner eye is opened. I should have stayed innocently sensitive, like you.' She turned, and Grace saw the look of sorrow in her grief-stricken face. 'Don't be tempted to try this line of work,' she said. 'That's advice I'd give my younger self.'

'Why the bell and the threads?' asked Grace.

'Communication. I thought someone with your creden-tials would understand.'

Lady Foster lifted the handle of the bell yoke and held it in front of the sunbeam. The tightly strung threads sparkled. 'Silk is one of the few substances that a spirit can interact with or be contained by.'

'Like your gown?' said Grace. 'I saw the blow to your side—'

'The door to the dead can open without warning, and something else was desperate to come through—a boy trying to communicate, but not with me.'

Grace swallowed hard. 'If you know how to summon them,' she said, 'can you also banish those that appear, unwanted?'

Lady Foster raised a manicured eyebrow and replaced the bell yoke into its socket on the table.

'Spirits only appear for one of two reasons, unless they are directly brought back through death's doorway by forming a connection called *the joining*. The first reason is vengeance, like the spirit our friend Henry Jellicoe will shortly encounter with any luck. Hate and anger are powerful seal-breakers.'

'And the second?' asked Grace.

'A spirit can be bound to a place if it has some unfinished business or seeks to reclaim something or someone,' said Lady Foster. 'They often impart or communicate something important to the living.' She studied the tense young woman opposite. 'Which of these scenarios is plaguing you, I wonder?'

'I do not know,' said Grace. 'He appears to me when I am most anxious.'

'Who is he—your illegitimate child?'

Grace looked away and gripped the arm of the chair, regaining her composure.

'No,' she said. 'His name was Arthur. He was my handsome little deaf ward until he died.'

Lady Foster folded her arms.

'He has powerful feelings for you; I sense it.' She leaned over and reached out an open hand. Grace glanced down, unsure whether to take it. Lady Foster reassured her with a smile. 'Would it comfort you to know he is not here for vengeance and is trying to tell you something?'

'But why?' said Grace. 'All it does is remind me of my failure to protect him, bringing my grief and guilt to the surface.' She rubbed at her wrists.

Grace placed her hand upon the smooth porcelain hand below. The burn-marked scar was clearly visible, and Lady Foster rubbed at the healing blister with a profound look of sympathy. Grace flinched with the intimacy, then relaxed as the touch became comforting.

'I couldn't save him,' she whispered, aware of her openness in front of a total stranger. She felt a little of the burden lift with the sharing; the noblewoman was a keen listener and counsellor.

'Take your time,' whispered Lady Foster.

'The fire was too intense, and Arthur couldn't hear the alarm. It's all my fault for not checking the lamps. I'd received the telegram from his sister about him being killed in action and went out into the garden just for half an hour, maybe longer I don't recall—'

'You don't need to say any more,' said Lady Foster. 'It was an accident.'

She laid a hand on Grace's matted blonde hair, smoothing it with words of comfort. She offered the other hand, and Grace took it.

'We all have our scars, Grace,' she said, gently twisting her wrists until they were visible. 'Some metaphorical, and others physical.' Grace glanced down at the white translucent scar tissue on Lady Foster's wrists, a testament to the many cuts made in the distant past.

'Yes,' said Lady Foster. 'I understand more than you think.

Pain banishes the past and what it brings forth, for a little while. But it always returns, unless we deal with it and find the strength to accept it.'

'It's so hard to forgive myself,' said Grace. 'I don't deserve it.'

'I think the child is giving you permission to forgive what hurts you, but not to forget what it has taught you.' Lady Foster joined her exposed wrist to Grace's. 'We will speak of this to no one, is that understood?'

Grace withdrew her hands and nodded. She glanced over at the sepia pictures in silver frames on the mantelpiece.

'The woman on the left in the oval frame?—she was the one that was here.'

Grace pointed to a faded image of two young debutantes posing in front of a large country house. The standing figure was dark-haired and bare-footed, and moodily looked out, not engaged in posing for the picture—Lady Foster as a younger woman. The left figure perched upon a fallen oak tree and Grace saw the blonde-haired beauty smiling back, just as the spirit had done so.

'Who is she?' asked Grace.

Lady Foster moved to the mantelpiece and lifted the oval frame. 'Florence,' she said. 'She was my sister and the joy of my life. This photograph was taken when the old oak came down in the park when we lived in the country. Is she still youthful?'

Grace nodded, recalling the face of the spirit in the parlour, and behind the bell. 'A little older, but recognisable all the same.'

Lady Foster replaced the oval frame. 'She died the following autumn.'

She winced from a spasm in her ribs. 'Aches and pains plague me, and the spirits I can no longer see.' Grace helped her back to the button-backed armchair, knocking over the umbrella perched on the side.

'He gave you this?' said Lady Foster, pointing for Grace to sit in the chair opposite.

Grace handed her the calling card from her papers on the tray. 'Yes, and this. He said you would help me.'

Lady Foster looked down at the word on the back of the card:

Tomorrow

'He was incredibly handsome, and I was just a silly infatuated teenager ...'

Grace pressed the issue. 'The duke said he was righting a wrong by sending me. He seemed to suggest he wasn't worthy of you?' She sat back, nervous with over-reaching in her familiarity. 'I'm sorry if—'

Lady Foster smiled and held up her hand to stop the apology.

'I thought that particular wound had healed long ago,' she said. 'It was I that wasn't worthy. I was wild, unladylike and about to elope with a man twice my age. I don't blame him anymore, and he did the right thing for his family by not meeting me at the station and marrying the woman his parents approved of.' She sighed, looking Grace intently in the eye.

'And now, he sends you to me. A girl who can see the spirits of the dead, sitting in the house of one who brings them forth. Why are you here?'

'I lost my previous two situations because I allowed my worries and past to interfere with my work,' said Grace. 'I have nowhere else to go, and the money the duke gave me is gone. I need a situation, and I'll do anything.'

'Be careful with that final sentiment; it's likely to land you in all sorts of misadventure,' said Lady Foster, squinting, eyes lit with a twinkle of mischief. 'You are a governess, one used to teaching deaf and dumb children to speak?'

'I prefer the term mute,' said Grace. 'There is little to prove they have any less intelligence than those born without the disadvantage of speech.'

'Don't you mean advantage?' said Lady Foster, frowning in the shadow.

'Language is complex and enriched by much more than what we say. Facial expressions, gestures, even the way we stand, for example. My specialism is to bring out the voice within, whether that be vocal or by any other means.'

'And what would you do to encourage a silent child to speak again, one that once sang like a nightingale?' said Lady Foster, taking a silver key from the mantelpiece and unlocking a nearby bureau.

'One that chooses not to speak, rather than one limited by physical misfortune?' said Grace.

Lady Foster nodded, withdrawing a tiny antique hourglass and setting it up on the table next to the bell. 'How quickly could it be done?'

Grace continued, curious as to the new addition to her side. 'Speed plays no part; it comes later, bursting out and speeding up once the child allows it—like your doorway to the dead.'

Lady Foster flinched with the reminder. 'Go on.'

'I must gain the child's trust and confidence. Without it, I can do nothing. Whatever is causing the silence lies within the child to reveal, not for someone, even as trained as I am, to force it into the light.'

Lady Foster sat down, staring at the hourglass. 'And if the child has little time to live?'

Grace frowned. 'You know of such a child?'

'Yes,' she said. 'You said you would do anything to gain a situation; what would you do to save a child in your care?'

Grace paused, trying to comprehend the question.

'To atone for my mistake?' she said. 'Whatever is within me—give my very life if necessary.'

Lady Foster lowered her veil and reached across, gripping her hand and abruptly turning the hourglass with the other. 'You have until the sand runs out to convince me you have the strength for the task I speak of, or I will throw you back into the street. Do you understand?'

Grace struggled to free herself from the sudden grasp and looked over at the grey sand filtering into a small pyramid within the lower glass.

'Shut your eyes!' commanded the medium, before closing her own, hyperventilating and beginning a new ritual.

Grace froze and obeyed.

'Show me the past,' said Lady Foster, between breaths. 'Show me the teaching of one who does not speak.'

Grace felt the lightest of urges as Lady Foster made the connection. The gentle nudge to recall the institute where she had learned and loved. She thought of Christopher in his soldier uniform, setting off at the dock.

'Not him,' said Lady Foster. 'He has passed on; I sense this. Show me the children—focus on the school.'

The urge to recall happier times rose strongly and washed away the intangible memory of her fiancé. She felt the medium's observance as she recalled the early years of her training and saw the rows of silent children and the repetition of her gestures and mouth placements, mirrored in the figures at their tiny wooden benches. Grace heard them once again, hoarsely and without refinement, expelling air through unfamiliar shapes of their lips and tongues, trying to form the sounds of speech. She tenderly recalled the beautiful and often painful transition in their loving faces from silence to sound and the sad day of their graduation, never to be seen again, but ready to face the noisy world outside of the institute on their terms.

She squinted open an eye to discover Lady Foster was staring back, oblivious to the physical world. Her pupils dilated so wide as to obscure most of the whites of her eyes. They blinked back, unseeing, and Grace closed her eyes once more as the memories returned, watched by the medium a few feet away.

She saw the kindly face of her beloved mentor, congratulating her for achieving her ambition and readying for the sad farewell—Pennington and a new life, waiting for Christopher to return from France. Her heart leapt with the first meeting with little Arthur.

Grace stiffened, unable to scan past the memory. Something else was controlling the narrative, and Grace could not tell if it was Lady Foster or something else.

'Don't fight,' said Lady Foster. 'It is necessary.'

Grace recalled the beautiful young boy being chased around the long table in the grand hall of the house by the new governess, her blonde hair streaming out of control as she collapsed in a fit of giggles and exhaustion in the centre of the room. Arthur sat down between her gown and parted legs, panting like a young buck.

'R ... Rabb ... it?' he said, overworking his mouth to form the word.

Grace glanced down at the past and whispered the recalled words from her memory:

'Very good, Arthur. Ma-ma will be pleased. Tomorrow I will teach you another animal, but perhaps one not so quick ...'

The young boy was scooped up into the arms of the formal gown and tickled until a joyous and untainted sound emerged from his lungs and through his innocent voice box.

Grace felt an overwhelming desire to remain, but the memory changed.

Something else was coming.

The image faded, but Grace saw herself still splayed on the floor, desperately searching around the room. Her senses sharpened, and she smelled the acrid smoke coming from the nursery wing.

'I can't get up,' said Grace, fidgeting in her armchair in the London townhouse, a hundred miles away from the room in her memory. 'I need to sound the alarm, get to the bell, wake everyone up ...' Her heartbeat thundered in her chest as she saw the first tendrils of flame enter the room. The tongues of fire slithered beneath the doorway, and emerged behind the tapestries and mirrors, making their way to her—guided by the sole purpose to ring and trap her.

She pulled away from Lady Foster and opened her eyes, glancing across at the hourglass still pouring out its contents, moments away from emptying.

'No!' said the voice of Lady Foster. 'Do not fear it. It is but a shade of what was or what may come to pass; I must see!'

Grace looked back in alarm as the room in her mind changed. The medium no longer gripped her hands, but that of a young girl whose pallid face stared back desperately for help as the fire consumed the walls, floors and ceiling, no longer the bohemian salon but a wide, circular panelled room. A spiral suspended staircase swung majestically up and out of sight, wreathed in flame. Silken threads and rope wound through and across its intricate railings, and many bells tinkled and swung freely with the updraught of the all-consuming conflagration.

'No!' said Grace. 'We have to get out—I can't move!'

'Wait,' said the voice of Lady Foster from out of the

flames. 'The sand is still running, and the moment of your trial is at hand.'

'The fire,' screamed Grace. 'I must get her out!'

Grace heard a loud snap of metal from above. A wrought-iron chandelier with a burning oil lamp hung on a mighty chain, wrapped in silken cloth. The chain broke, and the heavy circular cage tilted, suspended only by its outer silken sheath.

Grace looked down in horror to see the face of Arthur, solemn and calm, gripping her hands. The marks on her wrists lit up with burning bracelets of fire.

'No, please! Get out; you have to—'

The boy released a single hand and pinched his forefinger and thumb together, just as he had across the pond in the park earlier that day. Grace looked over at the hourglass, now appearing within the inferno of the memory room in its final moments of spilling. Time slowed, and she saw the single grains tumble onto the pinnacle of sand. The fire in the room gave off no heat and writhed in slowing, sinuous flame, licking at the staircase and the web of threads. The bells rocked slowly and deepened their peal. Grace heard her breath clearly as she looked down at the boy signing with a single hand below.

His pinched fingers drifted towards the bridge of his tiny nose as though underwater. From the side of his nose, high on his pale cheek, the fingers brushed across the bridge to the other side. He repeated the sign, mouthing the word slowly and laboriously:

ROSE ...

'Rose?' said Grace, watching as the little boy nodded and put his fingers to his lips, kissed them and reached out, tenderly, towards her face. Grace felt the lightest of touches before the remaining grains of the hourglass emptied, restoring time to its natural order.

From above came a great tearing sound as the silk wrappings of the chandelier tore apart, sending the great weight of wrought iron down upon her. Grace threw out her burning hands, pushing the spirit from the impending calamity, and screamed as the free-falling mass of metal came crashing down.

She shut her eyes, just as the hourglass emptied.

CHAPTER 7

Grace tugged her hand free and instinctively covered her head, cowering into a ball within the confines of the leather armchair. She opened an eye to see her host's drawn face, back in the half-lit salon, safe in the sumptuous surroundings belonging to the medium of Mayfair. She clutched her shoulders, trying to make herself as small as possible.

'It's all right, Grace. It's over,' said Lady Foster, retrieving a small handbell from beneath her armchair. She rang for the housekeeper, and Grace assumed the worst. Not only had she been traumatised and tested by the twisted woman on the calling card, but now she would be thrown out into the street to face a desperate future.

The housekeeper arrived promptly.

'Bring some tea, Edith,' said Lady Foster, 'and some caraway cake.'

'Very good, Your Ladyship. Shall I turn the mirrors and open the curtains?'

'Yes, air the room too—Miss Meadows is quite flushed.'

The housekeeper drew back the curtains and opened one

of the large bay windows. The view spread wide onto the leaf-strewn lawn. A gust of wind moved the light opaque muslin curtains, billowing like phantoms, ready to commune with the medium within. Edith bobbed into a curtsy and respectfully closed the door of the salon.

'What was it I last saw?' said Grace, relaxing into a more dignified position. She blinked with the sudden light, dim as it was on such a cloudy autumn day.

'What has also been in my mind this past year,' said Lady Foster. 'The future.'

Grace wiped the sweat from her brow. 'Whose?'

Lady Foster leaned on the umbrella and got up stiffly. 'I don't know,' she said. 'But I know that one of us may not survive, at least unchanged, if things are not done to prevent it.'

'But how would we know if in trying to prevent this fire we wouldn't actually cause it?' said Grace.

'We don't,' said Lady Foster. 'But I am out of options.'

'I don't understand,' said Grace. 'I came to get my life and career back on track. Have I done enough to convince you I am trustworthy and competent to get a more conventional situation?'

Lady Foster shuffled to an antique world globe in a far corner and rotated the lid to reveal a crystal decanter and glasses.

'You have,' she said. 'I have looked into your spirit, and can't imagine how you live with such torments. My struggles pale into insignificance, and they are indeed a burden to me. One thing is clear—you understood the child's sign, where I could not.'

'He said "Rose"—is that the name of the silent child in peril?'

'It is.' Lady Foster poured a large measure of brandy into a crystal tumbler. 'Rose Hemingworth-Ferris, only living daughter of Captain Charles Henry Ferris Esquire.' She glugged at the amber liquor, spilling an Armagnac tear from the side of her mouth. 'But for how long?' she whispered, wiping away the liquid.

'You said she was sickly, unwilling to speak?' said Grace, hearing the housekeeper emerge from the door behind. Lady Foster nodded for Edith to remove the hourglass and bell frame for the tray.

'Yes,' said Lady Foster. 'A debilitating illness connected to the madness and death of her mother nigh on twelve months ago; she stopped speaking around the same time.' Grace's stomach rumbled with the smell and sight of the freshly cut caraway cake, regal behind the rising steam of the china teapot. 'The house is unquiet, and she might be experiencing or encountering things unfamiliar, adding to the trauma.'

Lady Foster invited her to eat and opened a brass-inlaid wooden box containing thinly rolled cigars. Grace grabbed a plate and rattled among the cake with the silver tongs, still unsettled by the earlier experience.

'You think she sees spirits?'

Lady Foster nodded. 'Her age, illness, and emotional state caused by her mother's passing would suggest a strong possibility. Unless you are sensitive, like yourself, the only other way is by using strong narcotics or when close to death—at those times the veil between worlds is thinnest and most malleable. Charles Ferris is not in the best of health, and I have committed to care for the girl's education, and governorship, should anything happen to him. He trusts me, and I knew his mother, once upon a time.'

Lady Foster smoothed a hand down the gentle curve of her stomach. 'I know little of how to raise a child, least of all how to teach them without speaking. I think someone with your empathy and communication skills could make her understand and not be frightened of the shadows.'

'Why do you turn the mirrors?' said Grace, lunging at the cake and forcing it into her mouth while Lady Foster's back was turned. The ache in her stomach cried out for haste.

'Superstition, mostly,' she said, lifting a pearl-inlaid lighter and sparking a flame into life. She leaned into the brightly burning gas and puffed at the cigarillo.

'An old wives' tale about spirits becoming trapped in the quicksilver, like putting down grave-dust in front of doorways to prevent the spirit from re-entering. It doesn't hurt to be cautious, I suppose. It may well be that old tales keep in memory things once needful to know.'

Grace reached across to pour the tea into the delicate porcelain cups.

Lady Foster winced and raised her hand to her chest.

'Are you unwell?' said Grace, rising to be of service. 'Shall I fetch the housekeeper?'

She shook her head and lifted a silver pill case from the mantelpiece. The carriage clock chimed for two o'clock.

'My heart,' she said. 'It does not run as smoothly as that German timepiece.' Lady Foster grimaced as she swallowed the pills and replaced the case behind one of the picture frames.

'Years of exertion, excess and experimentation with certain opiates,' she said, turning to Grace. 'I recommend you avoid the former.' She drew on the cigarillo, reflecting the glowing gleed in her dark-mirrored eyes.

Grace blushed and looked away, surprised at the lady's honesty, wondering if she was still playing the part of the medium and embellishing her reputation. Grace concluded the woman was capable of anything, with her resources and talents, as well as the truth.

Lady Foster exhaled, setting off a sweet and sickly cloud of tobacco smoke. 'Can you communicate with them, too?' she asked, staring out at the yellowing leaves of a wisteria clinging to a decaying garden arbour. She refilled the glass with fortifying brandy, ignoring the offer of medicinal Earl Grey.

Grace gulped her tea, spluttering with the effort. She looked down at the crumbs and mess of the rapid dismembering of the caraway slice and glanced up at the silhouette of the strange woman. Unlike any other of the nobility she had met, Lady Foster was a peculiar and beguiling force smoking a thin cigarillo and sipping at strong alcohol in the middle of the day, despite the wisdom to avoid such damaging pastimes. It was a chance meeting between two women, lady-like and submissive when society demanded it; human and untamed when privacy granted it.

'Yes,' said Grace, 'though only when I am already extremely anxious. It's not something I choose to do.'

Lady Foster turned to the asters placed haphazardly in a fluted glass vase. 'That is a rare talent, indeed. Of the handful of drug-addicted sensitives I have met, none could do both.'

Grace watched as she arranged the flowers. 'I never thought about it before, but—'

'But what?'

Grace thought on the growing idea. 'The night I received the news that Christopher had been killed in France, Arthur tried to comfort me, despite having no understanding of what the letter contained or why I was crying—even the worst of children have an innate compassion for another.'

'I've yet to see that,' said Lady Foster, 'but I defer to your experience on the matter. What is your point?'

'Arthur was a gentle child, always empathetic and warm. I hadn't thought about it before, but he appears *after* I become agitated, and not before.'

Lady Foster snapped off a bent flower head. 'He is trying to comfort you?'

Grace nodded and looked at her wrists. 'I'm sending him away every time he tries, aren't I?' she whispered to herself.

The curtain billowed inwards with a cool breeze, and Lady Foster shivered and turned to put on a cotton shawl.

'I think you may have learned something to your advantage. Do the dead still appear as we are?' she said, watching Grace in deep thought. 'I barely remember anymore.'

'If you mean substantial and material,' said Grace, 'then, sometimes. It is difficult to know, but there is always something intangible about them, if you know what I mean.'

'I do,' said Lady Foster. 'They do not see or interact with the world as we do. Contrary to popular belief, they do not walk through walls or wail through the air covered with bedsheets. They remain bound by earthly convention, unable in the most part to communicate.'

'Unless they are summoned or encounter someone like you?'

'Like us,' corrected Lady Foster. 'But yes, though if they interact with the silks, then even the most hardened sceptic will be aware,' she said, narrowing her eyes and twitching her nose. 'I love to watch their faces when their materialistic worldview crumbles.' She gazed into the central yellow heads of the blue daisy-like flowers. 'Where did you get these?'

'The flower seller in the cemetery,' said Grace. 'When you were not at the address on the card, I wandered for several days until I chanced upon the Foster family stone.' She thought of the signals from Arthur: fire, train, and flower. 'Though I think it wasn't chance at all.'

Lady Foster drained her glass and stubbed out her cigarillo. 'I don't believe in coincidences either,' she said, raising the handle of the umbrella and pointing the tip to the vase. 'He used to bring me these.'

'Who?' asked Grace.

Lady Foster returned to the open bureau, and Grace

feared the return of the hourglass. The woman slipped a hand into a side letter compartment and withdrew a printed calling card and a faded leather wallet.

'Mr unworthy,' replied Lady Foster finally, tossing over the umbrella. Grace caught it with both hands as it sailed above the tea tray. 'Keep it. It belongs to you now along with this—'

The leather wallet opened and Lady Foster withdrew a fifty-pound note together with a sheaf of pound and ten-shilling notes. She placed the card on top and held out the large sum of money to Grace.

Grace frowned, uncertain of the gesture.

'Take it,' said Lady Foster, insistently. 'I honour the duke's request—for aid.'

'What is it for?'

'A new life,' said Lady Foster. 'The family on that card needs someone with your skills. It's not overly glamourous.' She looked down at the sorry state of Grace's appearance. 'But you will need new clothing, boots and a bath, I think?' She glanced over at the photograph in the oval frame. 'My sister was petite, and there may be something I can loan you for a formal introduction, though the style may be somewhat "Victorian". I believe she would want me to help you, and a closet full of her gowns is a little macabre, even for one such as I.'

Lady Foster extended the money again. 'Consider it an advance. If you are honourable, you can repay my generosity at a later date, so that others like yourself may benefit from my altruism.'

Grace trembled as she delicately lifted the copious sum from her outstretched hand. 'I don't know what to say. I can't accept this,' she said. 'I came for a situation, not charity.'

'I urge you to take the family I am offering then, and the money,' said Lady Foster. The woman stood tall, imposing and impressive. The exterior world and expectations had entered the room, and she spoke as one with the authority and confidence of nobility. 'You may live longer than the alternative, even if you can never truly come to terms with your past.'

Grace rose and glanced up at the towering figure of powerful femininity.

Grace thought of the silent child, the fire, and Arthur, and the prospect of a safe but anxious future wrestling with her inner demons.

'What alternative?' said Grace, noting the rapid dilation of the noblewoman's eyes.

'To act as my eyes and ears while you care for and encourage Rose Ferris back to health and speech, as well as to encourage hope and action back into poor Captain Ferris.' Lady Foster looked up at the ceiling with an expression of concern. 'At whatever cost to yourself—you said you would do anything within your power, did you not?'

Grace followed her gaze, recalling the fire and the falling chandelier.

'There is another who might be more suited to the role,' said Grace. 'The woman you saw in my memory of the Cambria Institute.'

'The tall, fair-haired teacher?'

'Yes,' said Grace. 'My mentor and one with longer time-served than I—Jane Urquhart.'

Lady Foster sighed. 'Miss Urquhart is the one you will replace at Hemingworth. She is no longer—employed. The household has trouble keeping staff.'

Grace detected a note of finality to the conversation but continued.

'I don't know how I could do more than Jane could accomplish? She is brilliant and a key influencer in oralist techniques among the very young; I learned everything I know from her.'

'Then you had better remember what she taught you,' said

Lady Foster, picking up the handbell and ringing for the housekeeper. 'You have until tomorrow morning to decide. If you do not return with your belongings, then I will assume you have chosen the former situation, and my reference to your new employer will follow in due course.' She handed Grace the letters of reference that had been on the nearby table but withheld the time-worn calling card. Grace curtsied as the housekeeper came in.

'Call a cab to return Miss Meadows to her lodgings, on my account.'

'Very good, Your Ladyship,' said the housekeeper, leading Grace from the room.

Grace folded the papers and money into her pocket and glanced at the Chelsea address on the card.

'If I take this conventional position nearby, will I be haunted for the rest of my life?'

'That depends on how you intend to live it,' said Lady Foster. 'It's not fire you are afraid of; it's failure. I do not believe you can truly be free of what grieves you unless you accept it or face the prospect of it happening again and defeating it. Goodbye, Miss Meadows.'

Grace nodded and left the room. With a last glance, she turned to see the medium of Mayfair hold up and turn the duke's card. It may have been a draught as the outside door opened, but Grace saw a slight shudder in the silk of her dress on her lightly clad shoulders. The quiver of someone holding back emotion before her reserve holding back the doorway to tears was breached.

The cab waited while she ran to the cemetery, joyful despite blisters and lack of food, to haggle with the flower seller for the return of the embroidered purse. The old woman looked suspiciously at the pound note as if expecting the out-of-breath young woman to be followed closely by policemen seeking the return of pick-pocketed money.

Grace held out the note—more than a weekday's takings for the flower woman—in exchange for the sentimental object.

'Someone's luck just changed,' called the old woman, stamping her feet with the cold as Grace sprinted out of the gates and back to the waiting driver. 'Did the witch reveal your fortune, then?'

The horse-drawn cab meandered its way through the exclusive borough and on to the working district of North London. Grace called a halt, half a mile from the boarding house, and got out with the umbrella, giving the man a warm smile. 'Good luck to you, miss,' he said, raising his hat. 'They don't all come out of Wellington Avenue in such spirits.'

She watched the horse retreat, and her nose led her to a nearby bakery, just closing for the day.

Grace counted the change from the ten-shilling note. The end-of-day buns would keep until tomorrow if they made it that far. Her stomach rumbled after its recent re-introduction to food, and she leaned against an empty stall, devouring two buns quickly before her shrunken stomach begged her appetite for mercy. A chestnut seller setting up for the evening lit an iron brazier and placed a wide skillet upon the growing flames. Grace moved on, uncomfortable with the proximity of the open fire, despite being out of doors.

She wandered into a shop, appropriate in her present dishevelled state and fitting her idea of what a new outfit should cost in the real world, north of the Home Counties. She bought a canvas bag to hold the shirtwaist, blouse and long, flowing skirt, together with the buns and a set of under-garments. The ready-wear clothes were of simpler design and materials than the home-sewn clothing she usually bought patterns for. They also offered a slimmer profile and the simpler, frugal styles demanded by the war; in London 1918, they had become the dominant fashion.

She was conscious of Lady Foster's generous advance, rolled tightly in her skirt pocket, and the cost of the latest fashions in the capital. Grace was a skilled seamstress, but even the patterns and cost of cloth made it uneconomical to make a single outfit. The money was close to five months' wages, and Grace decided she would pay it back in instalments once settled into her new position.

She held out the card and rubbed at the printed name and address. The cabby had informed her it was a good neighbourhood where many wealthy business people held property. There would be no repeat of her self-harm this time, she was sure of it. Questions would be raised about her lack of conventional references, and Grace would have to deal with them from upstairs, and downstairs, in the new household. She would be bolstered by Lady Foster's character recommendation and begin again; life would return to normal, with all the positives and negatives that represented.

She turned down a narrow street, narrowly avoiding a gang of boys merrily playing soldiers among the stacked crates and detritus on the pavement. A larger boy stood on the summit of a barrel, waving a tattered silken flag on a makeshift pole following the capture of an invisible German fortification. He waved his brigade onwards to the offal house's basement steps to mop up the remaining enemy soldiers in the imaginary trench.

A solitary boy remained, dragging a much dirtier fragment of material. The red, white and blue were barely distinguishable, but it was finely made. He twirled the silken rag in the air, and it slipped from his grasp, twisting and winding through the air, coming to rest as though buoyant, three feet above the ground further down the otherwise deserted street.

Grace stiffened as Arthur materialised and held out the silken fragment to the approaching boy. There was a hesitation before the youth snatched his war standard from the uncommunicative child and re-joined his victorious troop far down the end of the street, oblivious to his brush with the afterworld.

Arthur turned to watch the play, unable to take part ever again in such earthly rough-and-tumble. Grace approached, but he raised an open hand and glanced back, meaning she should go no further. He pointed at the card in her hand and gently shook his head.

'Arthur, I need this new position, please—' she whispered, cut off by the raising of his little hands.

A new sign was coming, and one Grace knew she could not ignore. The future she had briefly chosen slipped away as the tiny hands formed the words.

She will die without you.

The spirit imparted its message and dissolved in the melee of the returning children. Grace stood in the street, blankly looking down at the muddied cobbles and the fallen calling card trodden in by the passage of children's feet.

CHAPTER 8

The train thundered through the tunnel, plunging the private first-class carriage into darkness. Lady Foster hummed gently in the dim light opposite and looked up from her almanack, waiting for the November sun to return, pince-nez reading spectacles perched upon her nose.

Grace dozed, rocked by the movement of the locomotive and the soothing sounds of the lullaby. The echo of the tunnel roused her from sleep, and she glanced across at her benefactor, no longer dressed in exquisite and provocative silk. The sombre brown tweed seemed somehow alien to Lady Foster's personality, but socially acceptable as the outward-facing appearance of an understated noblewoman. Grace looked down at her admiral-blue silk gown, on loan from the sanctity of the guest room, and belonging to Lady Foster's deceased sister. She looked and felt like a governess, though one belonging to an earlier time. The matching bonnet was uncomfortable, and Grace fidgeted, unused to wearing such an outdated piece of head-wear.

'It took fifteen minutes to get that straight, Grace,' said Lady Foster, as the carriage blinked into the open air once more. 'It's a traditional family, and you can return to less formal attire when convention allows. Are you nervous?'

'I'm always nervous, ma'am,' said Grace. 'I feel more like a debutante than a governess.'

Lady Foster removed her spectacles and folded the periodical in her lap.

'You can drop the honorific titles until we are at Hemingworth Hall,' she said. 'You look much improved from your week's stay; even Edith seemed sad you were leaving, and that woman shows little emotion unless there's a mouse in the kitchen.'

'I do not know how to repay you,' said Grace, now reacquainted with sleep, safety and food. 'More than the money, I mean—'

'When all this is over,' said Lady Foster, 'I may end up owing you. I'm still a little surprised you came back.'

'You know why I came back,' said Grace, looking out of the window, trying to forget the message in the back street.

Lady Foster shrugged. 'Have you seen the spirit of the child since his message?'

'No,' said Grace, turning to the corridor at the approach of footsteps. The concierge knocked on the glass compartment from the narrow aisle to inform them that the Warwickshire station was approaching.

Grace rose and collected her battered trunk with slight embarrassment. It sat next to Lady Foster's small, lacquered case in the netting above the dinette.

'How long will you be staying at the Hall?' asked Grace, collecting her umbrella and offering a hand to Lady Foster now that the train had slowed towards the station.

'Just a few hours,' she said. 'I must return on the four o'clock train.'

Lady Foster struggled to her feet. The injury caused by the unseen force during the seance with Mrs Jellicoe had thankfully only resulted in bruising. Still, Grace had not failed to notice the labouring in the woman's breath as they strode down the platform at Euston Station to board the departing train. Grace had also espied the pillbox and its contents quietly and secretly swallowed before it was returned to the hidden fold in Lady Foster's sleeve.

The train came to a squealing halt, releasing steam like a great sigh, glad to be at rest. Several passengers alighted, and Lady Foster took out a pocket watch and checked the time against the station clock.

Grace collected the belongings and shuffled behind the noblewoman in the direction of the station gate. The largest man Grace had ever seen stood behind the white picket fence. A rough greying stubble covered his striking face. A pair of bright blue eyes sat beneath a lightly lined forehead, and his greased hair gave a dignified look to a man whose unadorned hands betrayed the callouses of someone having spent a life in manual labour. His giant frame barely fitted his morning suit, and he seemed as uncomfortable in the formal uniform as Grace did herself. To her surprise, he nodded to Lady Foster and opened the gate.

'This is Bishop,' said Lady Foster. 'Captain Ferris's man-Friday.'

Bishop bent a full three feet in a deep bow, collecting the cases and umbrella from Grace's tiny hands. Grace looked into the beautiful eyes as he glanced across at eye level before returning to his near seven-foot upright position. There was a keenness in them, and she felt his studious glance appraising her like an insect through a magnifying glass.

'Thank you,' said Grace, watching him struggle to get his massive fingers through the luggage handles. There was no reply or hint of acknowledgement.

'He's mute,' said Lady Foster, following the giant to the waiting car. 'He can hear well enough, though. Not afraid of anything and good for keeping family secrets—isn't that right, Bishop?'

The chauffeur turned and nodded respectfully, catching another side-long glance from Grace, who rapidly took the chance to put a closed hand to her mouth and remove it in a downwards motion.

'*Thank you*,' she mouthed, seeing recognition, if not emotion, on his face. Bishop directed them to a beautiful burgundy canvas-hooded motorcar and opened the rear door.

'He's let you play with the Sigma 10, has he?' said Lady Foster, getting into the rear, shortly followed by Grace. 'We are honoured.'

Bishop beamed in reply, and several more creases appeared briefly on his early-middle-aged face as he secured the luggage to the side racks. The driver's seat was modified to allow for the giant's frame, and it protruded into the rear, close to Grace's knees. He got in with difficulty and started the car, knees bent and wrapped on either side of the leather-bound steering wheel.

Grace was glad of the warm cab as the car sped along the country lane towards the Hall, a distance of four miles, but otherwise isolated from the nearest village. Lady Foster pointed out the country as it passed by.

'Wool,' she said, pointing to the rural landscape dotted with sheep. 'It's how the Hemingworths made their money centuries ago when they weren't hiding Catholics and clerics. I hope you're not looking for any entertainments outside of the library or nursery because there isn't much in any direction until you hit Warwick or Stratford-upon-Avon. Not much to see at this time of year in any case.'

'I'm not one for social occasions,' said Grace.

'You'll fit right in then,' said Lady Foster.

Bishop slowed the car over a hump-backed drover's bridge. The muddied water of the stream flowed from the higher wooded ground to the right, and disappeared into a lazy, spilling flood across the open fields beyond. After half a mile, Bishop slowed and turned in to an understated drive bordered by two rusted and immobile gates. Curved retaining walls of loose and unsettled stone completed the once-grand entrance, which had long ago fallen into disrepair. The car gathered speed through the woodland that crept over the pot-holed drive, unmanaged with the disappearance and unlikely return of many of the men from the Warwickshire Regiment who had taken slaughterous sabbaticals at the Somme. Grace looked at the great back of the driver, wondering if he had escaped conscription or played his part.

The woodland became thinner as the car wound to the left, revealing a straight section of weed-infested drive ending several hundred yards ahead in a grand stone and timber-framed mansion ringed with a moat and accessed by a single-arched stone bridge.

'Welcome to Hemingworth Hall,' said Lady Foster. 'The grand seat of a once great and powerful family.'

Grace struggled to see past the bulk in front of her and peeped out sideways at the brick and timber-framed castellated facade. The woodland to the sides became sporadic and failed altogether, opening up into a wide and unkempt lawn, mossy and tufted with patches of uncut grass. Bishop drove the car over a crossroads connecting a stable yard with garages and outbuildings to the right and a large walled garden to the left.

Crossing the narrow bridge, Grace glanced up at the tilted, narrow windows in the three-storeyed, fortified manor house. Ivy clung to large areas of the western front, emerging from the silted moat and drinking deeply from the stagnant pools that peppered the deeper regions of the former defences. It draped over the entrance arch and brushed over the canvas roof as they entered the wide and empty courtyard.

Bishop stopped the car at a wide and shallow set of steps leading to the main hall. He got out and opened the side doors, allowing the passengers to alight. It was noticeably cooler in the courtyard where little direct sunlight would reach until the summer months when the sun was directly overhead. Several other doors leading to sculleries, kitchens and storehouses completed the stone-lined lower floors. A series of horse-mounting steps lay slippy and unused next to a dripping hand pump, and Grace glanced up at the sky for relief from the mournful and decaying appearance of the once magnificent building.

A great circular tower on the north-eastern corner rose above the adjoining wings. A narrow leaded-window dripped with interior condensation, and a raven sat on the ledge, croaking for its partner in a nearby stag-headed oak along the drive. A shadow within the dark chamber moved, as though glimpsing the arrival below. Grace put her hands to her eyes to shield out the bright background of the cloudy sky, and the shadow retreated as Bishop put his fingers to his mouth and whistled loudly. A work-clothed youth in his mid-teens appeared from a door, and Bishop gesticulated for him to bring the cases as he led the ladies up to the double oak-studded entrance portal to Hemingworth Hall.

Grace glanced anxiously at Lady Foster, as though visiting the Bastille would have made for a more pleasant afternoon call. She was surprised to find her hand entwined with her own, followed by a soft squeeze of encouragement. The noblewoman stared ahead and breathed in deeply as though preparing herself for the encounter, and Grace detected a slight nervousness in her countenance. Grace wondered if the squeeze had been for Lady Foster's benefit as much as her own.

Bishop led them through an impressively wide and panelled hall, closely followed by the young man who placed the luggage near the base of the polished oak staircase that ran alongside the opposite wall. Grace's eyes adjusted to the Jacobean interior and the flickering sconces on the coarse plaster walls. Her anxiety lowered from its initial spike and the fear of naked gas or candlelight receded when she noticed they were electric lights struggling under load—infinitely preferable to fire. Great framed mirrors lay turned to the walls. Grace glanced across at Lady Foster, who nodded in acknowledgement; superstition resided here, along with an oppressive sense of melancholy and decline.

Bishop clapped his great hands, and the echo resounded around the ground floor. Several doors opened and servants appeared to their left and right, bobbing in rapid curtsies as Grace and the Lady passed by towards the room ahead. Grace noted the absence of any men other than the valet and the luggage boy and the look of apprehension in their eyes as they glanced upon the newly appointed governess walking stride for stride alongside, not behind, the noblewoman. Lady Foster's reputation preceded her, even here in an isolated corner of the country. The servants lowered their heads and retreated into the shadows of the rooms beyond as though trying to become invisible, incorporeal, and safe from rumour and speculation.

Bishop pushed open the doors in front and ushered them into a richly furnished drawing room illuminated by mullion-stone bay windows overlooking a perimeter of rough grass sloping into the barely discernible moat.

'Let me do the talking,' whispered Lady Foster, watching Bishop pull the manual bell cord for the room, 'and remember your manners; despite being barely in his thirties, Captain Ferris is old school.'

CHAPTER 9

A distant ring echoed through the silent house. Grace had never known such quiet. Households were always busy with some activity: the sound of chatter, crockery and cleaning, a gramophone in the principal room, or just the day-to-day sounds of a cheerful and noble house. Hemingworth Hall seemed neither of these; even the open fire of the otherwise pleasant room, guarded by a screen, much to Grace's relief, seemed reticent to crackle or offer any welcoming heat.

Bishop stood, immobile and mute, within the thick walls of the casement doorway. His great arms held behind his back, tense with great tributaries of veins protruding from his ruddy skin. The house held its breath, and all within suffocated with the oppressive atmosphere.

A door to a nearby room opened, and the sound of slow and solitary feet approached from the hall. A dour but well-dressed woman with a heavily blemished face emerged, pushing a hunched, dark-haired man in a wheelchair. His hands rested on the corners of the bronzed cane chair, and he waved the housekeeper away as he wheeled the remaining few yards to offer a shaking hand to Lady Foster.

'A pleasure to see you, Lady Foster,' he said, stealing a glazed-eye glance at Grace. 'I trust your journey from London to our humble backwater was pleasant?'

Lady Foster removed a glove and the paraplegic's hand gripped the offered hand.

Lady Foster returned the shake and nodded.

'You look well, Charles,' said Lady Foster.

'I look terrible,' said Charles. 'But thank you all the same. You remember Mrs Stanton, my new housekeeper, from your previous visit in the spring?' he said, pointing a wavering finger over his shoulder at the tall, middle-aged woman curt-sying behind.

'Yes,' said Lady Foster. 'A most attentive woman—I don't know how she puts up with you.'

Charles wagged a finger. 'If you try to lure her away to one of your cronies in London, I shall come back and haunt you.'

Grace saw the pockmarked face of Mrs Stanton stiffen as she wrapped her fingers tightly around the handles of the wheelchair once more.

'In which case,' said Lady Foster mischievously, 'I shall be pleased to offer you an appointment anytime between three and five in the afternoon.'

The noblewoman took off her remaining glove and placed them both into her purse.

'May I introduce Miss Grace Meadows, alumna of the Cambria Institute and new governess to Miss Ferris.'

His eyes widened momentarily at the mention of the institution.

Grace curtsied as Mrs Stanton wheeled the chair closer. Grace feared the vibrating hand, but he did not extend it. The war-wounded captain peered into her face, squinting to see detail.

'Bring me light, Bishop,' he said, and the stone giant lumbered across the room to bring an oil lamp.

Grace's eyes squinted with the closeness of the bright light, and she stifled a gasp as she stared into the cataracts of the clouded eyes of her new employer. Charles Ferris studied Grace's face and brushed a shaking hand against the blue silk. He waved away the lamp.

'Young to be so brilliant,' he said. 'Welcome, Miss Meadows. Forgive my scrutiny of your appearance; my eyes are weak, and I am somewhat ... incapacitated, following my return from France.' He waved the housekeeper away to arrange refreshments.

Bishop replaced the lamp and returned to his station between the doors, a look of sadness on his face at the mention of the war.

'Lady Foster tells me you can make Rose talk again?'

Grace glanced at Lady Foster, who sat down and nodded for her to speak.

'Her Ladyship is correct in that I can encourage communication in those willing to engage with the techniques and—'

'I want my daughter to talk again, Miss Meadows, not communicate with arms and gestures like an idiot.' Charles flailed his arms in front of himself.

'I understand, sir,' said Grace, glancing across at Bishop awkwardly. The manservant showed no signs of offence, and Grace continued.

'It is the right of every child and individual to communicate in whatever manner or method is meaningful for themselves.'

Bishop flashed his eyes as she spoke.

'Miss Ferris will speak when she is ready, or never, and that is a possibility. The decision will ultimately be down to her, not me, not my teaching aids, and not through any other externally imposed constraints. I have to make that clear from the start.'

Charles tensed his hands as though trying to rise, ready to counter the words with some choice ones of his own.

Lady Foster rattled her cup, tilting it, so it tipped, empty, onto the floor. Charles twisted round to locate the source of the sound, and Grace saw the deliberate distraction and the fierce glance in her eyes, demanding caution and contrition.

'But,' said Grace quickly, 'I understand the necessity and your urgency in restoring Miss Ferris's ability to do so through speech. I will endeavour with all my skill to achieve that goal.'

Captain Ferris turned. 'Do so, with all haste,' he said, relaxing back into his chair. 'I am not a well man and unlikely to see her wed. She is the most important thing in my life, and I will not have her silent and trapped when I am gone, with only an unquiet house for company.'

The immaculate Mrs Stanton returned with an older housemaid carrying a tray of tea. They set about the ritual of laying a side table with refreshments. The housekeeper gripped the wavering wrist of Captain Ferris and carefully placed a cup and saucer before squeezing the hand momentarily.

'Leave us,' he said, 'and make sure that Miss Meadows' things are delivered to the first floor, next to the nursery.'

Bishop closed the doors behind him as the housekeeper and maid left the room.

'Do you play the piano, Miss Meadows?' the captain said.

'I do,' said Grace. 'Would you like me to play something for you?'

'No,' said Charles. 'The house should remain quiet.' He turned in her direction.

'*At all times.*'

Captain Ferris wheeled over to the window. 'I used to see and hear things when I was a child here,' he said. 'The house is old, and I no longer have any doubt that things still lie

99

hidden or trapped among the warren that riddles this place; I urge you, for your sake and the well-being of my daughter, to remain quiet, vigilant, and in your room after curfew.'

'I will, sir,' said Grace, unsure of his meaning. 'I'm eager to start.'

'Mrs Stanton will give you your responsibilities as befits your privilege. My friend, the doctor, will be here this afternoon, and he is as close as you will get to a psychoanalyst in these parts. He can shed light on Rose's condition. Apart from that, you are free to perform your duties as you see fit, providing they are quiet and do not overtax my daughter's fragile health; I prefer for her to remain indoors and safe. There is a curfew bell at eight o'clock, and unless otherwise engaged, you should remain in your room following this, no matter what you see or hear.'

He spun round. 'Pray look after my daughter if anything should incapacitate me, or prevent an able-bodied man to defend against those things that would seek to do us harm.' Charles fingered a small crucifix around his neck. 'And as a precaution—' he looked across at Lady Foster '—the tower and north-east wing are out of bounds. They contain sensitive things belonging to my wife, and I wish the room within to remain as it once was. Do you understand?'

'Yes, sir,' said Grace, apprehensive about so many restrictions and the joyless atmosphere compared with the Soames' household.

'Mrs Stanton arranges Rose's medicine on the good doctor's instruction, and I will be available to discuss your progress each morning after my letters if that is convenient. Your teaching aids and books arrived yesterday and should be in the nursery; I think Rose is looking forward to meeting you.'

'As am I, sir,' said Grace.

'Then leave us now, and locate Mrs Stanton, who will

introduce you both,' he said. 'Lady Foster and I have some things to discuss.'

Grace curtsied and nodded to Lady Foster in farewell. She opened the door, glad to be out of the mournful room and eager to absorb herself in labour to work through the mounting anxiety of the new situation.

She shut the door and looked down the hall in search of someone to direct her to the location of the housekeeper's office. The door clicked back open, marginally allowing a streak of light to peep through. Grace thought of pulling it shut, but her curiosity got the better of her.

'A small thing, isn't she?' said the voice of Charles Ferris. 'Wherever did you find her?'

'She found me,' replied Lady Foster, over the rattle of a teacup.

'Are you sure she is up to it—a breath of wind might break her?'

'She stood up to you just then.'

'She has spirit, I'll grant you that,' said Charles. 'What was it that forced her to come to see you? Pregnancy, alcoholism perhaps?'

'Redemption, Charles,' said Lady Foster. 'Redemption.'

'I should see you myself, then,' he said. 'She will not find it here. I fear it is already too late for either of us. Dr Croswell believes there are some small signs of improvement in my daughter, but I know he humours me. It's what happens next that I fear. The bells in the tower are ringing nightly now, always after curfew.'

'That's what the curfew bell is there for,' said Lady Foster. 'The room remained locked, I hope?'

'Of course,' said Charles. 'I'm not mad, unlike Sophia. Will she ever leave us alone?'

'Not while Rose lives. Your wife is bound to the house, and you know what she wants, as do I. You can go on believing things will get better as you and your daughter spiral into ill-health and oblivion, listening to Elizabeth Stanton's ignorant nonsense about leaving things as they are, or—'

'Or what?' said Charles, hopefully.

'The option I spoke of.'

'No,' he said. 'Not until there is no other way. Does the governess know any of this?'

There was a long pause as Grace struggled to hear the whispered reply, even in the intense silence. Her heartbeat thudded in her chest and rang in her ears.

'Not all of it,' said Lady Foster. 'She would not have come, otherwise. I told you she is sensitive to certain phenomena?'

'In your letter,' said Charles. 'I don't know if that makes me more nervous. You still hold to your word to take my daughter, should anything happen to me?'

'Of course, but I wish you would send Rose away,' said Lady Foster. 'The change might do her good.'

'I'm a soldier,' said Charles. 'Always defend yourself from a place of strength. It's too late in any case; the doctor doesn't want Rose travelling in her delicate state. He fears she will deteriorate rapidly as a result and who knows where that leads us, far from aid.'

'Then tell me, is all secure in the tower?' asked Lady Foster. 'It will only slow her down. You know that, don't you?'

'Enough time to set the final act in motion,' he said, 'if it should come to it.'

Grace heard the wheelchair squeak across the floorboards within, and she stepped back. She listened to the fumble of his hand against the wall before he pulled the bell rope. It was a different tone, deeper and more resonant, and Grace concluded it summoned the great manservant.

'Come, I will show you,' said Charles, 'and then leave me be. I wish to be alone with my thoughts.'

'And your whisky,' said Lady Foster in a tone of matriarchal scorn. 'A dead father and a dead mother are no use to Rose.'

'It's my way of coping with all this,' said Charles. 'Anyway, Mother told me you're no saint.'

'No,' said Lady Foster, 'but I prefer martyrdom to self-induced destruction.'

'You sound like a proselytising Catholic,' said Charles. 'Are you sure we aren't related? Come, I'll show you the defences, and Bishop can take you back to the station.'

The conversation ended, and Grace turned, striding into the bosom of the waiting housekeeper, Mrs Stanton.

CHAPTER 10

'Have you no manners, etiquette or decency?' said Mrs Stanton, dragging her away from the door. 'If you've quite finished, follow me, and I will escort you to your room.'

Grace nodded, conscious of the heat developing from her blushing cheeks, and looked down from the cratered visage to the housekeeper's marred fingers, unadorned by any ring. Smallpox had disfigured the once beautiful face, surely making the spinster hard and cold when all chance of marriage or child of her own had faded. Grace wondered if any smile or warmth of spirit could ever broach the middle-aged, stricken face ever again.

'The master likes a quiet house, free of gossip and hearsay,' she said as she turned and strode away to the stairs. 'As do I.'

Grace followed and climbed the stairs to the first floor in pursuit, listening to the litany of rules and expectations. She paused, catching her breath, and looked to her right across at a barricaded door to the north-eastern wing. Great iron bars stretched between the double doors' deep frame in front of a tangled mass of web-like threads.

'Please keep up, Miss Meadows!' barked Mrs Stanton from the end of the north-west corridor.

'What's beyond the doors?' asked Grace, hurrying to the open doorway and the disappearing housekeeper.

'None of your concern,' she replied. They reached the corner of the first-floor wing. 'Your room. Please try to avoid using the electric light as it puts a strain on the household economy and the system. It is an old house, and I like to run a tight ship. The curfew bell is at eight o'clock until daybreak or five in the morning, whichever is sooner. I encourage you not to wander the servants' floor until the morning bell. Male visitors are strictly prohibited.'

Grace frowned. 'That seems a little draconian, Mrs Stanton?'

The housekeeper's eyes lit up. 'You are new here,' she said. 'Please follow the rules of the house, or I will inform the master.'

Grace took in the words' finality as she surveyed the plain but cheery day room with its single window overlooking the hazy walled garden and dilapidated glasshouse. Within the productive and protected walls, the young man who had brought in the luggage pushed vigorously and mechanically back and forth with a garden hoe over many rectangular beds of overgrown vegetables.

Mrs Stanton joined her at the window. 'Be careful of Billy,' she said. 'Leave nothing valuable lying around. He has a reputation before coming to this house of being wayward and light with his fingers and is under Mr Bishop's jurisdiction. I would keep interactions with both of them as brief as possible.'

'Mr Bishop seems a very dedicated valet,' said Grace.

'That's as may be, but I wouldn't trust either of them,' she said. 'Thick as thieves; in every permutation.'

Grace turned to see a bureau and a worn but comfortable-looking armchair in front of a modestly stocked grate. A coal scuttle and kindling lay nearby along with a hessian string-wrapped bundle of tallow candles.

'You handle your own fire, and the emptying. The house does not have enough staff to provide a house service to servants, but I monitor the liberality of the coal used.'

Grace's fears were allayed as she would not have to pretend to light fires and bring in cold ash as at the Soames' estate.

'Why do you have so few staff?' said Grace, half-expecting that the housekeeper's strict adherence to regulation was to blame. 'The war is all but over.'

The housekeeper smoothed the front of her skirt and hesitated.

'They don't have the fortitude,' she said. 'May I speak plainly?'

'Of course,' said Grace.

'It is my opinion that Hemingworth does not need a governess. I am happy to manage Miss Ferris's education and her return to health,' she said, jutting out her chin. 'Unfortunately, I was overruled by Dr Croswell.'

'We are both on the same side, Mrs Stanton,' said Grace, 'and I am here to protect and nurture the child back to speech, not to challenge the status quo or your authority. Isn't that a good thing?'

The housekeeper narrowed her eyes and creased the side of her mouth into the semblance of a smile, and walked into the adjoining panelled bedroom. A simple crucifix and framed embroidered sampler lay above the bed and a washbasin and stand sat in front of a window overlooking the drive cutting through the dense woodland that pressed in on either side to reclaim it.

Several trunks and the case belonging to Lady Foster lay stacked in the corner.

'Some of those aren't mine,' said Grace. 'That case, for example, it belongs to—'

'It was specifically requested to be brought up with your things, by the woman herself.'

Something in the way the housekeeper described Lady Foster made her defensive of her benefactor, and she opened the lacquered case to discover the polished ebony yoke and circular stand of the spirit bell. There was a note covering the brass bell:

Might you find this useful as a teaching aid? Don't be afraid of anything, or anyone. Be my eyes and ears. E F.

'What is that?' said Mrs Stanton, watching as Grace lifted out the yoke and fixed it into the socket of its stand.

'A spirit bell,' said Grace, not bothering to turn.

Grace heard the sharp intake of breath behind her, as intended. 'There'll be no musical instruments in this house while I breathe,' said the housekeeper.

Grace quickly stifled a smile and turned to puff up her five feet in the manner of Lady Foster.

'This is no musical instrument,' said Grace. 'It is used by those who no longer have any need for speech or breath.'

Mrs Stanton signed the cross against her chest and stared at the young woman in the outdated silken gown and bonnet. Grace locked horns in a battle of wills, and it was the house-keeper that looked away first. Grace rattled the bell, setting it tinkling.

'You know by whom I am protected and supported?' said Grace, pressing the issue. 'I will abide by your rules, providing you do not interfere with my teaching and mentoring of Miss Ferris. Pray you do not have cause to discuss my methods with Captain Ferris, and I will ensure that Lady Foster is kept unaware of your interference.'

Grace released her grip around the bell-yoke handle, amazed by the boldness of her words. She trembled with the conflict, hoping it had put down a marker. The governess was not under the jurisdiction of anyone but the house's principal; a servant, yes, but one outside the normal hierarchy.

Mrs Stanton's brown eyes narrowed with the challenge and clarification of the country house convention.

'Then let us make sure neither has cause to affect the other?'

Grace nodded. 'Agreed.'

Mrs Stanton shook her head almost imperceptibly and pinched her lips into a momentary semblance of a smile. 'Then I wish you more success than the previous governess; a failure in one's duties and overt curiosity are not good bedfellows.'

Grace frowned. 'What do you mean by that?'

Mrs Stanton raised a close-lipped smile. 'You mean, you don't know?'

Grace shook her head.

The housekeeper pointed to a stack of unfamiliar and battered trunks, the topmost of which carried the initials 'J.U.'

'These belong to the hall now, as is the convention when there is no next of kin. You may use them in your endeavours in the hope you will be more successful.'

'Jane died?' stammered Grace. 'I was told she was no longer employed—'

'An unfortunate accident,' said Mrs Stanton, chin up and chest out. 'It seems that the woman you are protected and supported by has been less than candid with you.'

Grace put her hands on the cold trunk as though touching the coffin of a loved one. Opening the chest, Grace saw the remains of a gifted life: clothes, half-finished needlework, books and an antique chess set. Grace dug her hands into the items as though seeking some final communion with the woman she called mentor, teacher and friend.

'I'll send Kate to fetch you when you have had time to settle in,' said Mrs Stanton with a formal nod of her tightly plaited head. 'Welcome to Hemingworth Hall.'

The door closed, and Grace fished through the jetsam in the trunk, fishing out a sepia photograph. The scene was familiar: the lawn in front of the institute. Numbers of friendly and known faces stared back, and Grace closed her eyes, spilling tears as colour returned in her mind to the photograph, taken on a sunny day in late May several years ago. A chance meeting with a photographer, offering several prints at a bargain price during the peak of the war. Several older men and woman stood proudly behind many children, one or two whose blurred faces revelled in the day's excitement and chance to escape the classroom, unable to stay still for the exposure. In her mind, she recalled the moment the photographer had lifted the cap off the lens, and Grace had mischievously tickled the hand of the woman next to her.

She opened her eyes and saw Jane Urquhart looking back with breaking mirth upon her surprised face, and the genesis of a term-long cat-and-mouse game to repay Grace's tomfoolery.

The sound of the motorcar crossing the moated bridge came from below, and Grace looked out from the window. The car came to a gravel-skidding stop on the other side, and the giant frame of Bishop got out, ready to open the rear door. Lady Foster stepped into the drive and ushered the man away. She crunched along the driveway as though aware of something unseen. The noblewoman stepped to the gateway of the walled garden and out of sight. Grace moved to her sitting room at the corner of the house and looked over the wall to see Billy leaning on his hoe. He raised his cap and returned to weed the beds of beetroot and brassica.

Lady Foster scanned around, passing over an indistinct figure in the woodland beyond a damaged section of wall.

Through the thick undergrowth, it looked back, watchful and hesitant, in the tower's direction and then up at the window where Grace stood. It shrank back into the gloom, but not before a lingering glance in Grace's direction. Lady Foster turned and returned to the car, looking up at the governess's window in silent farewell, pointing to her eyes and her ears in a nod to the words in her note. She spoke briefly with Bishop before returning to the cabin of the car. Bishop looked confused, and Lady Foster repeated the instruction with some agitation. The giant glanced up at the window and signed with his large hands:

'*Be careful. Something stirs.*'

Grace unpacked her meagre belongings and searched through items of practical use from Jane's trunk. A worn case revealed a hinged chessboard and a plush-lined compartment of carved wooden pieces. One of the black rooks was missing, and Grace emptied the trunk's remainder in an unsuccessful search for the missing tower piece.

She removed the bonnet and longed to comb out the tight weave of her hair and soak in the bath across the corridor. The room grew colder as the light outside waned with the passing of noon, but there would be no fire tonight, not with anxiety and many meetings with Rose and the other household members planned before supper.

Glancing through the simple books next to the black bible on the sitting-room shelf revealed common household texts and books of instruction, some of which could be recited at need or request. Desperate for a distraction, she stepped timidly along the quiet corridor to the back staircase and the third floor, eager for any company that might somehow be taking an all too brief period of rest. A long corridor ran back to the north-east wing and ended at the double doors to the tower. Iron bars were set within the frame to deter any notion of unlocking and opening the doors inwards while great clasps of iron, secured by heavy padlocks, completed the impregnable portal. However, there was one thing it could not restrain, and Grace leaned forwards into the chink of light escaping from the voluminous open space beyond.

A beam shone like a great torch from a single cobwebbed circular skylight in the opposite wall. It illuminated a wide spiralling staircase, intricately balustraded and defended by great webs of faintly reflecting rope. Small silver bells dangled dusty and motionless across the spiralled expanse. Grace glanced up into the glare of the thin November light to see an ornate ceiling from which a chain, wrapped in fraying and split silk, rocked, suggesting the great weight of some unseen lamp or chandelier below. The melted stubs of candles spilt over wall sconces and Grace stiffened in recognition of the room in her fiery trial with Lady Foster. She laid a hand on the iron bar, reassuring herself that the tower could not be accessed, and squinted up through the crack to a door that ended the run of suspended stone treads, a dozen steps further on. A shadow passed in front of the skylight, briefly blocking the light, and the sound of a flap opening on the roof heralded a breeze whistling beneath the tower-room door. The bells swung gently, joining the swirl of dust as soft footfalls came from the room above. The lights flickered as the load increased upon the antique system throughout the house.

Grace tip-toed back to her door, meeting the housemaid coming from the stairs below.

'Begging pardon, Miss Meadows,' she said. 'I'm Kate, come to show you to Miss Ferris.'

The housemaid's appearance seemed in contrast to the

perfection of Mrs Stanton. Her tumbled greying hair swayed across her haggard face drawn in a perpetual squint from the dim light of the house.

Grace rose and followed the housemaid back down the stairs, who briefly hesitated, as though listening, at the barricaded first-floor door to the tower wing.

'The nursery and playroom are next to your own, Miss Meadows,' said Kate, acknowledging a maid carrying fresh linen. 'But her bedchamber is on the ground floor. She eats in there alone when the master is indisposed.'

'I've never known a bedroom on the ground floor,' said Grace, trying to spark conversation. 'A necessity as a result of Mr Ferris's infirmity?'

'You could say that,' whispered Kate. 'It's also as far away from the tower as you can get.'

'Is that important?' said Grace.

Kate halted and bent her head. 'The north-east rooms are out of bounds, and mustn't be disturbed. Miss Ferris goes hiding and adventuring when she should be asleep. It's the master's wish she stays safe in here on account of her delicate constitution,' she said, knocking gently and opening the door.

Grace took a deep breath and entered the sumptuous room. A great blaze warmed the duck-egg blue wallpaper above the shoulder-high linen-fold panelling in a wide and airy day room. A crystal chandelier glinted with the flickering of the electrics and against the window. A child of seven years old, white-smocked and fair-haired, knelt on a window chaise oblivious to the interruption and looked out at the returning headlights of the burgundy motorcar. She waved as it sped past on its way to the garage buildings, and Grace saw the large hand of Bishop waving back.

'Miss Ferris,' said Kate. 'Will you get down from there? Mrs Stanton will have a fit if she sees you climbing all over the furniture. Come and meet the new governess.'

Grace smiled as the pretty, but pallid, child turned and got down from the settee.

Grace extended her hand, noticing the child inquisitively looking at the scars on her marked wrist. 'You can call me Grace,' she said, kneeling to discover the child was taller than Arthur or Oliver had been. She smiled, genuinely delighted to see such a fey and fragile creature whose cobalt-blue eyes swam in the moment's uncertainty.

Rose bobbed into a quick curtsy and limply took the offered hand.

Kate turned to the circular table spread with plates and bowls of mostly untouched food. 'You haven't touched your lunch,' she said, tutting in disapproval. 'There'll be no cake for you this afternoon with your medicine when Mrs Stanton finds out.'

Grace recalled the earlier exchange with the housekeeper, and the crooked smile of triumph as the knowledge of Jane's death was made known to her. Knowledge was the currency of a closed household, and it reigned supreme here, with Mrs Stanton as its herald.

Follow your gut, thought Grace, recalling the advice from her mentor. *Don't follow a convention to make a connection—if you sense an opening, take it!*

Kate continued to tidy and re-arrange the crockery and chairs, unaware of Grace's hands retreating from the hand-shake. The new governess crooked her fingers, scrunched her fists and rotated them in mockery of shedding crocodile tears.

Rose's eyes widened with amusement at the mischief of the golden-haired governess. Grace snapped back into a solemn face as Kate turned and frowned, uncertain as to the source of amusement.

'Well, I'm glad you find it funny,' she said. 'Wait till I tell Mrs Stanton; you won't be laughing then—she'll tell Pa-pa.'

Kate returned to the plates, and Grace raised a finger to her lips as the girl glanced up, intrigued by the childish behaviour. The thickening clouds darkened the room, threatening rain, and Grace knotted her hands together into a mass of writhing fingers. She threw a gaze across to the far wall where a rabbit, casting its shadow puppetry from the glow of the fire, opened and closed its mouth in time with the grumblings of the house servant.

Rose clasped a hand to her mouth to stifle any sound, watching the shadow mocking the mutterings of the unaware housemaid.

Grace got to her feet after a moment. 'Kate, would it be possible to keep Miss Ferris company while she eats?'

Rose clutched Grace's hand and nodded vigorously in silent pleading.

'Well, it's not normally allowed, but as long as you promise to eat all this?' Kate pointed to a plate of unappetising boiled vegetables and fish.

Rose nodded unenthusiastically at the prospect as Grace tickled her clammy hand, smoothing out the child's developing frown into a giggle.

The housemaid grunted and muttered her approval, waiting until the pair of them were seated at the dinner table before leaving the room.

The little girl covered her mouth and pointed a wagging finger at Grace, as though telling off one of her many dolls, seated around the table in high chairs.

'It's not my fault we were nearly caught,' said Grace innocently. 'I heard there was a silent young lady that needed a new governess, but I see that I must have the wrong house.' She pushed back her chair, bluffing to get up.

Rose grabbed the nearest doll and raced over to place it in the rising blue gown.

'Well, all right then,' said Grace. 'Maybe I'll stay a little while longer if you can keep a secret?'

The little girl nodded enthusiastically, and sat down, wide-eyed with the responsibility.

'I can teach dolls to talk,' said Grace, lifting the porcelain plaything to her ear. 'What's that?' she said, frowning as though straining to hear the toy's words. 'You know how to talk already, but you don't want anyone to hear? Well, don't you worry about that—I can keep a secret, I promise.'

Grace placed the doll back into its chair, watching as her new ward grappled with the idea that such things were remotely possible.

'Do you want to know what the dolly's secret was?' said Grace, a plan forming in her mind.

Rose nodded and sat down, resting her chin in her hands, ready for her opponent's next move.

'Sometimes,' said Grace, 'they can hear voices and see things, just like me, even when there is no one around—aren't they and I special?'

Rose shook her head and sat back, stabbing a finger to her pale pink ribbon, tied to her waist. She raised her finger defensively in the tower's direction, returning it meekly to pick at her lips.

'You can see and hear them too?' said Grace in mock astonishment. 'I've met no one like that before. Shall we make it our secret not to tell anyone about them, except each other and the dolls?'

The young girl looked nervously around the parliament of porcelain faces as though waiting for the idea to be debated and agreed upon. Grace held her breath as Rose bit her lip and nodded.

'I'm wondering if you shouldn't be eating that food, now, before it gets cold.'

Rose lifted the flaccid kale on her fork and looked over for mercy.

'I'll give you a new shadow animal every three mouthfuls,' said Grace with a coy wink. 'And a dragon if you finish the fish fillet.'

CHAPTER 11

Rose napped after her meal and the excitement of the mythic beast flapping around the firelit room, threatening to eat any child with spinach remaining on their plate. Grace retired to her room and changed into her grey check skirt and white blouse, hanging the heavy gown carefully in the otherwise empty closet.

The afternoon passed uneventfully and calmly in quiet reading, despite Grace's urge to press on and discover the source of the child's silence.

One blundering false move and trust will wither, she thought. *Patience—she's smarter than you think.*

Rose sat within the folds of her lap, turning the pages of *The Phoenix and the Carpet* to study the colourful illustrations and point out words unfamiliar to her.

'Whooping cough,' said Grace as the little finger stabbed at the page like a manuscript reading stick. 'It's a nasty disease that affects the lungs.' Rose nodded and continued reading.

She was an attentive pupil but suffered several episodes of coughing later in the afternoon, which left her breathless, and unable to chalk her joined-up letters on the framed slate. It also left several flecks of blood speckled across the crisply ironed table cloth.

Absorbed in the familiarity of her teaching, Grace relaxed into a routine, well-rehearsed and successful, until much of the copied handwriting lessons were done. A young maid came in with tea and a plate of ginger biscuits that Rose eyed hungrily. The maid introduced herself as Ann and handed a small paper bag containing sugared nuts to the eager young girl.

'What's that?' asked Grace as Rose jumped up and down in excitement.

'Begging your pardon, Miss Meadows,' she said. 'It's from Mr Bishop. He has me smuggle them here, being as Mrs Stanton doesn't like him near the child or anyone passing along treats. Did I do wrong?'

Rose froze as sentence was pronounced.

'No,' said Grace, turning to the pleading, wide eyes of the little girl. 'Shall we add this to our growing list of secrets?'

Rose nodded and picked out several almonds, smelling them intently before offering one to Grace.

'Tell Mr Bishop to be careful,' said Grace. 'I have the distinct impression that Mrs Stanton would not approve of anything that brings pleasure to anyone in this house.'

Ann looked down and away. 'We all have to watch out,' she whispered. 'Walls have ears, but she's well in with the master, so it's best to stay on her good side. She had a go at my Billy just for smiling at me this morning.'

'Well you can tell Mr Bishop he can trust me to keep the contraband a secret, providing he acts in moderation of course.'

Rose yawned, and her head nodded to her chest as the bell rang for the main door, startling them into wakefulness.

'That'll be Dr Croswell,' said Ann, hurriedly setting out

cups and saucers and glancing across as the clock chimed four o'clock. 'Mr Bishop will show him in because Master's indisposed in the study.'

Heavy, purposeful footfalls in the corridor arrived at the entrance and the great door opened. A cheery voice, warm and genuine, echoed through the hall as the doctor was admitted, closely and briefly followed by Mr Bishop, acting as the first footman. The giant appeared around the door and winked at Rose.

Grace stood and smoothed down her skirt, brushing back a wayward strand of hair as the clean-cut, smiling and well-dressed country doctor appeared from behind the door, carrying a heavy Gladstone bag.

'Miss Meadows?' he said in greeting. 'James Croswell. A pleasure to finally meet you.'

Grace bobbed courteously and smiled back, infected by his buoyantly handsome face. Words failed her as the whiskered, solemn and aged country doctor stereotype she had envisaged vanished to be replaced by this striking young gentleman with an unruly mop of short, curly hair. He readied his stethoscope from around his neck and proceeded to examine the hearts of several of the porcelain dolls.

He put his fingers to his chin, addressing the static painted face of the smallest doll. Rose giggled as the doctor continued his charade.

'I think you look a little pale today,' he said. 'How about a nice vitamin tablet?'

Grace smiled as the child nodded as though agreeing with the diagnosis.

'And how is my favourite patient?' he said, turning to Rose, placing the headset within her ears. She giggled as he raised the bell at the end of the tubing to his breast. 'Am I still ticking?' he said.

Rose's eyes widened with the beating sound coming

through the headset. She nodded as he retrieved the device and began to examine the little girl in front of him.

'Is the new lady nice?' he whispered, loud enough so that Grace could overhear. The distraction worked, and Rose nodded as he moved the bell to her lungs. 'Ready to breathe in and out like a bellows?'

Rose puckered her lips defiantly. Grace gave her a stern glance, and the child relented, rattling in great breaths while the doctor listened intently to the brittle lungs. He glanced over at the speckles on the tablecloth and a spasm of sadness clouded the sunshine radiating from his joyful countenance. Dr Croswell examined her eyes for quite some time and waited while she swallowed two brightly coloured pills with a glass of water.

'Well done. You are getting better each time I see you,' he said, turning to Grace. His honest face barely contained the lie, and his hazel-coloured eyes sought for absolution. Grace saw the setting of his jaw as he fought to return to his earlier jovial self.

'Why don't you have your tea while Dr Croswell and I have a little chat?' said Grace, sensing the relief in the medic's face. 'Make sure all the dolls in the secret club get something, too?'

Rose nodded and dived into the ginger biscuits.

The doctor flashed a thankful glance. 'That was skilfully done,' he whispered, collecting his bag and escorting Grace from the room. 'She usually wants to follow Mr Bishop or me everywhere. I think you've made an impression already.'

'Subterfuge is a speciality of mine,' said Grace, catching the doctor's raised eyebrow and smile, 'especially with children.'

'I must remember that, and be extremely careful around you,' he said, offering his manicured hand.

Grace shook it and halted in the centre of the hall.

'Is everything all right?' he said.

'Forgive me,' said Grace. 'You're not what I expected, that's all.'

'Feeling's mutual,' he said, avoiding eye contact. 'We were both expecting the same stereotype, were we not? Fusty, dry, rigidly formal and devoid of emotional warmth—is that about right?'

'You forgot "warted",' said Grace playfully.

The doctor blushed and slapped a hand to his head. 'Shall we?' he stammered, opening the drawing-room door.

'Does Rose's silence have something to do with her illness?' said Grace, taking a seat near the window.

'Possibly,' said the doctor, placing the bag between his legs and falling into a nearby armchair. 'Rose has a pernicious case of anaemia, but it doesn't respond to any traditional forms of treatment. Her immune system is compromised as a result, and she is prone to all sorts of infection.'

'Like the cough?' said Grace.

'Yes, though that is a lingering reminder of tuberculosis she suffered eighteen months ago.'

'Forgive me,' said Grace, 'but shouldn't she be in a hospital?'

'She's been in and out regularly, but we have to be careful of this damned Spanish flu. She revives for a time, but the treatments are severe and only temporary; she returns here, and the cycle of sickness begins again.'

'Is there anything I can do?'

The doctor removed a small brown bottle from his medical bag and placed it on the side table.

'Mrs Stanton gives her a dose of this,' he said. 'It's a tonic and expectorant to help fight infection and ease her airways. There's also an oil burner in her room for a balsam vapour that helps her sleep.'

'There's a candle left burning all night?' said Grace in alarm.

'It's quite safe and out of reach,' said the doctor calmly. 'Is there a problem?'

Grace rubbed her palms together and watched the dark liquid settle within the smoky glass. 'Are you willing to observe patient confidentiality?'

'Of course,' he said, maintaining eye contact. 'I'm willing to join the dolls in your secret club if you'll have me?' He placed three fingers together in a cheery mock scout salute.

'I have a problem with fire,' she said.

'Arson?' he said, raising his eyebrows.

'No,' said Grace quickly. 'Fear of fire and intense anxiety in knowing that a child would be sleeping in an unattended room with a naked flame.'

'I could arrange for an electric replacement, but it might take a few days to arrive. I've been harking on about burning lamp oil to Charles for months—it's not good for the child despite the benefits of the balsam. Fresh air is good, but it tires her out considerably.'

'You would do that, for me?'

He nodded. 'I won't pry, Miss Meadows. It's quite a reasonable apprehension to have, and I think it really would be better.' He leaned forwards to whisper, despite the empty room. 'I admire your courage in bringing it to my attention, but would insist on a return of a favour, however.'

'Name it?'

'Give my friend Captain Ferris some hope; he has little left in the way of it.'

'What's the prognosis for Rose?' said Grace.

The doctor rested his mouth on the steeple of his fingers. 'Not good, I'm afraid.'

'Hence the urgency of my appointment and the eagerness of Captain Ferris to encourage her to speak?' she said.

The doctor hunched forwards and nodded. 'He is a man with little left. He is alone, with dwindling health and an uncertain future, not to mention the sickness of his daughter. The house is falling apart as you've likely gathered, and the staff don't stick around long enough to get everything back on its feet.

'I, on the other hand, am an optimist.'

'Then we have something in common,' said Grace, comforted by the smile that returned to his face.

'You trained at the institute, didn't you?'

'Yes,' she said. 'Though I've been in private service for a short while.' Grace rushed at a question, desperate to start an explanation of Jane's death.

'Did you know my predecessor?'

The cloud of sadness returned as he fumbled in his open case.

'Yes,' he said. 'Only for a short time, alas. I was Miss Urquhart's physician and chess partner; do you play, Miss Meadows?'

Grace detected the diversion and danced around the subject.

'Badly. I play cards, though.'

'Bridge?' he enquired.

'No,' said Grace. 'Cards that gentlemen play when ladies retire to the drawing room.'

The doctor glanced up, his bemused countenance now returned, tinged with a little shock.

'Good heavens,' he said. 'Did Jane—I mean Miss Urquhart—teach you to play?'

'No, she insisted I learn nobler pursuits. It was a former employer that encouraged me to learn brag, poker and rummy; he had a wicked sense of humour and modern sense of propriety for one advanced in years.

'Are you able to shed any light on what happened to Jane?

We were very close, and I only discovered she had passed away this morning.'

James exhaled deeply. 'It was at the beginning of October, and I got a call about the accident; it was very early in the morning. Miss Urquhart had been unwell for some time—'

'Jane was ill?' asked Grace. 'She didn't mention it to me in her last correspondence over the summer?'

'It was a malady of the mind, I'm afraid.' He wrung his hands. 'I feel guilty because all the signs were there. Maybe she'd still be alive if I'd seen it sooner.'

'Seen what?'

'This may come as a shock,' he said, 'but the night she died, Jane had taken an overdose of laudanum. She fell from a great height attempting to climb along a dangerous ledge; if the fall hadn't killed her, the strong opium would have.'

Grace clasped a hand to her mouth and shook her head. 'That's not possible, Jane was no addict, and she was terrified of heights. I don't believe it.'

'Kate, the housemaid, found an empty bottle in her room. I'm very sorry,' he said. 'I feel partly responsible.'

'How so?'

'She had been complaining about cramps, hallucinations and feelings of being watched—all symptoms of paranoia brought on by regular use of opiates. I should have listened to her, talked through her illness or even referred her to a specialist.'

'If it's of any comfort,' said Grace, 'she wouldn't have listened. Don't torment yourself.'

The doctor snorted and pursed his lips. 'You knew her well,' he said. 'Do you have any idea what regret does to a person?' He formed two fists, and the blood drained from his knuckles with the exertion.

Grace leaned over and gently laid a hand on his shoulder.

'I know only too well,' she said. 'We carry those we

couldn't save with us, heavier than any Gladstone bag. Am I right?'

The doctor stiffened and ran his hands through his hair. 'Something like that,' he said. 'I think perhaps we should exchange places; you have an intuition I don't possess.'

'I think you would make an excellent governess.'

He laughed. 'I think you are humouring me,' he said. 'I think I would be dismissed for encouraging bad behaviour.'

'That's likely another thing we might have in common,' she said. 'You mentioned that Jane was killed in the tower—is that the reason it's out of bounds?'

'Something like that,' said the doctor. 'It's not safe in there for several reasons.' He glanced at his shoes and fiddled with the handle of his bag.

'Captain Ferris told me to remain vigilant,' said Grace, 'as though he feared for Miss Ferris's and my safety?'

Dr Croswell stretched out his hands. 'Charles is not a well man,' he said, examining the lines in his upturned palms. 'He believes that a spiritual malaise is causing Rose's condition. I'm a man of science, but I only mention it because it is a source of contention between us. I wouldn't want to worry you unnecessarily; it's all nonsense in any case.'

'What does Captain Ferris believe is happening to Miss Ferris?' asked Grace, staring into his rapidly blinking eyes. 'I've spent a week in the company of Lady Foster, and I'm the leader of the *secret dolls club* if that makes any difference?' She held up three fingers to the side of her head.

The doctor held up his open palm.

'Forgive me,' he said. 'I should not have patronised you. Charles believes that the house is under some form of spiritual attack, emanating from the tower. People under stress believe strange things, and beliefs can inform actions even when those beliefs are misguided. I assure you there are no such things as ghosts, but that doesn't stop people from being frightened by them.'

'Is Miss Ferris aware of this?' said Grace.

'Her head is full of it, and so is everyone else's in the blasted place,' he said. 'You can see it in many of her drawings, and the housekeeper is positively encouraging it. She's a spiritualist, and her ridiculous beliefs are being reinforced by the sudden appearance of—' He hesitated and sat back, folding his arms.

'Lady Foster and the strange new governess?'

He sighed. 'You see my reticence in bringing it to your attention?

'There's nothing in that tower to explain why she climbed up there so high. Not ghost stories, not fairy tales or stories about hidden silver; there's nothing in there except memories and dust.'

'What stories do you mean?'

'The family used to hide Catholic priests and sympathisers during the seventeenth century when it was illegal to practise mass openly. The place is riddled with secret holes, false panels and many passages. It was supposed to be where they hid copious amounts of church silverware to avoid it falling into the hands of soldiers stripping the abbeys and churches during the Reformation. I spent my youth in and out of here, playing with Charles, especially in that tower, and there's nothing to the tale, just a few dusty holes for priests to hide from soldiers and the like.

'Superstition and nonsense, I'm afraid,' he said, wringing his hands. 'But it's Mrs Stanton that drives the notion. She's becoming the power behind the throne, if you will—a surrogate mother and carer. I think she must have been a puritan in a former life.'

He shrugged. 'If I believed in that sort of thing, of course.'

'She told me you overruled her on my appointment.'

'Yes,' said the doctor. 'One of the few occasions, these days. If staff didn't keep leaving, then Charles would probably have relented to her request; even he realises Mrs Stanton and the few who remain can't do everything *and* educate Rose at the same time. She is extremely diligent, efficient and loyal to the point of obsession, especially around Charles, I'll give her that. I think if truth be told, she'd sooner see Rose remain quiet; she doesn't strike me as a positive role model.'

'Unlike Mr Bishop, for example?' said Grace.

'You've noticed?' said James, smiling. 'Rose idolises him, as does the lad he saved from a life of petty crime. My only concern is that Miss Ferris thinks bad things happen every time she speaks. You need to break that cycle.'

'Such as?' said Grace.

'The death of her mother and Miss Urquhart. When your role model is a near seven-foot tall and allegedly invincible mute, then you can see the difficulties. Bishop's a good man and is the reason Charles came home alive by all accounts. I only hope he can handle the fact that it's Mrs Stanton calling the shots around here.'

He closed his bag and got up. 'If you need me, you can send Bishop round in the car. The telephone doesn't work here, along with a good many other things.' He glanced up at the dim, hungry chandelier, starved of electric.

'How often do you visit?' she said, joining him on his way to the door.

'Every few days,' he said, 'though I'm here tomorrow to check on Charles when he recovers from his bout of melancholy.' He glanced at the crystal decanter set on the sideboard. 'He's not without his demons, if you pardon the expression.'

'Thank you for your openness and advice,' she said. 'I look forward to seeing you tomorrow?'

'Perhaps you can teach me how to play cards one evening?' He leaned into her face.

Grace smiled and nodded as he returned to stand tall and upright.

'Just promise me one thing,' he said.

'Of course,' said Grace.

The doctor pointed to a wide photograph on the wall. A row of many household staff stood in their Sunday best in front of Hemingworth Hall in happier times. The giant form of Mr Bishop, replete with a wax moustache, stood behind a young and uninjured Charles Ferris. A beautiful dark-haired woman sat beside, beaming with a baby in her arms.

'Belief is a powerful motivator. This house affects people who are sensitive and open to suggestion.'

Grace frowned, unsure of his true meaning.

She held his gaze, basking in the genuine and honest feeling of protection, but this time, it was Grace who looked away first.

'I have a profound respect for Lady Foster, but—' He tapped on the glass over the image of Charles's wife. 'For Sophia's sake, and that of Jane, I'm asking you to be careful. Just promise me that if you see strange things or ghosts, you'll let me know?

'I don't want to lose anyone else.'

CHAPTER 12

Grace shovelled the remnants of shepherd's pie into her mouth, keeping pace with the silent hulk of the manservant at the other side of the long wooden table. Bishop put down his fork, glugged at a huge glass of milk, and wiped his frothy beard with his bare arm. He was dressed in his rolled shirt and braces, and Grace felt at ease in his solitary company, though he seemed intrigued by her appetite and incredible ability to clean plates as readily as he could. Grace had bumped into him several times during the early evening as he struggled to fix several electrical issues before sitting down to his evening meal.

'*Forgive me*,' Grace signed, with a mouth full of food. '*I haven't eaten since daybreak and watching Rose eat for an hour was hungry work.*'

Bishop smiled and pushed over his portion of dry fruitcake.

'Are you sure?' said Grace, swallowing the last spoonful of the pie.

The giant nodded.

She wrapped it into a handkerchief and placed it into the

embroidered purse. 'Do you prefer signing or speech?' said Grace. 'I should have asked.'

Bishop put his great elbows on the table and cracked his fingers with his broad hands. His fingers moved with great dexterity and clarity.

'*Either, and thank you. Hands are good when bellies are empty, and mouths are full,*' he signed. '*Silence sometimes has its advantages, wouldn't you agree?*'

'That depends on what is being kept silent, and the reason for it,' she said, deftly warming her fingers to converse with the mute. 'Why is sound so forbidden here?'

'*Master and Mrs Stanton say so, and that is enough. It wakes things that should remain sleeping.*'

Grace dabbed at her mouth with a handkerchief. 'What kind of things?'

Bishop exhaled. '*Just superstition,*' he signed, '*like the curfew bell I must ring in the grounds later.*'

'I thought curfew bells were all done with, these days,' said Grace, 'apart from a few north of the border?'

'*It has been rung here since I entered the master's service thirty years ago and is done to make sure the fires are covered and only those that have reason to roam the house do so after dark; it's important to make sure that the house is safe from fire—wouldn't you agree?*'

Grace put away her handkerchief, unsure of the inference, and studied his poker face: the manservant, valet, handyman, man-Friday, the saviour of the injured and battle-stricken Captain Ferris; here was a man devoted and loyal, testing the newcomer's moral compass. Perhaps he was investigating the rumour of her past? Had such information arrived already, here in the depths of darkest Warwickshire?

'Indeed,' she answered. 'Fire would be my chief concern alongside the safety of Miss Rose—she thinks a lot of you.'

Bishop smiled as though satisfied with the sincerity of her

response and the disarming counter-attack. He cradled his arms as if carrying a baby.

'*I brought her into the world alongside the previous housekeeper when the doctor and midwife were delayed by the floods nigh on eight years ago. I was the first face she ever saw—*'

He pulled a grimace that was at once grotesque and humorous. '*—and for that,*' he signed, '*I must endeavour to amend.*'

'You love them both, don't you?' she said. 'The captain and Rose. I saw how he might have offended you in the drawing room, but also how he must rely on you. I think the feeling is mutual and unconditional, if a little imperfect.'

Bishop looked puzzled by her openness and judge of character. '*I thank you for your correction to my master in the drawing room; it was brave of you to challenge Captain Ferris on my account, but unnecessary.*'

Grace smiled and lifted her hands. '*I didn't do it on your account, but for everyone not able, unwilling or not ready to speak. I have spent my working life challenging the stereotype that someone without a voice is without intellect or usefulness.*'

Bishop rose and bowed. '*You should have been a politician; you speak eloquently, and with great conviction—like Jane, like someone I could call a friend?*'

'I hope so,' said Grace, rejoicing in the mention of her former mentor. 'If Rose is any judge of character, I would welcome the chance to earn it. I have few friends.'

He raised an eye, amused by the sincerity. '*Be careful what you wish for,*' he signed, '*I've sworn to defend this family, even if it takes my life.*'

Grace rose and tilted her head to look into the kind face. 'So have I, to make amends.' She held out her hand in friendship.

'*To whom?*' he mouthed, clasping his palm into hers and closing his hand. '*Lady Foster?*'

Grace marvelled at the gentleness in the great man's grip. 'Yes,' she said, 'but also to someone now beyond any danger.' She released him from the handshake.

'*A powerful motivator,*' he signed, turning to go.

'Why did Lady Foster ask you to convey the message on the driveway, to be careful?' she asked hurriedly.

'*I would ask you the same question,*' signed Bishop. '*Don't trust anyone, at least not yet. Some are not who they pretend to be. I used to carry the master's favour, but someone else has taken my place, and my star is on the wane—be careful and follow your mistress's advice so that history does not repeat itself.*'

'What history?' said Grace, moving to meet him at the door.

'*Recent history,*' he signed. '*You have been told to stay away from the tower?*'

'I know about Miss Urquhart. It's all right,' said Grace, touching his forearm. 'The doctor told me she fell.'

He turned to go.

'Is that the reason everyone is afraid?' she asked.

'*It's the reason behind Rose's silence, and that is enough,*' he signed. '*Be careful.*'

Grace collected the embroidered pouch as the electric lights flickered, and brief darkness enveloped the room. Something shifted in the thick plastered walls separating the adjacent pantry. Fire was her greatest fear, but being stuck in the dark with vermin was a close second. The sound shifted to the ceiling and creaked a final time before it became silent. Grace raced to get out of the room and back to the light of Rose's room before the uncomfortable darkness overtook the whole house and her faltering spirit.

The rain outside in the evening darkness ceased, and a bright moon parted the clouds, announcing its torch-like beam on the nursery floor. Grace closed the book, and Rose clapped, begging for another. The fantastical short story was a success, and the colourful telling of it had taken all of Grace's considerable skill as an orator.

'Not tonight, Rose,' said Grace, 'it's close to eight o'clock. Tomorrow we must begin our studies, but perhaps we can learn a song together, for Christmas?'

Rose screwed her face into a look of rejection and denial at the prospect of speech and the cheap, glancing subterfuge from the governess. She shook her head and ran over to the nursery table to continue her drawing. Rose hacked a great cough, wheezing between asthmatic breaths until she calmed, soothed by the governess's rubbing hands on her back.

After removing a handkerchief from her purse, Grace caught several of the larger expulsions of phlegm, speckled with minute dark fragments of blood as the suffering child glanced wondrously at the embroidered pouch. The fit of coughing subsided.

Rose smiled as she touched the purse, marvelling at its colourful threads and forget-me-not buttons centred by tiny lustrous pearls.

'Would you like to look after this for me?' said Grace, disentangling herself from the shoulder strap. 'Will you keep it safe for me until I settle in?'

The child's eyes widened with the joy and weight of responsibility. Rose rubbed her pale fingers across the embellishments and hugged the purse like a doll, squeezing the wrapped cake within.

'There's a surprise inside for later when no one is awake.' Grace smiled and raised a forefinger to her lips in a gesture of secrecy.

Rose placed her hand on her chest and extended out her

fingers in an affectionate gesture. Grace repeated it, and they touched palms. 'Did Miss Urquhart teach you this? You are so clever to learn signs when you can speak.'

The girl nodded and then smiled, indicating another. She pulled her palm away to raise it above her fair hair, revealing a great height.

'Mr Bishop? He taught you alongside Miss Urquhart?'

Rose smiled bashfully.

'Did he teach you any other signs?' asked Grace, sensing an opening and connection.

Rose shrugged and twitched her nose.

'Go on,' whispered Grace, sensing some reluctance or prohibition against the use of such language. She recalled the father's strong views on the matter. 'It's all right if we are alone. I know Pa-pa wants you to use your voice, but you have such pretty hands and you sign so beautifully.'

Rose blushed and blew Grace a kiss. Grace pretended to catch it.

'Did Mr Bishop teach you that?' she said, laughing as Rose shook her head and broke into a series of hurried but well-rehearsed signs concluding with the spelling of her name.

Grace clapped, wondering if the ruse to use a silent and secret way of connecting and building trust had already been attempted successfully by her former mentor.

Rose continued, encouraged by the audience. Her small hands whirled in well-practised signs: rose, flower, chocolate, songbird, train, and finally raising both her hands upright to wiggle her fingers.

'Fire,' said Grace, clasping the little hands together to end the game. 'That's enough for one day.'

Rose glanced up, confused by the sudden departure of joy, and pulled out a hand to point at the drawings and pencils on the table.

'Just a few more minutes,' said Grace, letting go and

leafing through the crayon-covered pages. Scenes of house life, rainbows and gardens, a pony, bells and boats. Through them all, the tower and west face of the house seemed a common backdrop. Several contained stick figures and obvious references to the staff: an old gardener, leaning over a wheelbarrow full of brightly chalked carrots, several young and long-lashed maids, her father, sad in his chair and wheeled by a female figure with a brightly speckled face. The crudely drawn woman shouted out the word 'Silence!' from a red speech bubble. In the distant tower, a face looked out, frantically scribbled over as though to disguise or obliterate the image.

Grace picked up a red-cheeked doll and whispered into its ear. 'Who is this in the tower?'

Rose paused but did not glance up. Her tongue lolled from one side of pale lips in intense artistic concentration.

Rose slowed her crayon and glanced at the drawing without emotion.

'Is it a secret?' whispered Grace.

Rose stared towards the moonlit window, slowly and imperceptibly nodding her head.

Grace pulled another drawing from the table that provided little more than coloured abstract lines drawn over the edges of a series of boxes. It could have been a map of the house, but for the confused stripes and scrawls.

A final drawing showed the bright blue emblazoned dress of a straw-haired woman, smiling and holding the hands of a happy young girl in an Alice band akin to the one worn by Rose.

'Is this me?' said Grace, pointing to the similarity of her dress and hair. 'It's very good.'

Rose shook her head.

'Is it your previous governess, then?'

Rose put down her crayon and nodded.

'Jane looked after me, too, and taught me how to speak to people who don't want to or can't. Did she ever get you to talk?' said Grace.

Rose pursed her lips and swung her legs.

'I think she would have asked you to say "chocolate cake", that was her favourite.'

Rose grabbed a blank piece of paper and several coloured pencils. Hastily she drew several clouds that soon developed legs and bleated upon a green hill. The stick figure of a shepherdess appeared, carrying a smaller animal. Rose twisted the page and returned to her earlier masterpiece.

'*Mary had a little lamb*?' said Grace, putting down the doll and picking up the drawing. 'Why did you stop talking, then?'

Rose picked up a black crayon and pressed down on the centre of the page, forcefully snapping the wax in half. She grubbed out a spiral, forcing the splintered end into her fist. She seethed and began to hyperventilate. Her hand spiralled out, covering the paper until the furious action turned the drawing into a frenzied mass of circular lines. Rose glanced up, clenching her teeth through gasping breaths.

'Stop it, Rose. You're frightening me,' said Grace, seeking to calm the child by grabbing the seemingly uncontrollable wrist. Grace shook the stub free as the child suddenly cried out in anguish.

'*My fault for speaking! All my fault!*'

Rose covered her ears, and Grace saw the crescent cut marks in the young pale skin.

Rose shrieked and pulled herself free racing to the hastily opening door.

'Whoa, Miss Ferris, whatever is the matter?' said Kate, narrowly avoiding the child who raced back into the protective skirt of the governess upon seeing the brown bottle and spoon. The young ward wheezed and sobbed.

'Her wrists are marked,' said Grace. 'Are you aware of this?'

The housemaid put down the bottle and scowled at the whimpering girl seeking shelter from the impending medicine. 'Bad girl, Rose. Wait till Mrs Stanton finds out you've been hurting yourself with those long nails again.'

Realising that her revelation would cause the young girl some form of self-realising punishment and guilt, Grace sought to break the cycle.

'It's all right, Kate,' she said. 'I'll speak with Mrs Stanton myself.'

'Well, so long as you do. Red and raw we were a few weeks ago, weren't we? I thought you'd grown out of that, you naughty girl. Mrs Stanton will have to trim them, however much you struggle and whine.'

'Please don't,' said Grace. 'Please don't upset her or punish her; it only makes things worse.' Rose tightened her grip on the dress as Kate unstopped the bottle. 'What is that?'

'Medicine,' said Kate, approaching with the spoon. 'And I'll thank you for keeping your medical opinions to yourself.' She lunged for the girl, grabbing her forearm. Rose cried out then clamped her mouth shut as the housemaid attempted to force the wavering spoon down her unwilling throat.

'Stop it,' said Grace, disgusted by the rough treatment. 'You're hurting her.'

'Bad girl, won't take her medicine! Ma-ma will get you if you don't!' said Kate, oblivious to anything but the task in front of her.

Rose went limp with the threat as the liquid was forced into her stiff open mouth.

'Don't frighten her!' said Grace, seeing the fear in her ward's eyes. She knocked the empty spoon from the surprised housemaid's hand.

'What are you doing?' exclaimed Kate. 'She's sick and won't take her medicine—'

The curfew bell's tolling, distantly from the walled garden, interrupted the altercation and Grace instinctively looked out of the window onto the moonlit lawn. The figure of a boy stood there, staring back. Rose returned to the folds of her skirt.

'Curfew,' said Kate, turning to follow the gaze of the governess and the child to the outside lawn. She shrugged at the patch of illuminated grass, fading into empty darkness. 'Long past time for your bed, Mistress Rose. I'd be making way to your room too, Miss Meadows, if you don't want to upset Mrs Stanton.' The housemaid left the room without a backward glance.

Grace barely registered the instruction; she glanced at her ward, quaking with the sight of the child outside in the moonlight.

'You see him?' whispered Grace, hearing the bell tolling outside.

Rose nodded, watching as the boy lifted his arms to sign.

'It's all right,' said Grace. 'He's not here to hurt you.'

Grace turned with the realisation that Arthur's spirit was here, and wondered what warning was forthcoming, so soon into her appointment. She took a few fearful steps closer to the window, and Rose followed, clutching at her grey cotton pleats and burying her head in the coarse cloth. Grace instinctively dug her nails into her wrist, subconsciously trying to banish the apparition, and glanced down to see Rose doing the same with her free hand.

'He's here to see me, not you, Rose,' she said, forcing her fingers through the clammy hand of the shivering child. They clasped tightly, and Grace felt the grip and tenseness in Rose's grasp as she continued to clench her eyes shut. For a moment, Grace sensed fleeting memories that did not belong to her, the same feeling of joining she had experienced in the salon of Lady Foster, only this time they came not from her own experiences. Images of the dark-haired woman and Rose joyfully chasing each other around the lawn of the moated mansion. A memory of Bishop throwing her, high and giggling, into the air, before carrying her upon his shoulders. A sad image surfaced of a uniformed Charles Ferris, younger and able to walk, saying goodbye to her mother, who was on the edge of hysteria, at the bridge, before he and Bishop departed with a salute. A feeling of fear welled as a dark face appeared at the tower window, images of silver flickering in the firelight, and scurrying sounds in the small hours of sleep.

Then it came. A memory resisted and unwilling to be unlocked, no longer contained. Grace saw the face of her mentor and best friend, Jane Urquhart, terribly injured. The woman lay on a hard, tiled floor among fallen pieces of masonry, bleeding from her lips, unable to speak. Grace felt the shock of the encounter through the child's eyes and her sudden recollection that her best friend and greatest ally had not left the situation or been dismissed—she had been mortally removed from it.

Silently coughing and in shock, Jane grabbed at a tiny hand. Grace saw the nail marks in the skin and knew it was that of the terrified child grasping at her skirt below, reliving the memory and unable to avoid the flood of emotion and grief at the final parting. It was as though Grace was also saying goodbye, and she felt the tears begin to slide down her cheek. Jane opened her right hand and dropped a small black chess piece into the lap of the crying child. Opening her ward's left hand, and with her life streaming away, Jane made a sign upon the flat of Rose's palm. Jane's middle finger extended downwards and pivoted like a spinning top in the centre of the little palm. The image in Rose's mind faded as the small hand grabbed at the object and turned to see a rush of servants coming through the doors. There was a faint wail of grief and shock as Rose was dragged away.

The memory faded as the bell tolled for the final time, and Grace looked out at the spirit on the lawn. The boy opened his palm and extended his middle finger downwards, repeating the sign.

'Poison ...' said Grace. She glanced down at Rose, and across at the sticky and lint-covered spoon on the rug as Mrs Stanton came in to collect the quivering child.

CHAPTER 13

Sleep was an impossibility, and Grace tossed restlessly in the dark bedroom listening to the night noises of the old house: the shuffling and creaking of those in nearby rooms, the snoring and sleep-talking of the servants despite the thickness of the walls, and the scurrying of mice, rats and other nocturnal creatures within great cavities behind the panelling.

Greatest of all of these was the knowledge that Rose lay sleeping in the room below, insistent on the burning candle to banish all fear. The balsam burner was now lit, and naked flames ruled downstairs now that the clinking of Charles's crystal decanter was silent, and his drunken squeaking chair had retired the melancholic captain to bed.

Despite the conflict with the head of the household and the likelihood that the episode with the medicine would be relayed, embellished, back to Mrs Stanton, Grace desperately fought to calm herself with pleasant thoughts. Thoughts of happier times, being at the institute, with Jane.

Then there was the intense sharing of memory, and final

moments of the dying governess, Arthur's appearance, and the new sign.

The circular reasoning began again.

She poured herself a glass of water from the refilled jug. Crinkling her nose at the bitter aftertaste, she suddenly turned, putting down the glass quietly on the table.

The scratching within the wall caused a moment of panic, and Grace sat up, searching the shadowy corners for any sign of worse things to come. The moon cast its last beams upon the seconded silver spoon on the washbasin, and she rose to sniff at the sickly treacle-like smear on its smooth surface, wondering if something sinister lay in the syrup.

A new noise, heavier and near, came from within the walls as though something larger than a rat shuffled within, and Grace recalled the pantry and the shifting sound, as though something shambled through sand. The sound shifted slowly and stealthily, pausing as if to listen before sliding and stepping its way from beneath the floorboards and up to the other side of the panelling. Grace panicked and reached for the light switch. She flipped it several times, trying to spark life into the dusty, solitary bulb to no avail. She reached for the electric torch beneath her pillow, turned it on and grabbed an iron poker.

The thing in the wall paused, as though listening to the rapid breathing from Grace's heaving chest. The sound moved the length of the wall and into the sitting room. Grace followed it as it stopped on the other side of the dividing wall, right between two wide recessed wooden sections of panelling. A gentle thud came from within, as though whatever was beyond was forcing a way through. Grace gave in to fear and ran for the doorknob, rattling the worn lock furiously to get out. She twitched the torch across to the wall and saw the panel squeak open as though hinged. An unsuccessful attempt to withhold a high-pitched sneeze came from the other side.

Grace lunged at the wall with the poker, trying to close the opening panel as a small pale hand bearing the embroidered purse shot through, deflecting her stroke into the adjacent woodwork.

'Rose?' said Grace, shaking in her undergarments and bare feet.

The panel opened wide enough for the young girl to emerge, dusty and cobwebbed, from within the thick wall. She squinted into the light of the torch and beamed back with a smile.

Grace dropped the poker and pulled her through like a midwife bringing a stone-dusted child into the world.

'What are you doing in there?' said Grace, pointing into the narrow void and the thin passageway between the walls.

'*Lonely*,' signed Rose, pointing into the holes. '*Hiding place*.'

'Passages and priest holes?' said Grace, seeing the disappearing light from the torch and the top step of a secret stone staircase barely eighteen inches wide.

'This goes to your room?' said Grace, wiping the cold sweat from her brow.

Rose nodded. '*Tunnels*,' she signed. '*Secret*.' The purse opened, and Rose lifted out the wrapped fruitcake, offering it to Grace as though a midnight snack with a young intruder was just the thing the exhausted governess wanted most of all.

'Dear God,' said Grace, grabbing her by the hand and sitting her down on her lap in the armchair. 'You gave me a fright.'

Rose smiled, handed over the purse and picked at the cherries in the cake.

Grace examined the sorry and smelly interior of the

embroidered pouch to find other items within. A folded drawing from earlier lay alongside a heavier wooden item—the black rook missing from the chess set laid out on the bedroom's trunk.

It was the piece that Jane had handed over at the moment of her death.

'Why did Miss Urquhart have this, do you know?'

Rose shook her head and folded Grace's fingers around it.

'For me?' she said, putting it into the pocket of her night-dress. 'Thank you. Do you want to look after my purse forever? I think I might get a new one, one that doesn't smell of crayons and cake.'

The child smiled with the exchange, put down the lump of fruity sponge and twisted the torch against Grace's wrists.

'*Bad things?*' signed Rose with a pained expression.

'Yes,' said Grace, 'but I made a promise to someone never to do it again. It used to make bad things go away, but only for a short time.' She took the torch and lifted the grubby wrists of the sickly child.

'Are you trying to make bad things go away, too?' she said.

Rose nodded and turned to fold herself into the warm embrace of the governess.

Grace hugged the child as Rose began to pick at the fruit-cake again.

'Will you share my promise not to hurt your wrists again if I promise to keep you safe from bad things?'

Rose turned and looked into her eyes, trusting and inno-cent. The smudged face nodded.

'Can you tell me where the bad things are?' said Grace, pressing the point. 'So I can keep you safe?'

Rose bit her lip and nodded but seemed unsure of how to make the sign. She opened the purse and unfolded the drawing of Jane and the other figures in front of the house.

Rose pointed to the tower's window where the dreadful face leered out behind a tangled mess of furious lines.

'Something about the tower?' said Grace. 'Did Miss Urquhart know of this?'

Rose nodded.

'What makes the bad things come?' asked Grace.

Rose rubbed her eyes and sleepily lifted a finger to her ear, rotating it in the air before pointing at the yawning chasm of her mouth. She snuggled into Grace's arms.

'Your voice?' whispered Grace. 'Is that why you don't want to speak, to keep yourself safe?'

Rose pointed to the stick people in the drawings. She lifted her finger and gently pressed it into Grace's arm.

'To keep everyone safe?' asked Grace, glancing at the speech bubble bulging from the stick figure of the house-keeper. Grace looked down at the child's pale lips, recalling the encounter with the medicine.

Ma-ma will get you if you don't!

'Does Mrs Stanton want you to stay quiet so bad things won't come?' she asked.

The girl nodded and twisted a braid of the governess's hair.

A gentle sound of a tiny bell echoed as though from the passage within the wall. Grace glanced over at the ticking clock and saw its thin hands nowhere near the hour. The tinkle of another bell followed soon after, joined by several others.

Servant's bells? she thought as they continued to sound, randomly but always from the direction of the tower. Grace was suddenly aware of the silence in the room above, occupied by one of the maids. Even the vermin and creaks of the house seemed to be still, holding their breath as the bells rang for a few moments more, and then fell silent, replaced by the sound of sobbing from the ceiling above, and the trembling of the girl in her lap. A faint wind sighed through the open passage, setting off a thin cloud of dust and rustling the curtains.

'What is it?' whispered Grace.

Rose looked up, eyes dilated in the dark, and raised her trembling hands to sign.

'*Ma-ma.*'

'Your ma-ma is no longer here, Rose.'

Rose shook her head and pointed at the tower in the drawing. '*Ghost. Something stirs—*'

Grace froze, recalling the warning from the departing Lady Foster.

'*Because I shouted downstairs,*' signed the shaking girl.

'That's not true,' she whispered.

The bells continued ringing sporadically for over ten minutes, accompanied by creaking and scuffling in corridors and rooms as those now awake scurried for security or those asleep shifted in their slumber.

'Stay here, and I'll make whatever it is be quiet,' said Grace, determined to show boldness in the wake of her fears.

Grace disentangled herself from the frightened child, pulled on a robe and peeped around the narrow of the open door; the erratic timing of the bells came clearer from the end of the corridor.

'Stay here,' she said, turning to Rose. 'Promise me you'll stay here?'

Rose clutched at Grace's robe, shaking her head in panic and trying to prevent her from leaving.

'*That's what Jane said,*' signed Rose.

The noise ceased, and several anxious silent moments gave way to the normal night noises' return, comforting now that the bells rang no longer.

'Very well,' said Grace.

She was about to close the door when she heard the

146

padding of gentle feet and glanced out in the direction of the back staircase. A figure was hurriedly avoiding the centre of the floorboards to prevent the boards from creaking and flexing. Grace grabbed the torch and shone the beam full into the face of the young manservant, returning from the third floor.

'I'm sorry,' he whispered, wide-eyed. 'Please don't talk. Ann's in a terrible state what with the bells and all. I saw the candle in her window and came running.'

He rushed away before Grace had time for questions. He leapt silently down the main stairs, glancing nervously at the tower wing, and vanished into the basement to escape back to the stable-yard bothy via the tradesman's entrance.

After closing the door, Grace sat down in the armchair and opened her arms to the shivering child.

'You are safe now, didn't I say so?' she whispered, rocking the child and humming a lullaby.

Rose breathed deeply and buried herself into the confines of the comfortable but cramped armchair. She fell asleep, letting the purse drop into the dwindling beam of the small bicycle torch. Grace lay back and closed her eyes, consumed by grief and tiredness, oblivious now to the soft scratchings that returned beyond the panelling and beneath her feet. She breathed deeply, and shifted to ready herself into seated sleep, warmed by the comfort of her ward, snuggling alongside in the armchair.

The sobbing from above shifted into slumber, and the house slept, safe and shivering in the embrace of the chilly November night.

A creaking from the floor above woke Grace suddenly. Rose was gone, and the panel was pulled tight from the inside and could not be readily opened. In the darkness before dawn, she opened the door and glanced down the corridor as the mournful morning bell ended the curfew and called the servants to the start of their labours. The sounds of life returned from the floors above and the corridor beyond. One of the younger maids, fully dressed and carrying her case, rushed past and glanced sheepishly on her way from the third floor to the entrance hall via the back staircase. Grace followed to the landing and watched as she emerged from the servants' stairs and raced across to the doors. The maid left a note on the nearby table and left her situation with Hemingworth Hall.

Returning to her room, Grace saw the hurried departure as the servant scuttled across the bridge and along the drive in the dim light cast from the rooms below. She flicked a switch, and a buzz signalled the awakening of the electrical system.

Grace washed and dressed, gulping down the remains of the jug of water, bitter and cold. The black chess piece stood lonely on the scratched side table. Grace retrieved the prodigal tower and set out the chessboard and pieces to accompany it. A sudden cramp seized her, and she grabbed at the mirror to see the colour drain from her face. Grace breathed deeply, ready to vomit, but recovered, watching the colour return to her cheeks, and shivered with the cold sweat forming.

Too much food last night, she thought, almost gagging at the smell of the fruitcake as she opened her purse, left behind by the child. She washed and dressed, steadying herself from a sudden dizzy spell, and made her way onto the landing.

Downstairs, Rose was awake and recovered from a hacking cough as Grace knocked and entered the room, seeing the grubby feet and hands of the nocturnal adventurer. A strong oily smell permeated the room and left a cloying tang in the mouth. Grace looked over and blew out the burner.

'I thought I'd fallen asleep and dreamed that a fairy with cake visited me last night,' said Grace, wiping Rose's hands and feet with a towel, dampened with water from the jug. 'I suppose you'll be expecting me to keep your secret passage a secret?' She looked around at the panels within the room. 'Which one is it, may I ask?'

Rose twitched with the ticklish cloth and pointed to a panel beside the bed. A small cross, unseen until now, was visible in the upper corner.

'Well, you owe me something for a stiff back and a crooked neck,' said Grace, wiping a final smudge from the girl's frowning face. 'Three animal noises after I return from breakfast and I will brush your hair, ready for Pa-pa. Three farmyard animal noises of your choice whenever I want them.'

Rose shook her head and put a finger to her lips.

'It's not really speaking, Rose. Making animal noises won't bring bad things, I promise.' Grace held out her hand. 'Deal?'

Rose rolled her lip, unsure and resistant to the offer. She held up a solitary finger in response.

Never bargain with a child, thought Grace, remembering her education at the institute. She held up one finger in reply and rolled the dice.

'One animal noise *and* the quietest one-word whisper I ever heard,' she said. 'That isn't speaking either, is it?'

Grace glanced over at the panel, doubtful that the bargain was truly in her favour.

'When the wood is sealed, I'm going to be so lonely if you can't visit me after curfew ...' she bluffed.

Rose shot out her hand to shake on the deal.

'Are you all right?' said Grace, kneeling to rub at the cold, pallid cheek of the child. 'About last night, I mean?'

Rose ran to a new drawing on the table and held up the early morning work; she gritted her teeth like a warrior entering the fray. A straw-haired angel carrying a black chessman wafted above a tower upon which stood a blue-gowned figure baring her teeth and attacking a frightened-looking figure in the window with a sword.

'Is this me fighting the ghost in the tower?' said Grace, raising an eyebrow. Rose nodded, rolling her bottom lip.

'I don't own a sword,' she said. 'Will an umbrella do?'

The little girl held up her hands before swinging them expectantly behind her back.

'You forgot this,' said Grace, retrieving the purse from her pocket. 'Now, get dressed and wash your face and hands.'

Grace put down the drawing, staring at the face in the tower window. It was crudely drawn, but Grace had never seen such malice and evil in such a few short strokes.

CHAPTER 14

I n the kitchen below, breakfast was brief and rushed. Grace ate little in the joyless room, surrounded by grim, sleepless faces. Billy and Ann exchanged worried glances across the wooden table. Bishop munched his way through half a loaf of bread, liberally spread with golden marmalade, and stared unceasingly towards her.

A monastery has more chatter than this.

The few servants who remained got up with Mrs Stanton's arrival; she threw a dirty rag upon the table.

'It has come to my attention,' she began, chest out and shoulders back, 'that a person or persons were abroad last night after curfew.'

She lifted the rag. 'Footmarks, everywhere!' she said, glaring at the down-turned faces. 'Folk wandering from ground floor to the third floor, and bells ringing as a result. Don't you have any respect for Captain Ferris and the rules of this house? Do you have any idea how dangerous and stupid this was?'

Grace looked across at the bashful faces. Ann was visibly

shaking, and Billy adjusted his cuffs nervously. Bishop remained intently staring in her direction.

'Perhaps it was the maid that just left?' said Grace, unconvincingly.

Mrs Stanton raised her eyebrows so far that they disappeared into the prim fringe of her hair.

'Perhaps it was someone that is looking to join her in a new situation? I will lock the doors from this evening unless I hear right now who took to wandering and woke the unholy damnation in the tower last night.'

A murmur of discontent rippled through the room.

'You can't lock people in like a prison,' said Grace. 'What about fire?'

'Well, you would know all about that, wouldn't you?' squawked the housekeeper, pulling down the front of her smock. 'We can do very well without someone with your reputation and choice of guardian causing a stir and upsetting things that should be lying still.'

Anger swelled as Grace struggled to keep calm.

Be careful...

She thought of the momentary pleasure of giving the most important woman in the house a piece of her mind, and then the destitution of returning home to the coastal canning factory; there would be no support from London this time. She thought of Rose, hopeful in the nursery, and Arthur in the alley.

She will die without you.

'I apologise for speaking out of place, Mrs Stanton,' she whispered.

Billy shuffled and looked guiltily over at Grace. As if in readiness, Mrs Stanton turned knowingly in his direction, relishing the prospect like one who already knew the answer to a question asked.

Staring into the sorrowful man's eyes, Grace took a long breath as Billy scrunched his face, waiting for the inevitable. Grace closed her eyes and stepped forwards.

'It was me,' she said, 'and I humbly beg your pardon.'

'You?' said Mrs Stanton, unconvinced. 'And what were you doing on the third floor?'

'I was intrigued by the bells and then went to comfort the maid that just left.'

'More than likely you helped scare her away. Stay in your room next time, and we will all be safer without your nocturnal wanderings,' said the housekeeper. 'Captain Ferris will hear of this.'

Billy unscrewed his eyes and looked over as the housekeeper left the kitchen. A collective sigh of relief did little to lighten the mood, but he glanced at Grace.

'Thank you,' he whispered. 'For Ann's sake.'

A large, cupped hand from the giant behind struck the back of his head, tussling the young man's hair. Bishop gave him and the maid a disapproving and knowing look. He glanced over at Grace and exhaled a long, drawn-out breath between his weather-beaten, cracked lips. He smoothed his beard, expertly and stealthily ending in a one-handed sign.

'*Thank you.*'

The business of eating resumed. Grace's stomach ached, and the rushed, frantic bolting of food by the hungry servants did little to improve the situation. One by one, the servants left the room for a day of increased toil as the housekeeper hurriedly re-arranged plans to cover the shortfall after the maid's departure. Grace grabbed several rinds of dried bread and raisins, stuffing them into her pocket for later.

In the office, Mrs Stanton poured over a list of daily duties and called over the remaining young maid.

'Ann, take Miss Meadows and the morning trays with you

to the nursery; see that she does not wander off.' She looked over her spectacles. 'The master is indisposed this morning and will take brunch when the doctor returns.'

Grace brightened with the recollection that the interesting medic would be calling. She accompanied the young maid out of the kitchen, both of them now loaded with breakfast items.

'Master's not up,' said Ann, striding next to her. 'Sore head more than likely. Miss Ferris will have to take breakfast in the nursery.'

'No one seemed very surprised the other maid left,' said Grace. 'Least of all Mrs Stanton.'

They climbed the stairs from the basement, rattling the crockery and plates loaded with toast, marmalade and eggs.

'It's usually just a matter of time,' said Ann. 'I've only been here a year, and we've had four come and go in that time. Curfew, rules and—'

'And?' asked Grace, struggling to keep up as they crossed the hall.

'Unquiet house,' whispered Ann. 'You heard the bells last night?'

'It's only the wind,' said Grace. 'What are they and why do they ring?'

Ann paused and stared down at the buttered soldiers.

'Ask my Billy,' she said nervously. 'He helped Mr Bishop put them up, and he was mighty put out when he was finished —I'd have held him all night for being so brave.' Ann glanced away, her cheeks showing a hint of blush. 'We weren't up to nothing last night, honest.'

'We all need a little comforting from time to time,' said Grace. 'Especially when we get frightened.'

Mrs Stanton appeared in the hall and clapped her hands sharply at the delay.

Ann put down her tray and knocked on the door, opening it for the governess a moment later.

Rose sat at her mirror, combing her long blonde hair.

Ann stared at the tray. 'I hope you'll stay,' she said. 'Despite you coming with the medium and putting Mrs Stanton's nose out of joint.'

'I got the impression I wasn't welcome,' said Grace. 'What does she have against Lady Foster?'

Ann pursed her lips. 'Difference of opinion on spiritual matters,' she whispered. 'Mrs Stanton thinks we should keep things calm and quiet, not go meddling with anything in the tower.'

'And Lady Foster?' said Grace.

'Begging your pardon,' whispered Ann, 'but your guardian thinks we should be taking the more direct approach and get rid of it.'

'What do you think?'

Ann lifted her shoulders. 'The place needs a bit of hope, if you know what I mean. There must be something we can do? We can't always be running from what frightens us.'

Grace glanced momentarily at her wrists as the housemaid departed.

'I agree wholeheartedly,' she murmured, turning to the little girl at the mirror, ready to begin the day's lessons.

Grace watched Rose's head sink to her chest as she struggled to finish the handwriting lines on the slate. The lack of sleep and fragility of her condition was taking its toll. Rose sagged at the desk.

'Do you want a nap while I go get some fresh air?' said Grace, feeling the change would do her good.

Rose yawned, and her bloodshot eyes blinked like a well-fed cat's.

'That's what comes of being up all night,' she said, putting on her coat and gloves.

She carried the child downstairs, tucked her into bed, and made for the main door.

Outside, the air was chill and a light frost veiled the parkland drive. Grace crossed the bridge and took the mossy path that ran around the moated manor house's perimeter. In the partially drained ditch, patches of thick ice glinted in the low morning sun like a giant's footprints. Grace turned to see wisps of steam rising into the air from the warming slates of the roof. A funnel of heat haze emanated from the tower's top, and she walked up to the north-east corner to examine the fern and butterfly bushes growing from its many cracks and imperfections.

It lay opposite a dry section of the ditch, and a natural causeway of firmer ground led from the heavily wooded corner. Stagnant pools of rime and rot lay either side as Grace followed a pair of large footprints, only a few hours old, leading to a small door, hitherto unnoticed. Grace looked up at the immense height of the tower and steadied herself against vertigo. The dizziness returned, and she leaned against the door until her mind cleared and her stomach returned to its sedentary but uneasy state.

A covered frame led from the door around the rear of the wall, leading up onto the roof some thirty feet above. The dense woodland bent its branches across the ditch as though reaching out to the rotting timber of the external staircase canopy. Grace tried the locked door; the metal handle's mossy grime left a mark on her gloves.

She returned across the ditch and completed the perimeter. Rooks cawed along the overgrown trees hanging across the enclosure of the walled garden. The creak of a wheel, badly in need of oil, came from within.

Grace entered the heart of the estate's fruit and vegetable kingdom; two acres of overgrown beds, untrained fruit trees and long, unkempt grass. At the far end of the garden was the curfew bell, supported by a tripod of thick timber posts, its rope coiled upon a nail hammered into one of the ten-foot legs. From behind a nearby seasoned log pile, Billy loaded a small handcart.

'Miss Meadows,' he said, tipping his cap, sending it sprawling onto the damp grass below.

'Ann said I might speak with you out here,' said Grace, seeing the man stare at the log pile before him.

The young manservant smiled with the mention of the maid and straightened his collar and braces as though half-expecting the pretty young woman to come by. 'What else did she say?'

'She told me you were a good person, and that she was proud of what you did for the family, in the tower. She also told me you only had noble intentions last night.'

The young man looked away, bashfully. 'Mr Bishop gave me a right tongue-wagging. He knows I was with her—saw me coming back to the stables, he did.'

'You seem to get along well with him?' said Grace.

'He got me the job with the family, not six months back.'

'He seems a good man, devoted to the family, I mean.'

'He's the reason Captain Ferris came back alive from the war,' said Billy, wiping his hands down his trousers.

'How so?'

'Mr Bishop was Captain Ferris's orderly, responsible for his welfare, running errands like looking after his uniform or acting as his personal bodyguard.'

'I think Mr Bishop would be very good at that sort of thing,' said Grace.

'He is, especially as he can't be killed unless it's by his own hands. That's what the villagers that came back say, and I believe them after what he did.'

Grace frowned. 'Why do they say such a thing?'

'He got separated from Captain Ferris during a skirmish and went out searching for him against orders through a hailstorm of bullets. The men said he got hit several times, but he just got back up and disappeared into the smoke. He came back an hour later, wounded but still alive, carrying the master over his broad back; they nearly shot him until they saw who it was. Captain Ferris came back alive to the big house, thanks to Mr Bishop, even if he couldn't walk anymore.'

Grace glanced at the young man, sensing great attachment.

'You've likely heard I used to be a bad person,' he said, raising his palms, 'but he took me in and gave me a chance. I'm honest now, and I don't do any thieving, picking locks or cutting keys anymore.'

'I can see why you look up to him,' said Grace, 'but it seems like he isn't in Mrs Stanton's good books, or the master's either?'

'He and Mrs Stanton have never seen eye to eye, and Captain Ferris has got into such gloom that I think he blames Mr Bishop for bringing him back alive. If he'd died in France, then perhaps all the bad things that are still going on wouldn't have happened, and Mrs Ferris would still be alive.'

Billy took out a handkerchief and wiped his sweaty hands. 'Miss Rose just gets sicker, and the bells get more frequent. I don't know how long we've got before it's all over.'

'I'm sure all will be well,' said Grace. 'If it's of any comfort, I'm here to see that nothing happens to Miss Ferris, like Miss Urquhart before me.'

A noise, like a slate skittering down the buckled roof of

the hall, caused her to look round. Someone ducked beneath a castellated section of the roof-line before scurrying behind a broad chimney stack and out of sight.

'Who's up there with all this ice?' she said, turning to see Billy loading the cart.

He put down a log and raised his hand to his brow. 'I don't see anyone. Might have been a mirage?'

Grace followed his gaze to the corner turret of the manor house. The wide, solitary window at its summit dripped with condensation glinting in the reflection of the rising sun. The tower section stood proudly from the rest of the roof, like a great candle giving off a flickering heat haze.

'See that heat coming off?' he said. 'There's a great glass roof on the top with a small door, but no one is allowed in the room up there on account of it being the mistress's room when she was alive.'

'There's a way into the tower from the roof?' said Grace.

Billy hesitated. 'Yes.'

'What's the matter?' said Grace.

'It's just that Miss Urquhart asked me something similar, not long before she got killed.'

'What's in there that's so important to keep us out, frightening the whole house and keeping Rose silent?'

The young man pursed his lips and glanced over at the tower; another slate skidded to a smashing halt somewhere near the chimney stack.

'Not what, but who,' he said. 'It's Mrs Ferris what's in the tower. You came with Lady Foster; I thought you'd know that?'

'I thought Mrs Ferris died?' said Grace, stamping her boots to ward off the creeping cold in her toes.

'Killed herself more like. The mistress threw herself off the top landing inside there, mad and shrieking by all accounts, threatening to come back in death for what she couldn't have in life.'

'And what was that?' asked Grace.

'Why, a family of course,' he said. 'She was mad by all accounts. When Captain Ferris returned in the army ambulance, it knocked her over the edge. That's what the old housekeeper told me before she left.

'Then it happened to Miss Urquhart. I was there in the tower soon after it happened, and I don't want to go through that again.'

'Can you tell me what happened?' asked Grace. 'She was a friend of mine.'

'Not much to tell,' said Billy, coming round to stand before her. 'Only that she was poorly, and the place must have got to her. She slipped, climbing around on the outside of the bell staircase that's in there.'

'Jane feared heights,' she said. 'Why did she climb on the outside of the stairs?'

Billy fidgeted with his cap and glanced at the tower. 'Mr Bishop and I, we put things across the stairs to stop people going up, or down.'

'The ropes across the staircase?'

'So you've seen them?' he said. 'Ropes and cords made of silk. Lady Foster and Captain Ferris had us tie all the bells to them we took from the staircase railings so as nothing can come in or out without sounding the alarm. Mrs Stanton was in hysterics about it, terrified of setting off—'

From the gateway entrance came a wordless bellow, as though one of the stone lions guarding the pillar of the bridge had wandered in to hunt for idle prey. Grace turned to see Bishop clap his mighty hands in annoyance with his younger understudy's lack of progress.

'You are telling me the ghost of Mrs Ferris is up there

rattling her chains and scaring the place; no wonder Rose is sick and traumatised.'

'It ain't no laughing matter,' said Billy, head down and throwing logs at a rapid pace into the cart. 'She's bound to the tower and has come back. She's just waiting for Miss Rose to get poorly enough that her spirit can be got at.'

'Mrs Ferris is waiting to claim Rose for all eternity?'

'Yes,' he said, 'and anyone else that gets in the way.'

CHAPTER 15

G race stood nervously at the open window. The fire in the drawing room was without a guard, and every spit and pop made her jump.

'Everything all right?' said the doctor, opening his bag.

Grace nodded and held a hand to her stomach. 'Do you have anything for nausea and cramps?'

'You are unwell?' said the doctor, frowning and coming to stand next to her. 'Do you want to lie down?'

'No, thank you,' said Grace as the doctor removed a small magnifying glass and his stethoscope. 'I find standing near the window less nauseating.'

He spread her eyelids wide and looked into her eyes. 'How long have you felt like this? Your pupils are slightly dilated.'

'Since yesterday,' she said. 'I thought perhaps I had overeaten after a long fast, but it's like nothing I've felt before.'

'Any dizziness or fainting spells?'

'Yes, this morning, accompanied by the need to vomit.'

'May I?' he said, offering his hand near her waist. She

nodded, and he gently pressed at her abdomen, watching intently as she winced and pursed her lips with discomfort.

He put on his stethoscope and offered the bell to her as a courtesy. She placed it above her left breast.

'I have to ask a personal question—' he began.

'I'm not pregnant,' she interrupted. 'I've not eaten much today, and I didn't sleep well last night.'

'New place, new environment and new nerves most likely,' he said.

Grace nodded and breathed deeply.

'How's Miss Rose and Captain Ferris's health this afternoon?'

'Rose seems brighter for having you around but more lethargic than usual; I wouldn't overexcite her if you can help it, just while she is fragile.'

'I'll mention it to the dolls,' said Grace, wincing as he moved his hand to her waist.

'Any history of kidney stones?' he asked, glancing at her face.

She shook her head.

'Well, your heart is fluttering like a butterfly in a web,' he said. 'I hope it's not my bedside manner or magnetic personality because I'm spoken for.'

Grace blushed with hidden resentment.

'Miss Rose has demanded my hand in marriage—I was forced, against my will, to propose in front of a teddy bear acting as a witness earlier, just to get her to take her iron tablet. If the medical council find out, I'll be struck off.'

Grace smiled and gave a selfish sigh of relief.

'I can give you something to ease your stomach and something to help you sleep?'

'May I ask you a personal question?' she whispered.

The doctor took off his headset and looked around the empty room. 'Of course.'

Grace offered him a seat and joined him in the easy chair opposite the small fireplace.

'I need to be honest with you,' she said, 'and I need you to be honest with me.'

He opened his hands. 'Very well, though I don't—'

'If I told you I suspected that something malicious was being done to Rose, and possibly myself, would you hear me out?'

The doctor rose and closed the door. He turned.

'Go on?'

'Would you recognise the effects of poison, if you saw it?'

'That would depend on the substance,' said the doctor. 'Are you suggesting someone is poisoning Rose? Her condition is unusual but—'

'The tonic in the brown bottle,' she said. 'Could she be having some adverse allergic reaction to it, perhaps nuts too, or maybe someone's tampered—'

The doctor placed his hand on her forearm to pause the rapid flow of conjecture.

'It's a vitamin tonic fortified with iron,' he said. 'One large spoonful three times a day.'

'Do you have any with you now?' she asked. 'And a spoon?'

He got up and fished out the small brown bottle. 'Not a bad idea, but it may give you diarrhoea if you take it on an empty stomach.'

He poured out the thin colourless liquid onto the spoon. Grace sniffed at it and dipped her tongue into the mixture.

'This isn't what Kate gave Rose last night,' she said, swallowing the rest. 'The stuff on the spoon was darker, like treacle. I dipped my finger into it, and it tasted like almonds.'

'Almonds?' said the doctor, reacting quickly and taking back the bottle and spoon. 'You are sure it was from a brown bottle like this?'

'Positive, and I have the spoon upstairs with some of it.

It's very thick, oily, and has hardened onto the handle like a crust. Wait here.'

She left the room and padded up the stairs to the basin in her room.

The spoon was missing.

Grace searched the bedroom for any signs of the silverware, but to no avail. She looked around her meagre belongings for any other missing items, but after five minutes she returned to the drawing room empty-handed.

'It's missing,' she said. 'I can't understand it.'

'Maybe a servant picked it up?' offered the doctor.

'No one has been in there, not even to replace the water,' she said, sitting down and wringing her hands. 'I'm telling the truth.'

'It's a fairly serious accusation. Are you in any doubt?' he said.

Grace glanced up, confused and wondering if there really was anything different about the two medicines. The memories of Jane lying on the tiled floor and Arthur standing on the moat lawn came flooding back; both joined by the sign warning of poison.

'None,' she said, looking into his worried eyes. 'She was terrified to take it, and the housemaid was very rough with her until she mentioned her mother.'

The doctor removed his arm and sat upright. 'Oh?' he said.

'Kate said, "if you don't take it, Ma-ma will get you". What did she mean by that?'

'Nothing,' he said, 'and everything. I'll speak to Mrs Stanton about it; that's not acceptable.'

Grace glanced across the room, trying to avoid the doctor's eyes.

'You are going to think me silly, especially after what you said yesterday.'

He narrowed his eyes, listening intently.

Grace pursed her lips. 'I know about the bells in the tower, and last night I heard them ringing—so did Rose and everyone in the house before you mock me. Billy told me why Bishop and he set them up, to alert them to any passage of spirits. Will you at least tell me the truth about what you know, even if you don't believe it?'

Dr Croswell crossed his legs and hugged his knee.

'Charles's wife, Sophia Ferris, was fragile, unstable and prone to hallucinations,' he said. 'When Charles returned home impotent, beaten and broken, it drove her to breaking point, and she took her own life.'

'Billy said she jumped from the high landing in the tower?'

'I was not present, fortunately, but your information is correct. Charles does not like to talk about it, and I would ask that you observe the confidentiality protocols to preserve the family's good name. There are dishonourable repercussions with suicide that extend far beyond the moated walls of this place. What else did the young gossip say?'

'That Mrs Ferris was back for Rose, that she's wandering around, waiting for Rose to get sick to the point where she can claim her. That's why the bells are in there, it's why they are ringing?'

The doctor stretched out a hand to soothe her tense writhing hands.

'I told you this was nonsense yesterday. The place is falling to pieces, and there are enough holes in the roof to play a tune with the wind that whistles around in there.'

Grace relaxed. 'I heard several slates shifting this morning, and yesterday I saw the ropes moving when someone opened a flap or door to the tower room from the roof.'

The doctor retreated his hand and furrowed his brow.

'Someone was in the tower room yesterday?' he asked. 'Are you sure?'

'Yes, I've seen someone in the window several times now.' Grace glanced at his face, unusually fixed and contemplative. 'Is anything the matter?'

He bit his lip. 'No one's allowed up there, not since Sophia died. Can you describe the person—was it a servant?'

'I don't think so. I thought I saw someone on the roof this morning with Billy.'

'Would Billy know who it was, Mr Bishop perhaps?' he said, leaning forwards.

'He was loading logs at the time next to me and didn't see. Mr Bishop could have got down from there in time, and he came round the corner to the walled garden soon after. It could have been him but I'm not sure; perhaps it was someone else on the roof—'

A new voice approached the room, stern and slurred.

'Who was on the roof?' said Charles Ferris, knocking into the door frame as he drunkenly negotiated his route into the room.

'Charles—'

'It's all right,' said the master of the hall, holding up a hand to the doctor. 'Had a chat with Mrs Stanton, seems she thinks I ought to keep things quiet, but where has that got us, eh?'

Grace got up, eager to avoid any scene. 'I'll just check on Rose, Captain Ferris.'

'It's all right, Miss Meadows. I'm keen for us both to hear what the good doctor has to say about my daughter's health this afternoon—much improved, I'm guessing. Isn't that what you always say, James? You don't need to wrap me in cotton wool, I've been in the bloody war in case you hadn't noticed.'

Charles grabbed a nearby ashtray and whacked himself in the groin to prove a painless but embarrassing point. The doctor retrieved the glass dish and clung on to his friend's wrists. Grace rang the handbell, and Mrs Stanton came in, rushing over to calm her employer.

'She's unchanged,' replied the doctor, 'which could be an encouraging sign.' He let go of his friend and returned to the settee.

Charles put his hands on his head. 'When are you going to accept it isn't anything physical that's affecting her?'

'I refuse to listen to anything while you are distressed,' said Dr Croswell, folding his arms.

'Distressed?' said Charles, raising his voice. 'So would you be if your own flesh and blood was under spiritual attack!'

'Begging your pardon, Captain Ferris,' said Mrs Stanton. 'But shouldn't these things be discussed in private?' She stared at Grace, unaware that she was only too eager to oblige.

'You are quite right, as always, Elizabeth,' said Charles, soothed by her gentle touch on his brow. 'But let the good doctor deliver his assessment of my daughter's decline into madness. Has it been that long that you don't remember Sophia's silence before her sickness took hold?'

'I remember everything,' said the doctor, trying to avoid eye contact as the wheelchair clattered backwards into the umbrella stand. 'It's not my field, but her mind is still trying to process the trauma of her mother's—'

'Suicide,' said Charles gruffly. 'There, I've said it, and Miss Meadows can hear it from me before she hears it from the staff if she hasn't already. I'm fed up with hiding and lying to protect a woman that didn't love me.'

Mrs Stanton blanched.

'I'm sorry,' said Grace. 'There's no need to discuss your private affairs with—'

'With the governess?' said Charles. 'Perhaps I should have done that with the other one, eh? Maybe Miss Urquhart would still be alive and—'

168

'Do you mind if we change the subject?' said James, giving Grace an awkward but sympathetic look.

'Suit yourself,' said Charles. 'What have you two been wittering on about all afternoon?'

The doctor grabbed the brown bottle and looked over at Grace.

'Are you certain?' he said, glancing down at the medicine.

Grace nodded and closed her eyes.

'There may be an issue of security in the house,' he said.

Charles dropped his hands from the wheel. 'Security?' he slurred. 'What kind of issue?'

'Before I answer that, I need to ask you, Mrs Stanton, to get me a bottle of the tonic from the pantry stores. The very same that I delivered yesterday, and that the housemaid used yesterday evening.'

Mrs Stanton frowned. 'May I ask why?'

The doctor stood up with the bottle. 'No, not at this time.'

The housekeeper's eyes flashed with wounded pride, and she looked over at her employer lolling in the wheelchair.

'Get the bottle,' said Charles, 'and bring me something for my headache.'

The efficient housekeeper returned a few minutes later with two empties and the almost full bottle. She handed a glass of water and aspirin tablets to the man in the chair.

'Well?' said Charles. 'Are you going to tell us what this is all about?'

The doctor sniffed and wiped his finger around the rim of them all. He put his finger to his mouth and sucked at the clear liquid. He poured a large spoonful and held it to his nose before passing it to Grace, looking down and away.

'This is the tonic I prescribe. I'm sorry, Grace, nothing is contaminating it.'

Grace looked at the clear liquid and shook her head. 'It can't be—'

Mrs Stanton gasped. 'Are you suggesting someone is poisoning Miss Ferris?'

Charles spun to face Grace. 'Well, are you?' he said, his glazed eyes looking disturbingly awry.

'I'm mistaken, and I apologise,' she said. 'I have been feeling unwell.'

'And were you mistaken about the person or person's on the roof trying to access my wife's belongings?' asked Charles, gripping the side of his chair. 'Perhaps we should get someone to go in there and check—would that satisfy your assertions and fantasy?' He raised a hand and wafted it in the air. 'Maybe your Lady Foster could ask Sophia nicely if she'll tootle off for a bit so we can have a look? Mrs Stanton says you like to tour the place after hours.'

'I am so sorry—' started Grace, kneeling and fearing the worst.

Charles grabbed at the servant's bell rope, summoning the giant manservant with the sound of the deep and resonant bell.

'Charles—' said the doctor, coming over to remove his hand incessantly tugging on the rope. 'It was a misunderstanding and my assertion ...'

'Get it open!' he shouted as Bishop entered the room, panting and vested from his hot work on the boiler. Grace saw the dreadful bullet scars on his shoulders and torso as he struggled to comprehend the instruction.

'Open the tower, Bishop, and get the third-floor door open so someone can go check for intruders and ghosts. I'm done with hiding. Do it, man, now!'

Bishop opened his hands, looking fearfully up at the request, as if unsure if his master had suddenly lost his wits.

'I'll go see Miss Ferris is protected and cared for,' said Mrs

Stanton, glancing witheringly at Grace. She shook her head in disgust and left the room behind the frantic captain, leading a charge to capture a heavily fortified position through a developing minefield of servants, rushing to see what all the commotion was about.

'What have I done?' said Grace, turning to the striding doctor.

'It's my fault,' said the flustered medic. 'I should have seen the signs. You are acting just like Jane.' He paused. 'If there's nothing up there, and if I find laudanum in your urine, then I'm calling the police. For your safety, and the rest of the house.'

CHAPTER 16

Bishop threw open the double doors to the tower, and Charles wheeled in. He glanced behind himself and snorted at the household's hesitation.

'Come and look,' he said, beckoning the servants into the dusty chamber. They approached, wary of being in the space that they had so long been denied access to. 'Make as much noise as you bloody well like.'

Bishop retreated to the hall and to the third floor, dangling a large bundle of keys.

'For God's sake, Charles,' said the doctor. 'You're making a scene!'

Charles raised a hand and pointed vaguely in the chandelier's direction. 'Do you remember when you dared me to jump across from the first-floor landing to the lamp?' he said, snorting.

The doctor looked up at the metal crown and shuddered. 'I was a fool; it could have killed you.'

'I still have balls, even if I've lost my eyes, eh?' he said, puffing out his chest. 'Which is why no shade or spirit will

172

bully me.' He raised his head and bellowed into the empty air. 'Do you hear me!'

Bishop removed the bars on the third-floor landing, and his head appeared, dim and dusty, far above.

'Who's going up for a sovereign?' said Charles, shakily retrieving a leather coin purse from his trouser pocket. 'Or do I have to crawl my way up?'

The servants stood back and looked up, weighing the dreadful bargain. No one moved.

Charles turned and tossed the month's wages onto the floor. It spun and twinkled in the beam of sunlight before coming to a rattling rest on the hard, tiled floor.

'I'll go,' said Kate, glancing over at Grace with a furrowed brow, 'and begging your pardon, Captain Ferris, I won't take your money. I'll be glad to clear my good name. I ain't put nothing in Miss Ferris's vitamins.'

Charles wheeled out of the light. 'Then let it lie here as payment for my sins, and those of my forebears. It's the only bloody treasure in here now.'

The housemaid brushed past Grace with a steely glance and trudged up the main staircase where she joined the manservant on the landing. Bishop handed her the iron ring, sliding across an ornate key. Kate looked nervously ahead, then resolutely down at the upturned and fearful faces.

Clambering through the ropes and cords of the last dozen steps, she reached the door in a carillon of bells. They twitched and sounded throughout the chamber as she unlocked and pressed against the wooden door. It budged but did not open. She turned to see Bishop pretending to throw his shoulder against the third-floor doors.

Kate nudged at the door, lending more weight to the attempt until it swung half-open. A gust of wind ripped through the tower, initially from the bright, sunlit room beyond, which met with the rush of air from the vacuous and cavernous space below. The servants on the ground covered their faces, and several made the sign of the cross as Kate stepped into the chamber and momentarily disappeared from view.

'Is she up there?' said Charles briskly. He scanned the space above him.

'Yes,' said the doctor, squeezing him on the shoulder.

Kate backed out of the doorway and onto the small landing. She looked down and put her hands to her mouth, leaning against the railing.

'What am I looking for?' she called.

A murmur of relief circled the floor. There was no obvious portal to hell or fiend lurking within.

'For God's sake, woman,' shouted Charles. 'Just tell us what's in there.'

Kate nodded. 'Just a big bed, a painting and some boxes with some of the mistress's things in.'

'No sign of squatters?' said Charles, fidgeting with his hands.

Kate pulled the stiff door shut and locked it.

'None, only a dead pigeon, Captain Ferris. There's a small pane of glass missing.'

Charles sagged his head to his chest as Mrs Stanton clapped her hands to dismiss the servants back to their work.

'Happy now?' he said under his breath, wheeling past Grace and the doctor. 'Bloody pigeon is what you saw.'

Grace put her head in her hands. 'I'm telling you I saw someone ...'

Dr Croswell put his arm around her and escorted her back to her room. 'I know,' he said. 'Let's get you feeling better, some food inside you, and then some sleep. We'll talk about it in the morning.'

Grace lay on her bed, staring at the ceiling. The curfew bell was long past, and she wondered at the hour. A corner cobweb twitched as a spider raced to its centre to trap an unfortunate insect. The silken thread vibrated and then was still.

No bells to warn you, she thought.

She sat up, watching the moonlit rim of the clouds shine upon the chipped earthenware jug. Her mouth was dry from the evening meal, unwanted and half-eaten on the bedside table. She shivered as she drank, despite the room being warmed from the earlier fire. The doctor had insisted it was lit, and he had remained in the armchair, chivalrously guarding his patient against any threat of fire, until she relented from the sedative and fell asleep. Grace had snuffed out the warmth in the hearth as soon as the lights of his small Austin motorcar vanished along the drive, carrying with him the vial of urine to check for laudanum and lies.

She set up the bell yoke on its stand on the table in the small sitting room, wondering whether she would ever now have the chance to incorporate it into some productive or educational game. She lifted a king's pawn from the chess set and set it down two spaces ahead in a classic opening move. Jane had reigned supreme at the institute and had always opened in such a fashion.

Command the centre of the board.

Her grief came rushing back, and she clutched at the bedpost to stop herself fainting. Her position hung in the balance. The little girl's crying downstairs went on for an hour when the housemaid forbade any interaction with the governess or wanderings.

Grace returned to the bedchamber and wrapped herself in the woollen bed robe. She glanced at the new candle, virginal and smooth, begging to be lit and be of help. Just a little flame to banish the fear and perhaps to banish the pain ...

The spirit bell rang in the room beyond, and Grace swung around, feeling her way along the wall for support. For an instant, she saw the shadowed hand, a young finger plucking at the silken thread, before a gentle thud swung open the panel in the wall and it vanished into the narrow recess.

'Rose?'

Something rolled from the table and struck the floor. A chess piece rolled along the floorboards to the opening, coming to a halt against the skirting board. Grace glanced at the chessboard, upon which lay one of her tattered silk gloves, a birthday present from her fiancé.

Then she noticed it.

The board was re-arranged. Many pieces now lay out of play, tipped or standing at the field of battle. On the board lay several chessmen, all surrounding and attacking a central white pawn. A white king lay on its side while the black queen threatened to take the lonely pawn on the next move. A white knight threatened to counter the queen's move but was itself at risk by the black rook. A white bishop lay out of position, unable to intercede in a game already lost.

Grace looked to the closed door, locked while she changed, and steadied the swinging bell. The panelling's open square showed a dark passage to each side, cunningly concealed within the broad walls. She fished out a battery torch from her trunk and stepped into the opening. Dried sawdust and sand softened her footfall as she swung the light back and forth. The narrow passage stepped up and around a sharp bend to her left, avoiding the door and disappearing above the ceiling. She turned right, hearing the hum of a child at play out of sight.

'You'll get us both into trouble,' she whispered. 'You should be sleeping.'

Stepping over the mummified remains of mice and their droppings, she inched her way through the dust and descended to the floor below. Chinks of light through which braided electrical cable was fed showed various rooms. The sound of play disappeared down a further narrow flight of brick steps as she twisted sideways in places to follow the miscreant child. It grew dark, and she panicked, seeing a wooden panel blocking further progress. She shone her light upon it to see the engraving of a spiral upon its cracked surface. There were several small handprints in the dust to its side, and Grace gently pushed to discover the panel swung back, with a squeak, to reveal the cracked wooden lid of a priest hole, partially hidden beneath a layer of straw. Further ahead, the passage narrowed substantially and veered left out of sight.

The torch flickered and went out. Grace shook the rubber cylinder, trying to squeeze the life from its empty batteries. A dim glow emerged from the bulb, superseded by the faint hairline light surrounding a panel's reverse to her left. She nudged at the square, and it swung open, revealing the cold, dusty tiles of the tower-room floor. Grace stepped out and looked up at the staircase webbed with ropes and bells.

'Rose!' she hissed, turning to the panelled door illuminating the hall beyond through two small hand-sized windows of coloured glass.

She placed her hand upon a grandfather clock, setting the stopped pendulum clinking within the mahogany case, and pulled herself through the tight opening. Dusting herself down, she scanned the dimly lit room, coming to stand beneath the tower's central section, haloed by the floodlight of a moonbeam funnelling through the skylight. Grace glanced up at the gently swinging chandelier and staggered back, as the image of crowned fire from the vision vividly returned to her mind. High above, on the second-floor landing, stood Arthur. He pointed upwards to the tower room and the faint candle glow that peeped beneath the door. He raised a finger to his lips and stepped back into the shadow.

A gentle breath of wind emanated from beneath the door, scattering the dust and setting the bells swinging. They sparkled along with the reflected brightness of the exposed metalwork from a broken section of railing high above.

A single bell shifted on the uppermost landing as something smudged and shadowed moved stealthily from the high tower door. The bells sounded as it struggled through and against the silken ropes, and Grace became aware it was the shade of a woman, insubstantial, yet very real.

The spirit beyond passed through the moonbeam, and Grace raised a hand to her mouth, recognising the familiar face.

'*Jane?*' she mouthed, clouding the chill air with her breath.

The governess's spirit rushed as though desperate to escape something unseen from above, setting off further bells. Several of the smaller cords passed through Jane Urquhart's immaterial bed-gown as she gripped the handrail, scanning around for a means of escape.

Out of the corner of her eye, Grace twisted to see the panel, through which she had emerged, quiver and then open, revealing nothing but empty darkness beyond. She stepped back to the ground-floor doors, fearing the sudden appearance of something or someone unseen.

'What is it?' said Grace, calling out to the spirit of the boy on the landing.

The shape shifted, and two little hands struck out into the shaft of light.

'*The past and Rose's future.*'

The spirit of Jane Urquhart paused in her laborious descent through the webs of silken rope and raised its hands. It signed in the beam's light, becoming more desperate as it turned to look back at the tower door. Jane urged a child beyond the panel to hide, close the panel, and, most insistently, keep quiet.

The panel closed, and Jane's spirit retreated, swinging her leg over the handrail and placing her feet nervously at the edge of the treads. Slowly and fearfully, she clambered her way down on the outside of the deadly spiral.

'No,' cried Grace, powerless to stop the horror unfolding. 'Jane, please—'

The former governess glanced back at the door as the candle in the tower room went out, plunging the outline of the portal into darkness, and continued her descent, calling out calm words to the hidden child. Grace watched as Jane slipped and grabbed on to the railing, trying to gain purchase with her scrabbling legs. She dangled, trying to pull herself up, just as the barrier began to give way. The soft metal twisted and pulled away from the handrail, cracking the stone treads beneath. In a final desperate act, Jane threw her arms across to gain purchase on the failing filigree of the ornamental balustrade as the crumbling stone gave way, and the governess fell, flailing, into the air. Grace threw her hands to her eyes as the spirit struck the floor and vanished, followed by the ghostly section of railing.

When she looked again, the room was still, the bells silent, and only the gap in the glinting balustrade indicated its traumatic history.

A thud on the door above rattled the nearby cords, setting off several bells. Grace looked up at Arthur, who was signing urgently and loudly with large gestures.

'*Something stirs!*'

On the landing, next to the spirit of her former ward, came the figure of a woman, dressed in soiled cream silk. Her hair lay lank and matted around her grubby bare shoulders, and her hands struck out, beckoning him. Arthur retreated, and Grace saw a look of resigned sadness upon his face. The woman began a soft and mournful lullaby as he made his shuffling way towards her.

Grace watched in horror as the woman put the spirit child's neck into the crook of her arm, stifling its silent cries. Arthur struggled and went limp, as the woman dragged her steady way up and through the webs of the staircase, setting off the tinkling of bells. Several thinner strands passed straight through both mother and child as they made their way to the second-floor landing. The spirit halted and pulled the limp child to her bosom, pawing blindly at its pale face and golden hair. It turned and clung tightly as though disturbed by something entering the room from its past.

'*I will have my child*,' it cried, '*in this life or the next!*'

Grace saw the woman's eyes, blind and feral, as the ghost of Sophia Ferris clasped the child tightly. They tipped over the railing, colliding with the silk-wrapped chain of the chandelier, tilting it with such force that it swung and collided with the staircase railing, snapping a link within the tightly woven binding.

The pair vanished into the floor, setting off a tremor of twinkling bells.

Grace ran to the panel and hurried back to her room through the cramped passageway, slamming shut the board and barring the wall with the armchair. Her heart raced, and she gagged with the exertion and sudden adrenalin-fuelled chill of the encounter. That Sophia Ferris haunted the tower was clear. Bound by her madness and desire to reclaim her only child at the moment of death, an end that seemed likely to be soon and unchallenged.

Grace would fail, and a sudden fear gripped her. Would Arthur be trapped here by her incompetence, endlessly reliving the spirit's torment until Rose's spirit joined them for whatever eternal fate lay ahead?

She huddled, knees in arms, and rocked in solitude and

sadness. The candlestick on the window ledge offered peace, if only for a brief period. She raised her wrists, shutting out the vague memory of promises to avoid self-harm. She imagined it flickering and then recalled the candlelight beneath the door in the tower, extinguished as she had shouted out, unheard by the spirit of Jane Urquhart. The former governess had been pursued by something, but not a ghost; otherwise, she would have seen it.

She got up and rubbed her arms, shaking with the chill. The medicine and sedative were losing their potency, and she sat in the armchair overlooking the chessboard. A solitary black rook stood at its centre.

Something was or had been in the tower room, despite the housemaid's assertion to the contrary. If she was leaving, it didn't matter anymore. Better to find out herself.

Better to go down fighting, like Jane.

CHAPTER 17

A knock at the door woke the governess. She glanced across at the clock to see it was well past half-past six. She shot up and smoothed back her hair. The cramp in her stomach protested at the sight of yesterday's food as she opened the door.

'Are you all right, Miss Meadows?' said Billy. He stood, brows furrowed, next to Ann, who wrung her hands. 'We didn't see you downstairs, and the doctor said to come to check on you—he's downstairs with Mrs Stanton.'

'At this hour?'

'He's come to see you before his rounds,' said Ann. 'It's why we've come looking, and to bring you this—' The maid handed over a wrapped brown paper parcel of warm toast and marmalade. 'I can't stay, too much to do.'

She bobbed and left for downstairs.

Billy turned to go.

'Did he bring the police with him?' asked Grace, reaching out to him. He turned and shook his head.

'I think whatever is making you poorly isn't what he thinks it is.'

'How do you know?' said Grace, glancing down the corridor and pulling him firmly inside. He glanced over the upturned furniture and scattered chess pieces on the floor.

'Blimey, you had a bad night.'

Grace shook him gently. 'What did he say was wrong with me?'

'He doesn't know,' said Billy, shrugging. 'Only that it ain't what everyone thought it was ...'

'Laudanum, you mean?'

He nodded. 'Kate's mighty put out with you; she was hoping it would be the end of you.'

'She might still get her wish,' said Grace, folding her arms and closing the bed robe around her.

'I wouldn't bet on it, not until he's spoken with Captain Ferris. He's shouting Mrs Stanton back into her box as we speak to get you to come down.' Billy smiled, and his eyes widened. 'I'll remember what happened yesterday for a long time, in the tower, I mean. I ain't seen no one so bold or telling the truth as no one will listen to.'

'What do you mean?'

'I have seen them.'

'Seen who?' asked Grace, gently closing the door.

'Someone on the roof last night when I was ...'

'Making sure Ann was safe?' said Grace, raising an eyebrow.

Billy blushed and looked across at the barricade in front of the panelling. 'Seems you heard them ringing like a royal wedding, too?'

'Did you get a good look at them?'

'No,' he said, 'but whoever it is has been coming and going from the bothy in the woods. There are signs someone's been sleeping rough out there. Mr Bishop's gone off to see if it's some tramp or tinker.'

'Have you said anything to anyone?'

'Only to Mr Bishop. I didn't tell Ann because I didn't want to fret her.'

'Can you get me up there?' said Grace. 'Just to check that no one has been into that room?'

Billy blinked. 'You shouldn't go risking your neck so soon after what happened yesterday. Master's drunk himself silly last night; it's the reason Dr Croswell was called so early—Mr Bishop thought he'd killed himself dead this morning when he laid the fires.'

'But you could get me past the door outside, couldn't you?' she said. 'Like make a key or pick the lock, as a favour?'

'I don't do things like that anymore,' he said. 'I know you helped keep Ann and me here, but it's too risky. Last time I did that, it ended up with someone getting killed.'

'Jane asked you the same thing?' said Grace.

Billy nodded. 'She taught me how to write and read better. Without her help, I'd still be signing my name with a large cross.'

He stuffed his hands into his pockets. 'I wish I hadn't. I ain't told no one else but Ann, but it's my fault she went up into the tower that night.'

'What did she ask you to do?'

'She got it into her head something, or someone, was knocking about up there, like you, and wanted me to fashion her a key to get onto the roof through the door that leads around the back wall.'

'You stole a key to make a copy?' she said.

'Not really,' he said, kicking his boot against the kindling by the grate. 'I pressed the one in the pantry into a bar of soap to make the key. I only did it because she said it was important—a matter of life and death. I didn't think she meant her own.'

'Jane was right. It is a matter of life or death—will you do the same for me? I'll teach you how to read and write like a magistrate.'

'No need,' he said, nodding over at the scattered game pieces on the chessboard. 'Miss Urquhart was adamant about it, keeping it safe and hidden, which is why I fashioned it into one of the castles.'

Grace turned to the chessboard and looked at the solitary rook at its centre. She grabbed the tower and its sibling, weighing up the marked difference in her hand. She handed the heavier one to the reformed petty thief.

He twisted the castellated top until it popped off like a cork, revealing a crudely machined key wedged into the underside of the cap. A narrow sheath within the castle tower's body provided the recess for the notches of the blade.

'I didn't make this if anyone asks,' he said, replacing the tower's head into its body.

He smoothed back his hair. 'Ann overheard the doctor saying you and Miss Urquhart shared the same experience, seeing things that weren't there? I didn't know till she'd died, otherwise I would have stopped her getting into the tower. I'm asking you to be careful.'

'Can you tell the doctor I'm awake but will need some time to dress and get ready?' she said.

Billy narrowed his eyes. 'I might be illiterate, but I ain't stupid,' he said.

'Do this for Miss Rose, then?'

'If you ain't down in an hour, I'm telling everyone. Deal?' He wiped his grubby hand down his trousers and held out his hand.

Grace looked at the clock. 'Eight o'clock by the latest—I'll need the light. Tell them I need Ann to help me bathe.'

Grace hurried down the back staircase, dressed in her woollen bed robe over her casual workwear. Narrowly avoiding the housekeeper, she snuck out of the tradesman's entrance and hurried across the bridge, conscious of every sound. She turned right and followed the long perimeter to the tower to avoid the formal rooms' overlook. The damp grass soaked her court shoes as she crossed the narrow boggy causeway to the external tower door. Grace retrieved the chess piece and fumbled with the top. The sliver of metal slid into the lock, and she twisted it first one way, then the other, fearing it might break at any moment. Withdrawing the key slightly, she turned the castle tower's head once more. The lock clicked gently, and the door creaked noisily in the thick air. Beyond lay a slippy set of wooden steps and a rotting handrail. The covered wooden boards were pockmarked with holes as though cannon fire had peppered the rickety staircase.

Testing the wooden treads, she climbed until several boards were missing. Grace looked down at the thin layer of stagnant water far below and clutched at the wet side rail to control vertigo and rising nausea. She lifted a leg far across the void and pulled herself across, shivering with cold and fear. She thought of Jane, terrified and alone, traversing the dangerous structure. Thirty more steps led to a sharp right turn as the staircase ended and the firm lead of the roof, littered with broken slates and tiles, came as a welcome relief. She lost track of time and panicked, wondering how long it had already taken her and how long there was left before Billy sounded the alarm.

The tower lay close to her right with a small access hatch to one corner heralding a way in. Grace crouched, seeing far below and distant the figure of a large man returning from an abandoned bothy within the woodland. It was Bishop, and she crawled beneath the parapet wall, scuffing her hands and knees. A disturbed pheasant clucked and crowed nearby, and Grace paused, realising that the door to the staircase was still open. She checked her pocket for the chess piece and reached the tower door.

It was locked, and she retrieved the chessman, hoping that the same key served both locks. The sheath of the notched blade entered the lock and jammed slightly, forcing Grace to waggle the thin metal until it relented. The door opened, but part of the key sheared off as it was withdrawn.

Grace sucked on the cut to her finger as she retrieved the sharp sliver and pushed open the door, worried about the time, rather than what lay within.

A wave of heat struck her as she descended a short number of interior stone steps to a glass-covered room, overgrown with exotic plants and foliage, and filled with damp air. The acrid smell of sulphur, sickly compounds and botanical powders pervaded the heady scents of the room. It was as though Grace stood in the centre of a person-sized terrarium. The bars of two large electric heaters glowed menacingly as she glanced around the sweltering room, noting the condensation on the grimy bay windows. Grace peered out through the film of algae at the courtyard on one side, and the walled garden on the other, and soon began to sweat as she glanced across a large four-poster bed to the interior of the tower-room door that had been opened by the housemaid on the previous and embarrassing evening.

The sound of bells gently moving came from the staircase beyond. She turned and clicked shut the hatch.

She stifled a sneeze from the exotic anthers of plants unknown to her. The mould spotted the putrid and stained yellow wall above the rotting panelling, all but obscuring its former glory. She wandered over to a table and averted her eyes at several dead animals, birds and partly dissected creatures pinned to wooden boards. Next to these were several glass jugs and brown bottles, identical to those used for the doctor's tonic. She thought of the man below, for whom she felt more than a little admiration, wondering if his honest face hid darker and more sinister intentions. Various other apothecary devices and tubes lay scattered about a burner. Jars of dark and unhealthy-looking substances lined a shelf like a deadly spice rack. Most dreadful of all was the appearance of a pile of brown and deeply drilled teeth, some still attached to sections of human jaw bone. Glittering metal dust coated a hand drill and implements of some deranged dentistry.

A vine clung to the windows and the interior of the glass roof, desperate to escape the unholy Eden. It had some stems of purple, while others grew with greenish-brown blotches. Fine hairs clotted the sides of the long, thin branches. Their oval leaves, with smooth edges and pointed ends, curled and blistered with fungal mould. Bell-shaped purple and green flowers gave way to a rainbow of ripening berries. Grace rubbed a dark juicy globe between her forefinger and thumb; it gave off a sickly smell of toffee and almonds.

She turned, bashing into the large purple and palmate leaves of a castor oil plant, woefully out of season but still hale and fruiting in the tropical heat. Several hanging orchids and exotic, colourful mushrooms littered the base of its root-bound pot. The electric heaters buzzed as supply weakened for a moment. The sun emerged, setting off a section of shining metal, and Grace peered down to see the missing section of railing, free of its masonry but hacked by several cuts to remove the finely wrought leaves that spiralled within the filigree. The silvered metal beneath glinted back against the tarnished black paint that had been applied to its surface. She picked up a small piece and was surprised by its weight, placing it on a set of tarnished brass scales, which suddenly tipped over without a counterbalance. She stepped back, nearly tripping over a rolled army uniform, heavily stained and torn. It lay unceremoniously against a dirty flask as though used as a cleaning rag.

The sound of footsteps on the roof outside startled her, and she realised she was trapped. She peered quickly through the lock to see a figure bundled against the cold, making their way carefully towards the tower. Grace glanced around and looked beneath the heavy valence of the bed. A large case and several boxes were crammed beneath, making it a futile place to hide. She looked around for a weapon in fear of sudden violence; she picked up the largest of the lumps of metal and backed away to the interior door, rattling it mercilessly in the hope of escape. The door stood firm. Her hands travelled across the wooden panel behind her as the sound of footsteps grew closer.

Her forefinger snagged on an imperfection in the wood, and she turned to see the small cross-shaped engraving in its far corner. A shadow passed in front of the bay window, close to the hatch, as she dug her nails into the thin crack, trying to prise open what she hoped would be behind—a safe and secure hiding place. The panel juddered, but her nails could not gain significant purchase. With her heart in her mouth, she scanned around for a lever. The silver spoon, still tainted by the treacle-like syrup, lay on the floor as though tossed in by someone from the staircase beyond. Grace grabbed it and forced the handle end into the crack, widening the opening. There was a blast of cool air from the dark recess, and Grace put the metal lump into her pocket. As she withdrew her hand, the chess piece came flying out and skidded across to the hatch. There wasn't time to retrieve it, and she yanked open the panel, pocketed the spoon and stepped into the cramped dark of a priest hole. Grace pulled the board tight just as a key in the hatch turned. Grace had just enough time to turn and crouch as the door opened, heralding the unseen tenant of the secret botanical garden.

A small corner of the panel allowed a chink of light, and Grace stared through, able only to see the lower half of the person descending the steps. The figure was so heavily clothed within a great army coat that it was impossible to tell precisely whether it was a man or woman. They hastened to remove a bag from within one of the large pockets and replaced an empty brown bottle with one from the table's supply. A noise in the corridor below caused them to freeze momentarily. A foot stretched out to brush against a taut thread of fishing line beneath the door, setting off several bells that Grace knew must be connected.

Someone rattling chains, she thought.

A door slammed shut, and hurried footsteps made their way back to work and away from the tower. The figure continued to place supplies in the bag, including a small purple bottle that it took great care to place upright in a carry case. They took down a vial of silver liquid and mixed up a paste in a pestle bowl using an aromatic wax and scraped the residue into a small jar. They turned and trod against the black rook next to the lower step.

Grace held her breath.

The figure bent down, blocked by the foliage of a yellowing and necrotic-looking plant, and retrieved the object. Putting down the clinking bag, they returned to the room, and crept to scrutinise the space closely. The figure hissed and lurched towards the valence of the bed, throwing back the material to reveal the packed storage beneath.

Grace breathed out slowly, desperate to stifle the gurgle from a sudden cramp in her stomach. The lactic acid in her legs burned as she stooped, desperate for movement and relief. The figure hesitated and listened in silence that Grace barely thought possible until, far below on the drive, came the sound of a motorcar. After a moment, the figure moved over to the window and collected the bag. The sound of tyres on gravel receded and the figure ascended the stairs and opened the door, sending a back draught through to the room and staircase beyond.

Out of view, Grace heard the hatch open and shut as the person left the tower room, locking the door and the governess inside.

She shifted quietly within the confined space, waiting for the footsteps to subside, knowing that without the key she was trapped, like a fly in a spider's web.

CHAPTER 18

Grace thudded open the panel and emerged into the sweltering room, desperate for air and movement. The access hatch was locked and would not budge. She turned and raced to the internal tower doors, rattling them and calling out desperately. Nothing stirred beyond, and after several moments she returned to the priest hole to examine it further. The light poured into the confined cell, revealing a wooden floor upon which she had crouched. She levered at one board, feeling a rush of cool air from the darkness below. A thin wooden ladder lay stacked to the side of the well-like hole. She pulled the panel to, and descended into the black void, feeling her way down until she met the soft sand ten feet below.

A single low passage led away to a mass of electrical cabling. Fighting her way through, Grace reached another corner and descended, warily, as light coming from the corridor beyond began to illuminate the dusty passage.

She had lost all track of time and wondered if, even now, Billy had started a search; saving her life, but condemning her to a life away from teaching and the thing she loved. She paused, leaning both hands against the interior walls, and hung her head. How had it come to this, and what was she now supposed to do or say? Would they believe her enough to try a second time? Would the doctor refuse to listen about ghosts, people at windows and roofs, poisons, and paranoia? She wondered indeed if she wasn't suffering from some malaise, supernatural or otherwise, that had all started when she had got involved with Lady Foster.

The best way out is forward and through, came the memory of the duke's words.

'But there are barriers and obstacles everywhere,' murmured Grace, delirious with nausea.

She lifted her head as she thought of Mrs Tatton's words, back at the Soames' household. *The past teaches us how to be present and go forward with our lives.*

'I can't go forward,' whispered Grace. 'No matter which way I go, it always leads to the past. She'll die, won't she?'

'*She'll die without you!*' came the soft voice of a young woman, out in the darkness ahead.

'Jane?' said Grace. 'Help me. Will I be haunted for the rest of my life?'

'*That depends on how you are going to live it.*'

'Help me,' cried Grace. 'Help me!'

A sound of hurried footsteps in the corridor beyond the wall resulted in banging against a nearby door. Grace stumbled towards the sound and kicked at the panelling around the lower section of the wall, finding the panel in her room.

'Miss Meadows?' came the voice of the housekeeper from the corridor beyond. Mrs Stanton was hammering on the door.

Grace kicked out at the wooden square, sending it flying open and off its rusted hinge. She fell through and collapsed in a heap, knocking over the chess set and bell yoke. She got up and threw off the dusty robe just as the handle on the door began to turn. Grace looked back at the chaos in the room and lurched towards the opening door, barring the entry of the irate housekeeper.

'Are you mad, screaming for help and keeping everyone waiting with your antics and attention-seeking?' she said, looking disapprovingly at the state of the governess's hair and general appearance. 'You are not coming downstairs in that condition. Whatever have you been doing?'

'There's a rat in the room,' lied Grace, 'and I've been trying to—'

Mrs Stanton paled and stepped back into the corridor, watching around her feet. 'Close the door, you silly girl, lest it gets into the hallway, and be swift. Miss Ferris is waiting.'

'I'm not being dismissed?' said Grace.

The housekeeper shook her head. 'The doctor has confirmed you have no shame of opium, against my better judgement. You are to take medicine downstairs in the kitchen and continue your duties until Captain Ferris decides on your fate this afternoon. The doctor has left for an urgent appointment and was not best pleased to be kept waiting.'

'Will he be back?' said Grace. 'I may need some additional medication.'

'He will return this afternoon to check on your progress,' said Mrs Stanton, coldly. 'If you are still here, of course.'

Grace nodded as the housekeeper hurried away from the door and the threat of vermin.

Grace closed the door and set about tidying the room, jamming the panel into the void as best she could and making herself presentable. She retrieved the spoon and lump of metal from her pocket and hid them within the chess-set case before wandering downstairs to find something to ease her stomach and the growing pain in her side.

Ann came out of the basement with a handful of chalky pills and a glass of milk.

'Doctor says to take these, Miss Meadows.'

'Did he give them to you personally?' asked Grace.

Ann gave her a wink. 'I think he's sweet on you,' she said. 'He insisted I give them to you after he had a right old spat with Mrs Stanton.'

'Who's been looking after Rose, while I've been—'

'Indisposed?' ventured the maid. 'Kate, of course. But she isn't what you call child-friendly. Miss Ferris was over the moon when I told her you were taking charge of her this morning.'

'Yes,' said Grace, swallowing the pills. 'But for how long?'

Grace sat and watched as Rose picked through her elevenses with a lack of interest.

'How are you feeling today?' asked Grace.

Rose breathed deeply and rubbed at her chest, wincing but pointing outside expectantly.

'You want some fresh air? I don't feel so great myself.'

Rose grabbed at a bright red coat and scarf, imploringly.

'It depends on you finishing at least three more of those soldiers, but don't get too excited, it won't be for long because we need to make a start on your lessons before the doctor arrives.'

Rose brightened and looked out on a bright morning as Grace hunted through the wardrobe for something suitable. With the toasted soldiers stuffed into her bulging cheeks, Rose was outfitted as though for an expedition. Grace escorted the eager young girl out of the hall and into the sunshine. They crossed the bridge and turned to follow the line of the moat along the path to the walled garden.

Grace lifted the heavily wrapped child across several large puddles and they entered the estate's fruit and vegetable kingdom. Rose pulled at the rope of the curfew bell until Grace intervened.

'Don't do that, please,' she said. 'It's not a toy.'

From the gateway entrance came a wordless bellow. Grace turned to see Bishop clap his mighty hands in greeting.

Rose ceased her games and sprang over the matted strawberry patch towards the giant. Bishop's face softened as he knelt, retrieving something from his waistcoat pocket. Tipping over a shovel-like hand, Bishop deposited a paper bag into her eager young hands. He glanced over, losing his smile, and raised his hands.

'*I know you were up there.*'

Grace furrowed her brow as Rose returned, offering her the open bag.

'No thank you,' she said, taking hold of the bag and holding up a hand to stifle dissent. 'Mr Bishop should not be giving you things that might be bad for you,' said Grace, declining the sugared almonds. 'You can have them later, if I get my animal noise and the world's quietest whisper, as promised.'

'*What will you do?*' signed Grace as Rose went in search of a farm cat that had disappeared between the brambles and briar of a nearby blackberry patch.

'*Protect the ones I love,*' signed Bishop. '*Be careful.*'

He retreated beyond the wall, leaving a trail of breath like a steam locomotive.

***

Along the southern wall lay a glasshouse, abandoned and buckled, with a partially collapsed roof. Empty clay pots, with a heavy patina of moss and algae, sat on ram-shackled wooden benches, peeping above tall nettles and spent rosebay willowherb. Attached at one end was a dusty-windowed potting shed, its paint-flaked door ajar to a cobwebbed room beyond.

Rose tugged free of Grace's hand and followed as the governess entered the camphor- and sulphur-smelling garden building. Her eyes adjusted to the dim light as the fluttering of a caged black bird on a solid oak trestle table startled both of them. Grace studied the untidy songbird hopping and chirping upon its stained and barren perches. A bright mustard yellow band ringed its beady eye, which twisted to look down at a large pile of droppings at the base of its rusting brass-stemmed cage. An egg cup of dirty water lay fouled next to an empty seed dish. The creature squawked and trilled with the pleasure of company and the prospect of food.

'Who's a messy mynah bird, then?' said Grace, screwing up her face in sadness for the unloved state of the bird.

'*Ding-dong, curfew time!*' squawked the bird, turning his beady eyes towards her. Rose gasped at her side and pressed her face closer to the metal bars, setting the bird circling the top of the cage. Grace pulled her gently back, and the bird landed, mimicking the sound of the curfew bell.

Rose retreated behind Grace's skirt.

'It's all right,' she said. 'It only copies what sounds it hears. Do you know who it belongs to?'

Rose shrugged as the bird hopped about in the cage, desperate to recover the attention.

'*Sing for your supper, pretty boy?*' said the bird, causing the governess and child to gasp in amazement.

Grace studied the sad creature, and its stinking, sorry state.

'Shall we teach him how to talk nicely?' she said. Rose joined her at the cage, nodding eagerly. 'What about the animal noise you owe me? Do you think he could learn that?'

Rose rocked side to side and pinched her nose, wavering in her promise.

'What about a duck?' said Grace encouragingly. Rose bent her elbows and made gentle flapping movements. Grace remained fixed on the opening of Rose's mouth, desperate for a meaningful breakthrough.

'Go on,' whispered Grace glancing up at the bird; it tilted its head curiously at the animated child below. 'He thinks he's smarter than you.'

'Quack-quack,' whispered Rose nervously.

Grace knelt with joy, hugging the quaking child. Rose repeated the sound, louder, encouraged by the safety of the comforting embrace. The bird clicked and whistled, listening intently as Rose grew in confidence and repeated the phrase once more.

'*Quack-Quack*,' squawked the bird, mimicking the words. Rose turned and clung to Grace's shoulders, burying her face into her neck.

'Good girl,' said Grace, clinching her tightly. 'Would you like me to ask Pa-pa if we can take him to live in the nursery? I think he would be happier there than in this smelly, cold potting shed.'

Rose coughed into Grace's exposed neck and nodded. Her dilated pupils brimmed with tears.

'Let's go and ask,' said Grace, taking Rose by the hand and leading her through a tangle of spent rhubarb leaves and artichoke stems, back to the quiet warmth of the house.

CHAPTER 19

'Absolutely not,' said Mrs Stanton, sternly, 'and I'm sure Dr Croswell would agree that it would be a noisy and unhygienic intrusion into the household.'

The doctor stood, hands on the octagonal study table like a man in the dock. He glanced over at Charles and shrugged. 'It doesn't have to be if it's properly cleaned and cared for. I'm not proposing we let Rose sleep with the thing.'

Rose fidgeted on Grace's lap, waiting for any sign from her father's face that he would make up his mind in her favour and grant the wish.

'I don't want Mrs Stanton upset,' said Charles, 'and I agree with her on the racket the thing is likely to make. Who does it belong to?'

'I've never seen it before,' said Mrs Stanton. 'It should be set free or—'

'Billy says it used to belong to the old gardener, Captain Ferris,' said Grace. 'The one that passed away during the summer. Miss Urquhart cared for it before Billy took on the responsibility.'

Mrs Stanton seethed and gave her a withering look. 'Well,

he hasn't done a very good job of it, has he? Look at the state of it!'

'*Long way to Tipperary!*' squawked the bird.

'See?' said the housekeeper. 'We can't have that spoiling the peace of the house.'

Charles wheeled over and placed his hands on the cage. 'What else does it say?'

Grace lifted Rose aside and knelt beside the wheelchair. 'It's not what it can say now, Captain Ferris,' she whispered, seeing Rose engaged with attempting to repeat the shadow puppet of a bird with her hands, 'it's what it might say if Miss Rose teaches it.'

The clouded eyes turned to look somewhat in her direction. 'You mean you would use this to get my daughter to speak?' he whispered.

'Exactly,' said Grace. 'They share something in common. I'm happy to take on the extra responsibility.' Grace knew that his decision was forthcoming about her continued appointment, and she needed to stay long enough in the house to speak privately with the doctor about the tower. She still had no idea how to broach the subject or get him to listen without dismissing the idea as mental frailty or worse.

'What do you say, James? Is it unhealthy to have the thing in a room? It stinks to high heaven.'

All eyes turned to the doctor.

'I have no objections,' he said, 'but it's your call, Charles. Rose does seem to have perked up a little.'

'*I'll raise a bunion on his Spanish onion ...*' squawked the bird.

Rose giggled and clapped her hands with glee.

'I must protest, Captain Ferris,' said Mrs Stanton, blushing at the words from a bawdy music hall number. 'It's filthy both inside and out; what else has it learnt?'

Charles teetered with the decision.

'Think of the innocent, Captain Ferris,' pleaded Mrs Stanton, 'not to mention the distraction with the other staff; we have problems enough, and I don't want to risk any unforeseen nightly noise.'

Rose rushed over to her father, grabbing at his shirt sleeve, pleading for the bird.

'I'm sorry, Rose,' he said, 'but you know that it could be dangerous to make so much noise with—' He paused, glancing at Grace, and fell silent.

'Rose?' said Grace. 'you promised me something yesterday morning, didn't you?'

Rose stuck out her bottom lip and waggled her arms like a duck.

'No, not that one. You know what else you promised, give it to Pa-pa.' Grace raised her closed hand to her chin and withdrew it downwards in a familiar sign.

Rose understood and turned to cup her hands around Charles's ears. She leaned in and whispered the quietest word that anyone could give, but it was enough.

Charles's eyes sparkled with hope, and he opened his mouth with unbridled joy at the beautiful sound. Tears welled in his eyes as he turned to Grace in astonished gratitude, before grasping at his daughter and bursting into tears.

The bird hopped merrily in the makeshift basket as Billy scrubbed at the guano-encrusted bars of its cage.

'You earned your electric burner,' said the doctor, setting down his bag in Grace's room. 'I've seen no one so overjoyed before, let alone Charles.'

Grace smiled, recalling the teary-eyed doctor escorting her from the room. 'If one little word can have such an effect,' she said, 'imagine what humans could do with whole sentences if only we used the right words.'

'What did you sign?' he said. 'What did Rose say?'

'The most precious word in the world, perhaps,' said Grace, handing Billy the dirty Bakelite bird bowl.

'*Please.*'

The doctor tilted back his head and whistled with joy. 'You are smart, Miss Meadows, very smart.'

'Follow your instinct; that's what Jane taught me. I could never have planned such success, so early on.' She examined the cracks in the oak floorboards, deep in thought. 'It's the next move that's the trick. How is she?'

'Exhausted,' said the doctor, 'and taking her outside for a walk was a bad idea. She's pretty worn out from the coughing and excitement.' He leaned forwards to give the second-quietest whisper in the world.

'*She's going downhill, quickly.*'

Billy held up the cage for inspection, and Grace gave him a thumbs-up. He replaced the bird and refilled the bowl with water from the jug next to the basin. Grace opened the small bag of almonds and jammed several nuts between the bars. The bird dunked his head into the water, taking several long sips before pecking at the almonds ferociously.

'Now, you wanted to ask me something?' said the doctor, examining her pallid complexion and wandering eyes. 'You look sick, Grace, and in some state of anxiety. Did you take the—'

'I found the spoon,' she said, 'along with other things.' Grace got up and returned with the long-handled silverware.

'Where?' said the doctor.

Grace looked across at Billy, slowing in his work, and listening intently.

'The tower,' she said. 'If you don't believe me, then Rose will die, and everyone loses. I don't need your experience to see that. This is my final card from a bad hand, and I'm not bluffing.'

'It's true, Dr Croswell,' said Billy. 'There's someone been knocking about up there, and Mr Bishop has been out to the woodsman's hut. Someone's been out there too.'

The doctor examined the dried and sticky substance. He sniffed and pinched part of the residue, placing it on his tongue. He spat it out immediately.

'This isn't just laudanum or the tonic,' he said. 'There's something sweet and toxic in here; I can taste it! Kate, the housemaid, administered this?' he asked.

'Yes.'

He shot up and was about to rush out of the door when he turned.

'Did you take any of this?'

'Yes,' said Grace, 'but only on the tip of my tongue; not enough to make me ill?' She held up her open hands as though to emphasise the point. The doctor leapt towards her right hand, turning and sniffing at the dark stain on her forefinger and thumb.

'I've seen this before, on Jane's fingers the night she died. What have you touched or eaten recently?'

Grace frowned at the stains, as though seeing them for the first time. 'Water, a little tea and some dried fruit this morning; several others had the same. I had a dry cracker this afternoon, but I was already feeling worse by that stage. There are plants in the tower along with horrible things, an army uniform and brown bottles; I've seen it!'

The doctor clasped her shoulders like a vice.

'Describe the plant you saw, quickly!'

'There was castor oil, toadstools, orchids and a climbing plant with shiny black berries; the higher stems had purple and green bell-shaped flowers.' She gripped her side as a stab of pain hindered her ability to sit upright.

'What is it?' she stammered.

'Belladonna,' he said.

'Nightshade?' said Grace. 'Poison?'

'You're displaying symptoms of acute atropine poisoning. You've ingested or absorbed what Rose has been taking at a lower dose.' He slammed his fist onto the table. 'How could I have been so blind! It was right under my nose.'

'Will she be all right?' said Billy, coming over to hold her shaking hand.

'I don't know, it depends on how much she's ingested,' said the doctor, fishing out a small, labelled bottle and rubbing a grubby spoon down his tweed jacket. 'Take four spoonfuls of this and hold on tight—it's a purge.'

'What about Rose?' said Grace. 'Shouldn't we—'

The doctor grabbed at Billy's waistcoat. 'Get Captain Ferris and Mrs Stanton and meet me downstairs immediately. Tell them it's an emergency and to send someone out for the doctor over at Eastings.' Dr Croswell hurriedly scribbled down a series of instructions and medicines, and forced the list into Billy's hands. The boy tripped over his feet as he sprung away down the corridor.

The doctor turned. 'You are going to be very—'

Grace rushed to the bedpan and emptied what little remained in her stomach into the porcelain bowl. He ran over with a cloth and ointment, rubbing at her fingers to remove the dark marks.

'Good,' said the doctor, retrieving a small clear bottle. 'Take a good swig of this.'

'Is it as bad as the other?' said Grace, wiping her mouth with the back of her hand. 'I feel faint.'

'No idea,' said the doctor. 'It's pilocarpine, and the only antidote for twelve miles.'

'Pilocarpine?' said Grace suspiciously. 'Isn't that for eyes?'

He turned. 'Don't you trust me?'

'I feel so dreadful, I'm past caring,' said Grace. 'If you are poisoning us then I'll be back for you, like Sophia Ferris. I promise.'

Dr Croswell blanched. 'I'll be taking holy orders, then.' He took a swig and grimaced.

'My God that's foul. Your turn—take the damn antidote!'

Grace gave him a withering glance and chugged at the acrid liquid before spitting it out. 'I don't think I can—'

'By the looks of you, you've got about an hour before your organs start to shut down!'

She stifled a whine as the burning elixir overwhelmed her capacity to avoid the taste. She shuddered, lowering the bottle, and glanced up.

'Tell me that's enough?' she pleaded, heaving and writhing as her body became a battlefield between poison and antidote.

She waved him away once the stains on her fingers had been removed and reached for a glass of water.

She raised it to her lips, but the doctor's hand slammed it from her grasp, hitting her cheek. Fearing some sudden violence, she twisted, ready to defend herself. Instead, she saw the startled face of the medic shaking his head and peering through the brass bars of the cage at the lifeless bird below, the yellow beak still covered in its sweet and deadly last meal of almonds.

'Bishop ...' she murmured before passing into a swoon and hitting the floor.

CHAPTER 20

Grace awoke to the sound of an argument between two familiar voices.

'You have no concept of what lies beyond the end of your stethoscope,' said Lady Foster. 'It's about time you opened your eyes, Dr Croswell.'

'With all due respect—' began the doctor, turning as Grace struggled to her elbows in the bed, shielding her eyes from the intense sunlight streaming in through the bedroom window.

'It's so bright,' she murmured.

'It's the atropine,' he said, bright-eyed. 'It's dilated your pupils, and bright light is going to be painful for a while.'

'How long have I been asleep?'

'Since yesterday afternoon, off and on.' He placed his hand on top of her own. 'You are going to be all right, but it was touch and go until my colleague arrived. Your kidneys have taken a hammering.'

'Rose?' said Grace, trying to sit up.

'She's all right, but she's going to get sick from the withdrawal of the laudanum in the syrup, despite the substitute my colleague and I have administered. There's no telling how long she has been under its effects. We've got Bishop downstairs in the basement, locked in the wine cellar, just in case.'

'Just in case of what?' asked Grace.

'Either he's a poisoner, or he isn't. We should know in the next few hours. He's showing no hint of malice or emotion; we could have done with you translating, but when challenged, he made a grab for the almonds from the paper bag and swallowed most of them before he could be restrained. I thought it was a suicide attempt, but he's showed no signs of any ill effects as of this afternoon. He refuses to take the antidote, even from Billy, and Charles won't release him until I've checked him over and the results have come back on the samples we retrieved just to be sure.'

'What about the housemaid?' asked Grace.

'Kate's been dismissed and is down at the station, protesting her innocence,' he said. 'I was there when they arrested her.'

'Why did she do it?' asked Grace.

'The inspector thinks it may be an angel of mercy case,' said Lady Foster. 'Killing the child slowly to release her from suffering and end the binding of Sophia Ferris to the house. He's worked on several cases like it before.'

Dr Croswell shrugged. 'Ridiculous belief informs ridiculous action, even among the educated,' he said, frowning at Lady Foster. 'Laudanum has been used maliciously for centuries to keep children quiet and malleable under the care of nefarious nannies and mothers. It's a reasonable conjecture that Kate was compounding the effects of the drug with as much fear and superstition to keep Rose in a perpetual state of quiet.'

'To avoid the spirit of her mother finding and claiming her?' said Grace.

'Yes,' said the doctor. 'And to keep her situation along

with that of everyone else in the household, once the spirit was gone. Poor superstitious fool.'

'It isn't superstition,' said Grace, turning to Lady Foster for support. 'I've seen her, and what happened in that tower.'

'You were hallucinating,' said the doctor. 'The invincible Bishop is leaning me towards the notion that the nuts aren't what killed the bird, it was the water you've been drinking for days—the scum from the watermark attests to it being laced with the stuff.'

'You think she tainted the water that Jane and I drank, and planted the laudanum bottle in Jane's room, the night she died?'

'The symptoms are similar, and even a toxicology report might not tell them apart,' he said. 'I've mentioned it to the inspector, and he's going to investigate whether there's anything to it.'

The doctor slumped and covered his eyes. 'Jane knew about the poison and tried to warn me about it—I thought she was having a mental breakdown. That's why she was trying to get into the tower room?'

'Yes,' said Grace. 'She was going in search of proof when she fell, but I know she was coming down from the tower room, not climbing up.'

Lady Foster huffed and turned to assist Grace into a comfortable sitting position. 'Are you going to tell him, or am I?'

Grace puffed out her cheeks and stared at the linen sheets.

'I have a sensitivity to seeing things when under great stress —' she said, raising her hands to stop the doctor from interrupting. 'Captain Ferris is aware, and so is Lady Foster. In fact, it's probably why I am here despite certain things being kept from me.' She turned as Lady Foster bowed her head and looked away.

'This has been happening to me long before Hemingworth, and long before atropine. Do you remember when I asked you if poison could be a factor in Rose's deterioration and my own?'

The doctor nodded. 'You were feeling unwell and experiencing paranoia about people in towers, being watched and seeing things that aren't there—'

'The notion it was poison didn't come from me; it came via two other visitations: the spirit of a child that has haunted me for the past year, and one other.'

The doctor rubbed his face with his hands. 'Go on,' he said. 'But if it's Henry VIII or Genghis Khan, then I'm done with the both of you—I mean it.'

'The other was Jane Urquhart,' said Grace, looking to Lady Foster. 'Something happened when I touched Rose's hand on the first evening.' The doctor sat upright and held her gaze.

Lady Foster dragged a chair to the bed and sat down. 'You joined with Rose without any controls in place or thought for your safety and that of Miss Ferris?'

'I didn't have any choice, and I did not initiate it. Rose grabbed my hand when she saw the spirit outside on the lawn. We were both in a state of anxiety.'

'Jane Urquhart appeared to you?' asked the doctor.

'No,' said Grace. 'It was the recollection of a memory. She lay dying from the fall, and she made the sign for poison on Rose's hand. She didn't know what it meant until she heard me repeat it from the spirit outside.'

'How the hell did Rose get in there?' said the doctor.

'The same way I escaped,' said Grace, getting out of bed, against the wishes of the protesting medic, and shuffling over to the panel in the next room. She grabbed the umbrella and prised the panel door open with its tip. James peered into the hidden passageway, looking left and right into the disappearing darkness.

'Where the hell does this go?' he said.

'It links with other rooms in the house. Rose knows about them; they are in her drawings—scratches like an underground map. I can tell you it leads to a panel in the tower room, next to the grandfather clock.'

Dr Croswell stroked his chin. 'Charles and I used to play in a priest hole there, but it wasn't a passage.'

'There's a false panel blocking the route through. They are all marked with a small cross like the one here—'

Grace pointed out the tiny engraved cross on the open panel with the tip of the umbrella, and the doctor leaned over, squinting at the symbol.

'This one joins the network running through the house,' said Grace.

'Catholics,' said Lady Foster with a roll of her eyes.

'Rose hid behind the staircase panel, the night Jane found out about the poison and was chased down the stairs.'

'I thought she was climbing up,' he said. 'How can you know this?'

'Because it's being played out time and time again to those that can see or hear it, you fool,' said Lady Foster. 'Why do you think we covered the staircase in tripwires and the damn bells go off every night?'

'Did you see who was chasing her when she fell?'

'No,' said Grace, 'but it's not a spirit; otherwise, I would have seen it.'

'Kate?' said the doctor.

Grace shrugged. 'Possibly.'

She pointed to the drawing on the wall. 'There's a face in the tower. Rose has been drawing it over and over, and I thought it must be her mother. There are a lot more next door.'

The doctor got up and left the room; he returned with Billy and a bundle of drawings.

'I'm so glad to see you awake, Miss Meadows,' he said. 'Mr Bishop didn't poison you, I'm sure of it!'

She held out her hand to squeeze his arm. 'I don't think so too.'

'He's refusing to protest his innocence until he sees you,' said Billy.

'See me?' said Grace. 'Why?'

'A bond of trust, perhaps, or maybe he wants to confess to someone that understands his dumb language?' interrupted Lady Foster.

Grace frowned at the use of the term.

'I meant to say, sign language,' said Lady Foster, correcting herself.

'Whatever it is,' said Billy, 'he made me understand it's serious. Something more important than even his own life.'

'Well, I'm coming with you if he survives,' said Dr Croswell. 'But not until you've had rest.'

'What about those drawings?' said Lady Foster, taking a page and holding it up against the window. 'Bishop is carrying the child, *and* the faces in the tower are in this one, so it can't be him up there.'

'Faces?' said Grace. 'There's only one.'

The doctor held up another page. 'There seem to be two, in every one of them. One seems to be always crossed out unless you look at them with the light.' He lowered the drawing to Grace's lap.

She looked down at the heavy blots and marks, hiding the second face beneath the heavy crayon and pencil rubbings.

'Looks as though someone has been trying to remove themselves from the picture, quite literally,' said Lady Foster. 'I think the child has been trying to tell us all something, but we weren't listening.'

The noblewoman pointed to the dreadful face in the tower. 'There's two of them in on this, and I guess that we caught the apprentice trying to blot out her role, but not the master chemist.'

'Why not blot out both of them?' asked Billy.

Lady Foster tapped a finger against her cheek. 'Because it served their purpose to make everything appear as though Sophia Ferris was causing this. She's bound to the tower all right, but it looks as though she's been getting a little mortal help from someone in speeding up the decline in the child. She's not got long to wait, now. I can feel it.'

The doctor furrowed his brow. 'Do you know of anyone that she might have been seeing or related to, Billy?' he asked.

'She wasn't married, I know that. She had a brother that visited a few times and did a bit of gardening just before Captain Ferris went away; he's in the picture of the big house down in the drawing room.'

'We'll take a look,' said the doctor, turning to Grace. 'You rest easy now. Men are coming from the village to empty the tower room of its filth, and three of them are keeping watch tonight at the bothy. Charles is in his element, ordering people about like he's back on the front lines.

'I'd stay up here if I were you; there's nothing Kate Jellicoe can do to hurt anyone anymore.'

CHAPTER 21

'Y ou're sure of this?' said Charles. 'I only vaguely remember the man.'

Lady Foster stared at the notorious poisoner and murderer standing chest out, hand tucked into his braces, beaming beneath a bowler hat next to his sister.

'Positive,' said Lady Foster. 'I've seen him.'

'Where?' said Dr Croswell. 'Here?'

She shook her head. 'You won't like the answer, or believe it in any case.'

Charles stiffened. 'You think he had anything to do with—'

Lady Foster stared at the beautiful woman cradling the infant child. She placed a hand on his shoulder.

'Let's not go down that path, Charles. Not yet. Think of Rose and what we are going to do next.'

'I've had the place searched, top to bottom, and everything that can be locked down has been.' He glanced in the doctor's direction. 'How is she?'

'Not good, Charles. It's too late to move her, but I've got William Knowles coming over with as much medical firepower as my Austin can carry. The hospital is full of Spanish flu.'

'How long has she got?' whispered Charles, sliding his hands down to the side of his chair despondently.

'A few days,' he said. 'Maybe less. There's something I'm missing. We've stopped the purges, and we've both been up there to see what foul chemistry he has been practising. Grace mentioned a purple bottle he or his blasted sister were taking special care to keep safe. Unless I know what I'm dealing with, I could be doing more harm than good.'

'Then try harder, James!' said Charles, swivelling and heading for the decanter.

The doctor was about to open his mouth, but Lady Foster shook her head.

'You think he could still be around, Charles. Hiding out somewhere?' said the doctor.

'What? In a priest hole, you mean?' he said, feeling his way to a glass and unstopping the whisky. 'I've got a dog coming and several sturdy men to sniff the place out, but more than likely he knows he's been rumbled; more's the pity.' He gulped down the malt and slammed the glass into the table, shattering it into pieces.

Dr Croswell stood up and put his hands in his pockets. 'What I don't understand is why?'

'Neither do I,' said Lady Foster. 'Jellicoe is an evil bastard, but he's motivated by money as much as killing.'

'Well, he can have the damn lot, including my wife, for all I care. There's virtually nothing left, and I will have to let most of the staff go in the new year. Can't do it at Christmas, can I? The car's being sold and most of the tenanted pasture. No one is coming back from the war to farm it—not like they used to.'

'Does Mrs Stanton know?' asked Lady Foster. 'I'll be able to find most of them places, I promise.'

Charles nodded in thanks. 'Elizabeth knows, which is why she's been so damn protective about the place, trying to run it single-handed. Don't you think I haven't noticed everyone thinking she's plotting to take over? I'm blind, not deaf. She's refused wages for three months, and that sovereign I made a fuss over is counterfeit—got it from a fella in the trenches, cheating at cards. Bloody glad someone didn't pick it up. Well, there's a reason for it all, and now you know.'

Lady Foster poured herself a glass of the whisky and handed the captain a second glass.

'I think there might be more to it than that?'

Charles rested his hands on his lap.

'So what if she cares for me? Aren't we both struggling with our physical deformities? I say what matters is on the inside. The woman's a saint.'

He raised his glass to the light of the window, and Lady Foster struck it with her own in a toast.

'Here, here,' she said.

Grace descended the stairs alongside the doctor. The condensation on the arched roof dripped onto the polished flagstones as they made their way along the chambered passageway to the brick-lined wine cellar.

The doctor put down the candle in front of the iron bars and squinted into the makeshift cell.

'Bishop?' he said. 'Are you awake?'

A shadow shifted in the corner of the locked room, and the giant came forwards into the light. Dr Croswell took a step back, but Grace stood her ground.

'Are you well, Bishop?' she said. 'The doctor needs to know if you are unwell, even if you didn't—'

'*I did not poison you, or Rose,*' he signed. '*I am well. Tell the doctor to put his bag away.*'

'He's feeling fine,' said Grace, turning around.

Dr Croswell lifted the candle and shone it fully in the manservant's face.

'No sweats? No fever or cramps?' he said.

Bishop shook his head.

'I have to wait until the results come back from the hospital before Charles considers letting you out; I'm sorry.'

'*Rose?*' he signed.

The doctor glanced at Grace, trying to understand.

'Rose is not well,' said Grace. 'We believe that Kate and her brother, Henry Jellicoe, have been poisoning people here for a long time. Do you know anything about why that could be?'

Bishop smoothed the hair on his brow. '*I swore to protect the family, do you remember?*'

Grace nodded, relaying the words out loud.

'*I also swore to protect a family secret, one that I can only pass on in dire need or at the moment of my death. It was to Billy that I would have given this responsibility in time, but I fear that Jellicoe has discovered it.*'

'What secret?' said the doctor. 'Does Charles know about this?'

Bishop shook his head. '*I am its guardian; it was passed down to me from Mr Squires, the butler, in an unbroken line from its hiding. When the Hemingworth's last heir died, she passed on the secret to her chambermaid to avoid her cousin ransacking the house for its treasures. It's come down to me to decide what to do with it, now that Jellicoe threatens both secret and family.*'

'So what are you going to do?' said Dr Croswell, pulling Grace back as the man behind the bars stepped forwards.

He fixed his gaze on the governess and raised his hands.

'You have earned my trust and my friendship. Silence has its advantages, but the time for secrets is over.'

He bounced the little fingers of both hands together, sending the open hands away as though sending out an explosion of sparks.

'Silver?' whispered Grace.

Dr Croswell narrowed his eyes. 'You aren't serious? It's just a fairy tale ...'

Bishop raised a finger to his lips and gently rotated it in a grand spiral above his head.

'It's in the staircase, bits of the filigree,' said Grace. 'I've seen pieces of it cut up in the tower room—'

Bishop nodded and put his finger back to his lips.

'It's just pieces of scrap from the broken railing,' said the doctor.

'No,' said Grace. 'I've got a piece of it, hidden in the same place as I hid the spoon.'

She thrust her arms through the bars, and Bishop grasped them. Fixing her eyes on those that glittered black, bright and blue in the candlelight, she said, 'We'll get you out of here soon. I promise.'

Grace raced up the stairs to her room, leaving the doctor to tell Charles of the discovery.

Hope, she thought. *Hope for the future, for the Hall, for Rose if she survives.*

She threw open the trunk in the bedchamber and fumbled with the catch on the chess-piece box. It flew open, revealing the heavy hunk of tarnished silver.

A gentle thud in the sitting room was followed by the sound of the lock turning in the door; Grace poked her head around the connecting door to see the panel lying on the floor and the open passage in the wall.

'Hello?'

She clutched at the metal in her hand and tip-toed to the door. It was locked.

She rattled the door handle and opened her mouth to call out, just as the intruder re-emerged from the hole in the wall and cupped his hand around her mouth.

'You forgot this, you interfering little whore ...' said the deep voice of her assailant. The man held up the rook in front of her face and cast it aside. His free hand twisted around her throat and dragged her struggling and kicking into the bedchamber.

Grace tried to punch her elbows back into the heavy overcoat to no avail. The man spun her round and pinned her throat to the bed, revealing his dark and sallow face, weatherbeaten and worn, like a vagrant used to spending time destitute and on the run. The odour of sickly sweat and noxious chemicals surrounded the desperate criminal dressed in mismatched clothing. He wore a dirty, collarless shirt wrapped by a woman's silk scarf.

'Jelli ... coe—' she mouthed as he crushed her windpipe in a vice-like grip.

'Yes,' he seethed as he squeezed the life from her. 'This is for my sister, and for spoiling my beautiful work. Your little ward has quite a strong constitution. I'm done with toads and mice; perhaps when this is all over, I'll dig her up and advance my studies further!'

Grace writhed and clenched her fist around the metal lump, smashing it into the side of Henry Jellicoe's temple. He cried out and released his hand, allowing a sudden rush of air back into Grace's lungs.

Jellicoe staggered back, rubbing at the blood from the cut to his forehead, seeing the lump fall to the floor as Grace struggled to get up and into the sitting room. She cried out hoarsely for aid.

The poisoner picked up the lump of silver, watching as Grace lifted the ebony umbrella and flailed it in front of herself.

'You wanted this for yourself, did you? Is that why you came looking for it? It was a pure coincidence. If that other bitch hadn't fallen, I'd never have seen where it was hiding.'

Grace jabbed forwards with the tip of silver, keeping the man at bay. 'You killed her, and Sophia, didn't you?'

He shrugged his shoulders and looked down at the metal on the floor. 'It's all for science, and chemistry is an expensive hobby—I'm only trying to help humanity in the long run, but sacrifices have to be made. I was safe in that tower with all that bollocks my sister kept spouting about ghosts; till you poked your nose in.'

'What do you want, the silver?' she said. 'There are men with dogs coming; you won't get away this time.'

Jellicoe circled, sneered at the umbrella and shuffled forwards as Grace retreated towards the bedroom. She lunged out as he attempted to grab the makeshift weapon.

'I'll be long gone, thanks to your little revelation in the walls.' He glanced at the open passage.

'Come,' he said, taking out the small purple bottle from his pocket. 'This is only for special people, and little girls who need their balsam burning all night to breathe. Poor little thing's been enjoying some beautiful dreams, I'll wonder. Your doctor friend is as blind as that cripple.'

'You put it in her balsam? You're a monster!' rasped Grace.

Jellicoe licked his lips. 'Want to try some? I've never got the chance to try it on someone orally. I've only just realised the poetry in what I've created. A balsam giving off vapour from quicksilver made in a tower full of true silver; it's beautiful, isn't it?'

He shot a glance at the window. Grace jabbed at his stomach, but the blow landed on his side. He grabbed at the umbrella, wrenching it from her hands, and threw her to the floor. He knelt and grabbed at her throat, causing Grace to gasp for air.

Jellicoe unstoppered the purple bottle with his teeth and forced it to her lips.

'It'll be quick,' he said. 'More's the pity!'

Grace threw up her hands to ward off the liquid and grabbed his wrists.

A sudden wave of uncontrolled confusion and frenzy broke over her as something else took control. Jellicoe hesitated, and dropped the bottle to the floor, spilling its silvered contents. Grace clung on as the man dragged her to her feet.

She screwed her eyes tight, forcing through the thoughts from her assailant's past, uncontrolled and untamed as something from beyond the seal of death's door struggled to make itself known. Jellicoe lurched back as the faces of previous victims cried out to him for vengeance, held back by the most recent, who now claimed the right to collect. A drunken soldier appeared in his mind, guided and brought out by the untrained and unqualified medium.

The poor man leaned against a wall, in suit clothes ill-fitted and alien to him, watching as Henry Jellicoe put on the rough khaki uniform and exchanged identities. Jellicoe forced his wallet and ring into the man's hands, framing him for the murder of another. Policemen raced around a lamplit corner as the young man slumped to the street, turning on the slippery cobbles to see Henry Jellicoe, in soldier disguise, escape into the dark of a nearby alley.

'You!' said Henry.

Grace stiffened and fought against the urge to release herself from the horror of the poisoner's mind, desperately searching for the soldier's spirit among the souls, desperate to come through. Something stirred and came forwards in the room as though trying to take form. Grace and Henry writhed as the authorities rapidly convened a court and pronounced swift justice on the innocent man, for heinous crimes he did not commit. Out of the dark came the image of a hangman's noose.

A feeling of utter terror and foreknowledge of death, experienced through the innocent man, overwhelmed her as the noose was placed over the head and tightened around her throat. The jail room slipped upwards as the soldier fell beneath the wooden platform to his death, and Grace gave in to the urge to allow the summons to take place.

She opened her eyes. The seal between worlds shattered and a rush of uncontrolled rage and fury flowed through her, and into the midriff of Henry Jellicoe, sending him reeling. The man flailed to get up as the spirit of the soldier strode across the floor, unseen by his eyes, but not those of the governess. Henry grabbed at his throat as he felt the silk scarf around his neck constrict. The soldier's spirit gripped and twisted the scarf like a tourniquet as Jellicoe tried to attack the invisible strangler. Grace screamed out and ran for the door, unlocking it in a frenzy.

The life drained from Henry Jellicoe's eyes, arms sagging to his lap as he approached the moment of death. A dreadful splutter of rattling breath signalled the end as the doctor and Lady Foster burst in to see the man in the drawing-room photograph, Henry Jellicoe, dead. The lifeless body was being dragged across the floor by a length of silk scarf, towards the open passage.

'Get out!' shouted Lady Foster at the doctor, who stood gaping at the unbelievable scene. 'Get Charles and tell him to put Bishop back where he belongs.'

'He's trying to get away,' said the doctor, pushing past.

'He's dead, you fool! Get out; science and reason have no more use here.'

Lady Foster shoved him out, locked the door and raced for Grace's upturned wrists.

'I'm here,' she said. 'Let go. Let me seal the door.'

Grace looked blankly at Henry Jellicoe's corpse as it was jerked forwards by the soldier, intent on taking the body.

'He tried to kill ... me,' she murmured. 'The soldier ...'

Lady Foster slapped the governess's face, causing a sudden awakening to full consciousness.

'Listen to me, Grace. If we don't close the door, they'll be trapped here or worse, like Sophia. Do you understand?'

Grace nodded.

'Close your eyes,' said Lady Foster, dragging them both to kneel on the floor.

Grace felt a challenge, and the spirit stopped its tug on the silk, dropping the end of the scarf to the floor. The medium strained to remove vengeful thoughts from their minds and replace them with compassion, forgiveness, and justice. The spirit wavered, entreating the medium to allow him to remain, and faded as Lady Foster gained control.

The door opened with the sound of hurried feet, the doctor leading the charge. Grace leaned forwards into the arms of Lady Foster, unsteady and faint. She limply pointed at the purple bottle, and Dr Croswell ran to retrieve it.

'Rose ... hurry,' said Grace, falling into a swoon. 'It's quick ... silver, in the ...balsam.'

CHAPTER 22

G race opened her eyes, focussing on the dim outline of the doctor, seated beside the bed.

'Where am I?' she asked, glancing around at the unfamiliar surroundings.

'My room,' said Lady Foster. 'I thought it best under the circumstances.'

Dr Croswell checked her pulse and looked curiously at the scars against his thumb and forefinger. He turned the raised hand to Lady Foster, drawing the curtains.

'I know,' she said. 'Not a word to Charles, if you want me to continue with your wretched medicine while I am in the country, do you understand?'

'Lady Foster, are you ill?' said Grace, glad to see the noblewoman, but concerned about her unusually pale appearance.

'A minor fainting episode following the incident earlier, nothing more.'

'Low blood pressure, brought about by—'

'I demand patient confidentiality,' interrupted Lady Foster, removing a silver cigarette case from her pocket.

'Not in here,' he said defensively. 'Grace needs clean air, rest and regular purges to clear the remnants of the poison.'

Lady Foster screwed her face at the prescription and replaced the cigarette case. Grace blushed as she raised an eyebrow in the doctor's direction.

'It's Grace now, is it? It seems I got off lightly with a bottle of syrup and a tongue-wagging.'

Dr Croswell frowned, and Grace thought that he might stick his tongue out at any moment in reply to the noble-woman's childish behaviour.

It's a defence mechanism, thought Grace. The two bickering adults had something upon which to focus their anxieties. Despite being opposite sides of the coin, they had a common purpose—someone for whom they both cared.

They are worried about me.

'The balsam—' said Grace.

'Jellicoe processed a vapour of mercury into a wax that has been poisoning the air while she slept. I've administered an antidote, but it's too soon to tell if Rose has the strength left to deal with it.'

'Is he—?

'Gone,' said Lady Foster. 'In all senses of the word. Mr Bishop has kindly exchanged places with the body. We are all free of Henry Jellicoe, even his wife, Marjorie. It's what comes next that we need to concentrate on now.'

Lady Foster continued, as though sensing the uncertainty.

'The good doctor here finally has the solution to his puzzle; Bishop has revealed the wealth of melted down and refashioned silver in the staircase,' she said. 'It seems Hemingworth has given up all its secrets—all but one. Charles has something to fight for now and has finally decided.'

'On what?' said Grace.

'To go on the offensive, whatever the cost,' said the noblewoman. 'No more hiding from what haunts the place, no more waiting for Sophia Ferris, skulking in that damned tower.'

'Just for the record,' piped the doctor, 'I am totally against this ridiculous seance. Rose's ailments are physical or at worst psychosomatic. They are not spiritual in nature.'

'I am *so* looking forward to seeing your material world fall apart this evening, Dr Croswell,' said Lady Foster sarcastically.

'You mean *the* material world—it's the only one I'm aware of!'

'I love the way your voice deepens when you are agitated,' said Lady Foster. 'It's very appealing.'

'You aren't going to summon the spirit of Sophia Ferris?' asked Grace, pulling herself up to accept a glass of water and trying to halt the squabbling. 'Isn't that dangerous? I thought she was mad?'

'Not half as dangerous as letting her take Rose, come what may.'

'What are you going to do if she comes through?' asked Grace.

'Bargain with her,' said Lady Foster with a contemptuous glance at the doctor shaking his head in disbelief.

'With what?' said Grace.

The noblewoman approached the bed, fidgeting with her hands. 'Excluding Rose Ferris?' she said rhetorically, leaning over to whisper into the doctor's face:

'*Whatever the bitch wants.*'

Grace blanched at the language, and the doctor rose to protest as Lady Foster raised a hand in defence. 'Charles's words, not mine!'

'And if she refuses?' said Grace.

'Then we do things the old-fashioned way,' said the medium of Mayfair. 'Trap and lay her, once and for all.'

'There's no way I'm letting you get involved in this,' said James from the adjoining room. 'Doctor's orders.'

Grace brushed out the tangles from her hair and pulled on a robe, ignoring the instruction.

'Are you even listening to me?' he said.

The doctor's face peeped round the bedroom door. 'You and Lady Foster are treating this like some kind of game. You are both unwell, and this is only likely to end in disappointment for Charles or make things worse meddling with things you can't control or understand.'

'You saw what happened in my room earlier, with Jellicoe?'

The doctor fumbled for an explanation. 'Death throes, final moments of life—'

'If you don't believe in spirits, why are you so concerned?' she said, scratching at her wrist.

James glanced at the scars before she had time to conceal them.

'Precisely because of things like that,' he said, pointing to her hands, now at rest in her lap. 'Your mental well-being, and that of the rest of the house. Belief informs action, Grace, and that woman has been filling your head with nonsense.' He stuck his hands deep into his pockets. 'Rose needs a specialist doctor, not a medium. Don't do this.'

'I feel like a pendulum, Dr Croswell—'

'James,' he said, 'call me James, please.'

Grace turned to the mirror, seeing the concern reflected on his face. 'I feel like a pendulum, James, swinging between her world and yours. Two extremes with the truth somewhere in between. You remember the child I spoke of, Arthur?'

'The ward that died in the fire?'

She nodded. 'You are going to tell me I have been halluci-nating for the past twelve months and that his appearances result from intense grief or symptoms of my subconscious brought on during bouts of extreme anxiety?' She held up her wrist to the mirror. 'You think I would do this to myself knowing all that?'

He shook his head and combed his hair with his hand.

'No,' he said, coming to stand behind her. 'I truly believe you experience these things; I just don't believe they are what you think they are.'

Grace stared at his reflection.

'Do you exist in this mirror?' she said.

James frowned. 'Of course not. I'm a reflection of light interacting with a silvered surface.'

'But I still believe you are there, even if I can't turn round,' she said. 'You are right, belief informs action, and I don't have to choose between spirits or a poison-induced hallucination to act on my instincts. Whatever Arthur and the others are or were, or even if they don't exist at all, my response would be the same—do you see?'

James sighed and shrugged a single shoulder. 'And what is your instinct telling you now?'

Grace shivered, setting a strand of hair cascading across her dilated eyes.

'What is it?' said James, nervously glancing around the room. 'A spirit?'

She raised a hand to stifle a laugh. 'No, I'm just chilly. Can you close the window, please?'

He exhaled deeply, puffing out his cheeks.

'How irrational,' said Grace, lowering her hand. 'You are frightened by something you don't believe in.'

James disappeared from the mirror and parted the curtains briefly, letting in a sunbeam that struck the ebony umbrella. The curtains closed, and the shaft of light blinked out.

'With few exceptions,' she said, 'everything or everyone

I've ever cared about is connected with this situation, or with this house: Jane, Lady Foster, Arthur, Rose ...' She glanced at the gentle, pleasing lines of his cheekbones and returned to stare at her reflection.

'I made promises to a duke, an eccentric medium that saved me from ruin, and a child that has no voice of their own. My instinct is telling me that the best way to keep all of them is forward, and through.'

Men from the village laboured under the weight of the great mirror lowered from the wall.

'We needed more men,' said Charles, directing the placement of the heavy frame onto the dolly cart like a battlefield general.

'They came to search for a fugitive, not for a siege. They wouldn't have come if you'd told them the truth,' said James, observing the silence and the furtive glances of the farm labourers. 'I can see the fear in their eyes just by being here after sundown.'

A clock chimed the half-hour in the hall, speeding the men in their escort to the tower; not one of them wanted to remain after the curfew bell. James followed the captain as he wheeled through the candlelit hall.

'No luck in restoring the electrics?' asked James, reluctantly following his friend into the corridor to the tower wing.

'None whatsoever,' said Charles. 'Bishop's been at it all afternoon.' Charles gripped the edge of his chair. 'Those blasted electric heaters have added to the complications; the fuse board and interior cabling are a disaster. He's going to look at the old generator in the morning after the police officer returns to collect the body in the basement.

'I have the means to do anything I like, now,' he whispered, glancing in the staircase's direction. 'The lad has confirmed the leaves and wire of the filigree are silver, and he's kept his mouth shut so far. His colourful past has become useful. I'd give it all up if only Rose would—'

'She's a fighter,' said the doctor. 'Elizabeth and Bishop are with her now; they are going to stand watch whilst this silliness plays out. I never thought I'd see the day when they were both on the same team—seems we've been wrong about a good many people, wouldn't you say?'

Charles bowed his head and reached out a shaking hand to hold the cuff of his friend.

'Yes, myself included. Whatever comes next I want you to know that we'd both be beyond help without you.'

The doctor squeezed the hand and sighed. 'I think we might all come to thank young governesses that don't follow rules or curfews before this is all over.'

The doors to the tower lay open, streaming out golden firelight from every available sconce, candelabra and lamp. The great oil lamp and chandelier rose as men pulled on the chain on the staircase wall. Lady Foster, dressed in blood-red claret, bustled about the tower and around the three black silk cloths covering the great monolithic mirrors, propped upright by A-frames of cleft chestnut. The men laboured with the final panel, sealing in the noblewoman until a slight adjustment allowed her to squeeze through a narrow opening.

'She has a sense for the dramatic,' said James, wrinkling his nose at the pungent smell. Men stacked paraffin drums across the wall next to buckets of sand and several extinguishers.

'You aren't serious?' he said. 'Charles, I—'

'It's the final act. The ultimate solution if Foster fails,' said Charles, squeezing his fists. 'Better to live without a tower than a daughter.'

'But the rest of the house—?'

'It's all in order,' he said, pointing to the reinforced metal plates attached to the landing doors. 'Bishop ripped them off the garage doors earlier. It's a chance I'm willing to take.'

Lady Foster beckoned the last mirror into position. Four great slabs of silvered metal, covered with the darkest sable, formed a makeshift box room within the tower. At the centre of the mirrored box was a small table, stacked with items and surrounded by three chairs; one of which held a coil of silk rope across its carved wooden backrest. An antique brass hourglass stood next to the bell yoke, proud above a crystal decanter set and smouldering ashtray. A narrow gap at one of the mirrored corners allowed barely enough room to access the makeshift room. The final mirror was propped, and the men were dismissed, squeezing through the narrow opening. The foreman tipped his bowler hat and escorted the men out of the hall, promising to ring the curfew bell at eight.

'Is it secure?' said Charles. 'Will it work?'

Lady Foster retrieved her cigarette and passed the captain a tumbler of brandy, her hand shaking, from the table. She tugged on the tobacco and folded one arm in front of the other, fidgeting as she flicked the ash far from her exquisite gown.

'Apart from the circle of fuel around the oubliette,' she said, pointing her cigarette through the opening to her side, 'it's showtime.'

***

'You don't half look pretty, Miss Meadows,' said Ann, smoothing down the admiral-blue silk.

The gown hung majestically upon Grace's small frame, but she resisted the temptation to twirl in the small bedroom or take any pleasure in the dress belonging to the spirit of Florence Foster.

'Will you be all right?' asked Grace, holding still the shaking hand of the maid. 'Once the bell rings, it will only be safe for Mrs Stanton and Mr Bishop to be in the house.'

Ann nodded. 'You will be all right, won't you, miss?'

Grace lifted her head and clutched the handle of the umbrella. 'With luck, it will be over this evening.'

The mantelpiece clock chimed for the final quarter. 'It's time,' said Grace, puffing out her chest and breathing deeply like a bride about to enter a church.

Ann hurried along the corridor to the backstairs as Grace descended to the ground floor and the main hall. She squinted in the bright candlelight and made her rustling way to the tower wing. The smell of paraffin made her gag as she entered the brightly lit bell staircase chamber of Hemingworth Hall. She closed the doors and turned to the once beautiful tower room reflecting in the tangled webs of silk and silver bells, still and silent like cold stars against a backdrop of spiralled silk and dark polished panelling. The oil lamp chandelier shone like a crown above the narrow, mirrored chamber squatting beneath the finery of the suspended staircase. Lady Foster, resplendent in her bustle-backed claret silk, paced around the structure, muttering and preparing her thoughts for the trial to come. A ring of candlesticks circled the structure, and the noblewoman wrung her hands and glanced across at the governess.

'Lift your dress,' said Lady Foster nervously. 'There's lamp oil on the floor in between the candles. Charles is already inside; we are just waiting for you.'

Grace stepped over the stinking fuel. 'I thought you said the mirrors were superstition?' she said.

'We are about to find out,' said Lady Foster.

'You've not done this before, have you?' said Grace, furrowing her brow.

Lady Foster looked to the ground, trying to hide her frightened eyes.

'Not a word,' she said. 'Charles is scared; we all are. There should be four, but there we are, three will have to do.'

The medium held out her hands, and Grace took them firmly.

'What about the chandelier?' she said, glancing towards the iron crown. 'It's the one in the vision.'

'I don't believe in coincidences,' she said, wincing through a sudden twinge of pain. 'But this is not your time or mine; I can feel it.'

'You aren't well,' said Grace, gripping her hand tightly. 'You don't have to do this. Tell me what I must do, to—'

'No!' snapped Lady Foster, shaking her head. 'There isn't time to teach you, and you would see things you cannot unsee.'

Lady Foster recovered her composure and rotated her hand to show the scars on their combined wrists. 'For everything we have done, and we will ever do to ourselves, I say we stand and fight.'

Grace squeezed and shook her hands free. 'Yes, and for the woman I once was, before you, and the woman that I hope to be. Let's finish this; I'm done with being haunted.'

Lady Foster's dark eyes glittered, and she lifted her hands to cup Grace's cheek. 'You remind me so much of my sister, Florence, and not just because of the gown.'

She glanced down, amused by the umbrella in Grace's other hand. 'What's that for?'

'For luck,' said Grace.

The doors to the tower wing flung open and in burst the doctor, struggling with a foldable chair and his medical bag. He halted, and bowed his head, blushing wide-eyed at Grace as though expecting a governess but finding instead that a duchess had taken her place.

'Here comes Prince Charming,' said Lady Foster, rolling her eyeballs and addressing the latecomer. 'Why the sudden change of heart?'

'For the record, I'm here in a medical capacity to see you don't kill yourself or burn the place to the ground. There has to be at least one actor in this pantomime that's still rational.' James glanced across at the gowned governess. 'And to make sure that the pendulum remains centred.'

Grace fixed her unblinking eyes upon him and smiled. The curfew bell pealed softly from the walled garden without, and within from the house, several clocks chimed for eight o'clock. The doors closed behind them and clicked with the turning lock. The pockmarked housekeeper rubbed the nape of her neck and stared through the glass panels, wide-eyed, alongside the comforting face of Bishop. Mrs Stanton bent down out of view and slid a length of jute twine through the narrow gap between the tiled floor and the bottom of the door.

Bishop gave Grace a long look as though fearing never to see her again.

'*Be careful,*' he mouthed, before bolting shut the flaps to the small glass panels.

'What's that?' asked Grace.

'It's the key to the door,' said Lady Foster, allaying their confusion. 'If we are successful then withdraw it to pull the key through. We must keep Sophia within the tower at all costs.'

'And if it doesn't?' said Grace.

'Then, and only when there is no alternative, we fight fire with fire.

'Hurry,' she said, flashing her eyes, 'and watch you do not disturb the candles.'

CHAPTER 23

Grace glanced up at the amber glow of the burning chandelier, casting its quivering light upon the four people below. The single candle flame at the edge of the table bobbed with each long exhalation of the veiled medium, unable to penetrate the mirrored walls' black coverings. Its single flickering light cast its meagre glow upon the occupants of the seance.

From across the table, Charles Ferris clutched at Lady Foster's wrists bound to her chair by several lengths of silk rope at her waist. Bolstered by whisky and the final hope before him, his glazed eyes remained transfixed upon the brass bell at the centre of the yoke, suspended in miniature mockery of the staircase hidden behind the makeshift enclosure.

James fidgeted and fixed his gaze on the weave of hands and arms. His own, and those of Grace, crossed the table perpendicular to meet in a firm and clammy grasp. He pursed his lips and glanced around.

Lady Foster, eyes firmly shut, scanned the inside of her eyelids. Her breath became shallower, and she sipped at the air, searching for the malignancy of Sophia Ferris among the spirits still connected to the Catholic stronghold around her.

'So many, desperate to be heard,' she whispered. 'So few and so little time to listen.'

She twitched her right hand, and Charles closed his eyes as instructed. A breath of wind, faint at first, spiralled around the ceiling rose, descending the staircase in growing tumult. It set off the suspended bells, and they tinkled, unseen and unsettling beyond the blackness of the enclosure. The candles bobbed beyond the narrow open corner through which the medium and her assistants had entered the makeshift oubliette, marking the passage of one unseen, patrolling the new structure in its domain. The breath whistled through the narrow opening and wound itself around the mirrored box, disturbing the candle on the table.

'Will you commune with us, Sophia Ferris?' said Lady Foster. 'Once for yes.'

Grace shuddered with the sudden and stifling silence, listening to the short, sharp breaths from the hyperventilating medium beside her. She longed to pull her hand free and plunge it into the candle flame, banishing the fear of the impending encounter, and the fire that surrounded her. James frowned, but she gently shook her head to put him at ease and breathed deeply to regain composure.

'Are you among us?' repeated Lady Foster. 'Once for yes.'

The bell between the suspended threads twitched, and Grace felt the weave of arms stiffen.

'Do not let go!' said Lady Foster, labouring to remain calm.

From behind the seated medium, faintly at first, came the spirit. Its presence was palpable. The insubstantial suggestion of a woman smoothed her arms up and down the claret gown of Lady Foster, pawing at the fine fabric and yearning for its sensual touch.

'Something's here,' whispered Grace. 'Behind you.'

James twisted before seeing Lady Foster quiver and twitch, aware of the groping caress from behind.

Grace struggled to swallow, as fear gripped her entire being. This spirit was unlike the warmth of Florence Foster or the dull aching anxiety that heralded the spirit of Arthur. Here was something wild, filled with a madness that was untamed, and uncharted. The figure responded, growing in confidence with its appearance as though energised by the intense emotion building within the enclosure. Parts of its barely clad feminine form faded in and out of Grace's sight, visible only when necessity dictated. The ghostly miasma removed its arms and drifted around the claustrophobic space, raising an arm to pull at the coverings to the mirror and humming a deep-throated lullaby.

James twisted his head to follow the gentle ripple across the silk.

'I hear something,' he said.

'It's all right,' said Grace, squeezing his hands tightly. 'She's walking around. Focus on me.'

'Hush!' said Lady Foster, as the spirit completed its revolution, like a mouse examining its cage. 'Once for yes!' she hissed.

The spectre shot out an arm to tug at the thread, almost pulling the yoke from its socket. The bell swung wildly, time and time again.

Charles opened his eyes and searched for the ghost of his wife.

'Sophia?'

The bell came to a sudden stop, halted by the doctor's hand as he pulled his arms free from the governess opposite.

'James, no!' said Grace.

'It's nonsense, I tell you. How the hell does she—'

His hand released as the spirit tugged on the strings,

setting off the bell once again. Grace saw the spectral hand develop and grab hold of the threads immediately surrounding the golden bell. It twisted and jerked its wrist, ripping the brass bell from its web and casting it against the far mirror. The covering billowed as the glass beneath shattered, sending sliding slivers of silver smashing to the ground immediately behind Charles's chair. The captain clung on.

James wavered but did not get up. He scanned for any sign of illusion, desperate for a rational explanation, and looked over at Grace with an open mouth.

She nodded. 'It's Sophia, right by your arm, but I can't hear her.'

'Turn the hourglass,' said Lady Foster, turning with closed eyes beneath her veil. Her bright red lips twitched through rapid breaths. 'We have two minutes to get an answer; after that, we go to Plan B. Close your eyes and form a circle of hands. Quickly!'

Grace rotated the glass, and the sand began to run. Grace closed her eyes and searched for the delicate hand of Lady Foster to her right, and the shaking hand of Charles Ferris to her left. Fears and uncertainty rushed through as the joining began, and the spirit of Sophia Ferris merged, trying to gain access to the physical world through one of them.

Grace flinched and pushed away from the uncomfortable presence as Lady Foster fought to dominate the encounter. The spirit tried again, eager to possess her faltering will. She opened her eyes to see the wild eyes of beautiful madness staring back, inches from her own.

'No!' cried Lady Foster, digging her nails into the back of Grace's hand. The pain banished the sensation, and Grace felt the rush of the departing spirit as it turned and found a new host.

Lady Foster screamed with the exertion and forced the spirit's attention upon her. Grace saw the images in Lady

Foster's mind of Rose playing, laughing, and sulking. The spirit gravitated towards the pleasant memories, desperate to be part of them. Lady Foster joined the hum of the lullaby, and Sophia lurched towards the medium. The seal between worlds splintered, and the spirit collided into the body of the noblewoman, sending her chair toppling backwards towards the mirror. The ring of hands drew wider, but recovered and remained steady. Charles opened his eyes instinctively and was dragged upwards by the force, but he countered with long-forgotten strength and dragged himself back to a seating position, righting the chair of the bound Lady Foster.

The medium's eyes opened to reveal a horrid dilation of the pupils. The sound of the lullaby increased as the spirit took over her voice and body.

James opened his eyes in disbelief.

'Do not let go!' warned Grace. 'Not until the sand is done.'

'Sophia?' stammered Charles.

Lady Foster opened her mouth with a thin whine of anguish, ending in a grotesque smile.

'*I see you*,' said the voice of Sophia Ferris, thin and mad from the mouth of the one she possessed. She looked at them all, pausing upon the doctor. He glanced back, his body rigid.

'*James ...*' she whimpered, moving her head back and forth like a snake watching a flute. '*Do you desire me now? Why won't you come to me and give me your special medicine? We can be happy* —' The medium's eyes flashed sideways, leering into Grace's face.

'*A dirty little secret?*' said the voice of Sophia. '*You desire a common governess over me—she's still a girl? But you have a thing for clever girls, don't you? Like the other one trying to keep my baby from me. I can feel your passion for her.*'

'Stop this charade,' said James, turning away from the medium. Lady Foster spread her legs, possessed by the spirit, and pulled away one of her hands. She began to rub at her thighs, hitching her gown, and slid the hand beneath. Her head lolled back in mock ecstasy.

'Enough!' said Charles, glancing at the small pyramid growing inside the base of the hourglass. 'Why do you not rest and leave the house in peace?'

'*When I have Rose. I want my baby. You all keep trying to keep me from her.*'

The medium struggled under the rope and seethed, trying to free herself from the chair.

She shot out a hand and ripped down the black silk that had covered the mirror. The possessed Lady Foster screeched at the reflection.

'*What deception is this?*' she shrieked, rocking the chair from side to side.

'A bargain,' said Charles. 'For the love of someone I once held dear, will you not depart this place and leave us in peace? What do you want?'

'*Everything and nothing,*' said Sophia. '*I want to be happy with my baby. I will get well, and we can have more children, Charles. Through this woman, or perhaps the other?*'

Grace watched as the face of Lady Foster frowned, struggling in its madness.

'*Rose will be safe with me, give her to me!*' She sneered at her former husband.

'Never,' said Charles. 'While I still breathe.'

'*Why won't anyone make me happy? I'll get my baby soon, Charles, and nothing you can do can stop it. Even now I hear her; she is coming to me ...*'

'Take me,' said Charles. 'Why don't you take me and we can—'

'*I want my baby,*' moaned Sophia. '*Tomorrow we will all be together—*' She turned to stare fiercely into Grace's eyes. '*Even Jane and poor little Arthur!*'

'Over my dead body,' said Grace, rising with anger.

'*Of course, it will be my pleasure*,' whispered Sophia, grabbing at her hand. Grace felt the sheer madness and the unwillingness to comprehend any rational notion. The distant struggle of Lady Foster surfaced, and Grace glanced across at the emptying hourglass.

'*We are the same, you and I*,' said Sophia, fighting to remain in control. '*We both want to protect our children forever. Come with me, and you can be with the one you failed.*'

Grace looked down at the expectant face, reaching out from across death's threshold, offering something so perverse and yet so tempting that she shook her head, freeing herself from the confusion.

'You aren't going anywhere,' said Grace, ripping down the remaining silk cloths, sensing the return of Lady Foster to consciousness and control.

'There's no more talk here,' said Charles, wheeling over the broken glass and mirrored frame. He sped across and kicked over the candles, mere specks of light in his dying eyes, which sent a trail of fire circling the remnants of the mirrored enclosure.

'What the hell are you doing?' cried James, watching as Lady Foster struggled to turn and place a solitary hand upon the mirror behind. The hourglass spilt out its last grains as Charles returned to the table and grabbed the medium's arms, forcing them to the glass. Grace saw the burning of the ring and the empty frame reflected in the quivering mirror. She watched in horror as the face of Lady Foster began to droop, the stroke burning through her mind with the exertion of forcing the spirit into the silvered surface. Sophia resisted, desperate to escape before the hourglass emptied.

James saw the attack and fought against Charles, who was still forcing the flailing noblewoman's hands against the glass, desperate to complete the ritual.

'*I will kill her if you do not relent!*' wailed the voice of Sophia

Ferris, partway between the body of Lady Foster and the mirror.

Grace watched as James heard the words, turning to see the barely conscious noblewoman undergoing a horrific attack of heart and mind.

'She's having an apoplectic attack!' said James. He ceased suddenly in his struggle to remove the combined weight of Lady Foster and Charles's determination and saw the terrifying visage of the spirit twisting within the glass, moments away from entrapment.

He grabbed at the umbrella, and with an abject look of terror on his face, he lifted the tip and drove it like a lance between the fingers of the faltering medium and into the mirror, sending the panel toppling backwards and shattering the glass into explosive pieces. He threw himself across the exposed faces of Charles and Lady Foster as the glass showered his back.

Grace threw herself through the open frame and fell to the floor, covering her head. The freed spirit of Sophia Ferris surged towards the stairs, dissipating through the webbed threads of silk, and setting off the lower bells until she vanished from sight and the material world.

'Light the oil!' said Charles, wheeling away and knocking into the side mirror. The frame twisted and toppled over, knocking the captain, unconscious, to the floor and pinning him beneath.

'Get the door!' shouted James, dragging the noblewoman through the open frame and through the ring of flame, smearing the room with fire like a burning wedding train.

'We need Bishop to lift the mirror!' called the doctor, as Grace ran to pull the thread beneath the door. The key skittered back into the room as the doctor slumped over Lady Foster, applying pressure to her stomach.

'What is it?' she said, fishing for the key.

'Apoplexy or heart attack, probably a combination of both. I warned her.' He glanced up as though pleading for forgiveness. 'I saw it, Grace. I saw Sophia in the mirror. Where is she?'

'Gone, for the present. When Lady Foster passed out, it broke the connection.'

'What have I done?' said James. 'I couldn't let Emeline die.'

Grace grabbed the key and unlocked the door. Bishop came bursting through and surveyed the chaos.

'Get the captain free,' she said. 'Lift the mirror and get him out of here.'

Grace lifted the noblewoman's legs as the doctor swung his arms through Lady Foster's elbows. 'The study, quickly!' she said, taking the load.

She glanced only once behind to see the titan roar as he cast aside the remaining mirrors and frames to retrieve his fallen captain. Lifting him across his broad shoulders, Bishop stepped across the battlefield once again, littered with glass, splintered wood and pockets of flame, to deliver the casualty to the hastily convened field hospital in the nearby room.

The battle was over, and they had lost.

CHAPTER 24

Rose lay on the chaise longue, panting and fitful, as the poison and antidote coursed through her veins, battling for victory.

Bishop glanced up, tears in his eyes as he held the limp white hand. He let out a wordless cry of anguish. Grace wrapped her arms around his broad shoulders.

'We've done everything we can,' she said. 'Stay here. I'm going to check on James.'

He nodded and grabbed her forearm as she turned to go. The kneeling giant shuddered.

'I know,' said Grace as she released the grip. 'Whatever happens to either of them, it's not your fault, Bishop.'

She raced through the hall, its gleaming white tiles glinting in the abundance of candlelight, sparkling against the glass bulbs, impotent in their dead sockets. At the entrance, Billy hastily lit candles passed rapidly to him by Ann. They looked up briefly, and Grace saw the same fear in their eyes that would consume her own heart.

But they were there. Determined to stand and ready to fight.

She ran on, setting the candles dancing, and skidded into the study to see the anxious-looking doctor applying a cold compress to Charles's forehead.

'Will he—?'

James nodded. 'He's going to have the mother of all headaches and Emeline's over the worst. Thank God I acted when I did. Billy's back and the hospital ambulance is on its way. There's nothing more I can do. Has Rose regained consciousness?'

'No,' said Grace. 'Bishop is with her, and the colour in her cheeks has returned. Is that a good sign?'

James stroked the clammy cheek of his friend fighting against an enemy that no military training could prepare for. 'It's a start; it means the immune system is reacting, attempting to flush out the toxin. I just don't know—' He rose and smoothed back his mop of hair with his shaking hands and glanced over for guidance.

'I just don't know what to do next.'

Grace took his hands and kissed them.

'You have given them all a chance, and they are fighting back because of you. We will get through this, and when this is all over, you will teach me how to play bridge, and I will show you how to cheat at poker. Deal?'

James nodded.

'The ambulance will be here soon,' said Grace, gripping his hands within her own for reassurance.

He let out a small sigh of relief. Hope swelled in his eyes, but was extinguished as the clock on the mantelpiece chimed for eight o'clock. Outside, distant like the tolling for a funeral, rang the curfew bell.

The clocks began to chime within the house, setting up a harmonic that shimmered through the heavy air.

The servants' bells in the basement rang out, called by hands unseen. They would not be answered, except by one.

Lady Foster moaned in an armchair near the fire and twisted her tortured face to form the words only Grace could understand.

'She's coming,' said Grace, listening to the cacophony of bells, pealing in the house, sounding the alarm. 'What do I do?'

Lady Foster groaned and lifted her hand in the direction of the fire. Grace rushed over as the medium pointed to the chandelier and back to the flames. Grace grabbed at her wrists and saw the image of the falling chandelier, wreathed in flame.

In her mind, she saw Rose, limp and lying on the tiles of the staircase floor surrounded by encroaching flame. Hands whirled in front of her as though swinging something at the end of a long rope. She felt her body tighten as something wrapped and constricted itself around her.

'What is it?' she begged. 'What must I do?'

The sound of bells intensified as Grace saw her dilated pupils reflected by those of the noblewoman.

'F...*future...now!*' Lady Foster spluttered with urgency.

Billy and Ann came rushing in, pale and frightened.

'What is it? What's the matter?' said James, crossing the room.

'It's Miss Rose,' said Billy. 'She's been took.'

'Took?' said James. 'Taken where?'

'The tower. Bishop's took her there. I tried to stop him.'

'What the devil's he up to?' said James, shaking the boy. Charles twisted and cried out in pain.

Grace got up, breaking the connection, and looked down into Lady Foster's wide eyes.

'I said I would do anything, and I hold to my promise.'

James turned, seeming conflicted as to whether to remain or rush to the tower.

'Stay here,' said Grace, 'and wait for the ambulance. Science and reason belong here, with you.'

Charles began to twitch. 'He's having a fit,' said James. 'Go!'

Grace rushed into the hall, followed by the two servants.

The bells within the house reached a crescendo and then cut off, leaving only a fading harmonic and the sound of the curfew bell. It tolled for the last time to be replaced by the growing rush of a storm, ready to break and crash down upon the house at any moment. The sound intensified.

All the panels in the house, those known and unknown, swung open as though sucked outwards by the storm preparing itself for a mighty breath. Ann's skirt billowed as the wind returned with a fury, whistling through the walls and narrow places like a warren of interconnected chimneys. The candles flared as though fuelled by the approaching tempest and launched themselves up across the ceiling. Billy grabbed her arm in fear.

The spectral wind railed within the hall, knocking over candlesticks and setting the paintings and turned mirrors swinging. Fire spread across the wall like rivulets of frost on a freezing window, as a sudden and ferocious release of fury came like a breaking wave from the staircase, blasting open the doors to every room as it travelled towards them.

'Get down!' shouted Grace and she watched the approach of the storm front as it blew open the doors to cabinets and clocks. The revealed priest holes whistled and moaned as though terrified of their own discovery as the wind rushed up and through the walls, carrying the historic cries of many tortured souls.

The fury broke over them, cracking glass and mirror, forcing them to the floor and showering them with shards. For a moment, the candles went out then returned in a blaze brighter than new-born stars, spreading their fiery wrath across the silk wall coverings and igniting the coils of the light bulbs into life. They glowed brightly, their coils burning beyond any man-made limitations, causing them to explode and shower the hall with shrapnel.

Grace rolled over, feeling the line of blood from a cut mark on her cheek. She glanced at Ann, faint and covered with glass.

'Get her out, Billy!' she shouted. 'Sophia is coming for Rose. Get out and call for help, firemen, police, anyone—the place is going to go up. I think I know what Bishop's going to do!'

Billy hesitated. 'What about—'

Grace shook him into action. 'It has to be you, Billy. I can't drive, you fool!'

Billy got to his haunches, lifting his beloved, and looked back as the wall of furious anger reached the main doors to the hall. It rebounded once, then twisted into a vortex of such violence that Grace covered her ears from the sudden shock. The spiritual storm threw itself against the outer doors, and they splintered, drawing with it the flames and feeding it from the backdraught.

Grace feared for James, and the two in his care, but there was no time to help them. The seal between worlds was wide open. The force that had once struck Lady Foster so violently in the chest in the dimly lit London salon was here, dragging with it and fuelled by the countless souls rushing outwards to herald the arrival and madness of Sophia Ferris.

Silence fell as Billy crunched his way across the littered floor, bearing the maid, making for the doctor's room and then to the outside to raise the alarm. He would get the opportunity once more to drive the Sigma 10 tourer. He looked back to see Grace urging him on, framed by walls alight and dripping with incandescent beads of melting wire, silk and wax.

In the dead stillness, a whisper echoed through the hall, followed by the hum of a half-remembered lullaby.

It was the voice of Sophia Ferris, come to reclaim her own.

CHAPTER 25

G race got up and raced into the tower wing, dodging burning fragments of lining paper. The open doors slammed shut as she approached, commanded by unseen servants at their mistress's bidding. She banged against them, trying the handles to no avail, and opened the shutters to peer through the small stained-glass panels to the smoky room beyond.

Bishop stood, beckoning to something unseen in the darkness above. Rose lay at his feet, at the foot of the stair-case, in a fitting sleep. Grace banged on the glass panels, and he turned round.

'No!' said Grace. 'You swore to protect her!'

Bishop stared back, sweating profusely. His eyes mournful, but bright. He turned to look through the crooked hang of the chandelier and the tangle of broken threads, and opened his mouth, bellowing into the darkness in challenge.

'What are you doing?' screamed Grace. 'She'll kill you and take Rose!'

Bishop shook his head and signed back.

'*No time to explain. Have a plan.*' He coughed and ran

around the room stamping out patches of fire and smouldering embers. Grace turned to look back down the corridor filling with smoke and glowing ominously from the direction of the main building. The fire in the hall was spreading.

The doors to the uppermost room flew open in answer, and something glided from the shadows to the broken section of railings. The figure materialised briefly and then flitted across to the staircase's first threads, continuing to hum the dark melody in its passage through the silken web. The bells swung, excited by the movement, and accompanied the lullaby as Sophia Ferris appeared, silk-robed as though coming down to dinner. She brushed her dark, unkempt hair back from her pale, black-eyed face as she struggled through the threads. Each obstacle was brushed aside, and those thicker cords that resisted slipped through her ghostly body like cheese string, dragging her silken robe through it. The robe lifted and carried behind like a tattered train caught in the passage of the bell threads, revealing bruises and self-inflicted wounds to her legs and thighs. Her modesty was uncovered, and Grace stared in horror as she descended towards the child that eluded her eternal grasp, groping in front to register the bells and seek the soul that called to her from below.

Bishop scanned the upper stairs, seeing the bells swing, and threads move and snap, but Grace could tell he was blind to her.

'She's coming!' shouted Grace, banging her bruised palms on the glass. 'She's near the third-floor door.'

She glanced to the side to see the duke's umbrella, seized it, and stabbed at the antique glass until it shattered inwards. The spirit on the stairs looked over, distracted by the sound, but did not alter its descent towards her barely conscious child.

Rose murmured and turned onto her side as Bishop fell to

his knees to comfort her. The mad spirit on the stairs twitched with the sound and weaved through the threads at greater speed, like a malevolent spider.

Bishop lunged over to the silk-wrapped lowering ropes at the base of the stairs, setting the chandelier swinging. He untied the oil lamp cord and let out the long length in a clinking rattle of chain.

The spirit stopped its fearful lullaby and screeched with the sound as though driven with pain. Sophia Ferris let out a wail, igniting the sconces on the wall in sudden flame. A line of fire trailed down the handrail like a burning locomotive to greet her withered hand. Bishop looked up, seeing her passage now more clearly though not the spirit herself. He lowered the burning glass bowl of the lamp, and dragged it to the door, glancing back to see that the burning passage of the unseen spirit had reached the second floor.

His face pressed against the broken panel and twisted into a forced smile.

'Let me in, Bishop,' said Grace. 'What are you doing?'

Bishop shook his head and tossed the key from the lock into the room. He glanced back quickly at the trail of fire approaching the fitful movements of Rose, now lightly wreathed in smoke rising from the paraffin-soaked floor.

He turned and signed so quickly that Grace could barely make out the words coming from the room beyond.

'*Use as bait, kill ghost, save Rose ... stop bad things forever.*'

Grace watched as he whirled like a dancer, then swung his great arms like a highland games hammer thrower. He clutched at the end of the silk lamp cord and shook it so that it lay straight, then thrust his other forearm into the jagged hole of the panel, cutting great scratches along his mighty fist. The hand opened in a final display of friendship and Grace grabbed it, knowing that whatever he planned would be his last act as guardian.

'B ... by mm ... my own h ... hands,' he stammered, looking through the panel in the other door.

'No,' said Grace, as smoke and the fear of parting filled her eyes with tears. 'Whatever it is, there's got to be another way.' She looked over at the panelled wall within the burning room. He followed her gaze to the priest hole and secret passage.

'F ... full of ss ... smoke. No way th ... through.'

Grace clung to his fingers as he pulled his hand away.

'Bishop, please give me the key. Open the door!'

Smoke billowed from beneath the tower doors, stinging her eyes as Bishop turned to make a final sign.

'*Make noise, no more silence. Farewell!*'

The spirit reached the first-floor landing and hissed, scraping her nails against the silk wallpaper and setting the five-fingered trails alight.

Grace picked up the umbrella and twisted the handle through and downwards on the other side, trying to rattle the doorknob, desperately trying to lift the retaining latch to the other side.

From the corridor behind came the desperate calls of James, urging her to get out. The gallery filled with smoke and fire licked around the corner to the hall. She was trapped. Fear gripped her; the fire was behind and before her.

Bishop roared within the room, dropped the silken cord, and pulled on the chain, setting the chandelier swinging once more. It jerked under its failing links as Sophia reached the bottom of the burning staircase and Bishop kicked the key towards the centre of the room. Rose rolled over and attempted to sit up, her body instinctively climbing to get above the thickening smoke.

The trail of fire ended as the victorious spirit of Sophia Ferris reached the bottom tread searching for the source of the young girl's cough. Bishop grabbed Rose and retreated to the room's centre, swinging his free arm in front to beckon the mother closer.

Grace screamed as Sophia Ferris grabbed at Rose's silk nightdress, catching Bishop off-guard. He pulled back as Sophia screeched in the agony of a mother being parted from her child.

'*Mine*,' cried the spirit. '*Give her to me. I want my baby.*' She lashed out, and Bishop yelped with pain, letting go. Great weals of smoke appeared on his chest from the raking of Sophia's hand against his sweat-stained calico shirt.

Rose murmured and opened her eyes. She looked over to see Bishop lumbering forwards, grasping at her legs as she was dragged upwards out of the smoke and into the incandescent air by the ghost of her mother. Rose screamed out, and Bishop clung on, pulling against the unearthly strength of the spirit in a deadly tug of war.

She was freed by a sudden jerk, and Bishop flung her across the floor beneath the staircase. She struggled to sit up and cried out, seeing the face of the governess desperately trying to break through from the other side of the circular room.

Sophia Ferris turned and slashed at the giant shielding himself from her maddened and frantic attempts to remove the obstacle to her desire. Bishop staggered backwards under the onslaught and lifted the silken cord. He fell to his knees and grabbed out with a loop, leaving him vulnerable to an uppercut that sent him backwards and bleeding with burns. He held on to the cord and grabbed out into the fiery air for a final time, connecting with the wrist of his tormentor. The spirit screamed as Bishop wound the silk round and round the wrist until the spectral form could no longer shake off or pass through the bindings. Sophia lashed out, cutting his face to ribbons, but he rose for the last time.

Billy's legend would come true.

He would die by his own hands.

In one deft movement, he spun his former mistress into the fastness of his body, clasping his shredded arms about the spirit's waist. Sophia raged and struggled to escape, but the muscled prison remained strong. Bishop grabbed both ends of the oil lamp, still burning within the knee-high smoke, and spun round, wrapping the combined waists with a tough silken cord. Grace cried out, seeing the line vanish into the silk of the spirit's robe. His great arms lifted into the air, rotating the cord in great circular motions above his head before swinging low to drag the lamp ever closer. The binding wrapped ever tighter and thicker, trapping the flailing arms of Sophia Ferris like a spider wrapping a fly. Faster and faster swung his mighty arms as the lamp appeared out of the smoke and swung into the air, all the while coiling around the bound pair.

Fire leapt around the room as the spirit realised the trap. The mighty lamp swung inwards, on its terminal collision course, but Bishop did not waver. He cried out as the spirit frantically shifted to knock him off balance, but his great legs stood defiant and planted like lumps of oak.

Grace looked in horror as he glanced down and into her eyes in a desperate, agonising farewell. The lamp travelled its final rapid spiral and collided with the pair, smashing the glass and covering them both in liquid flame. Bishop staggered and fought to remain upright, clutching hold of Sophia Ferris lest she escape from the burning silk before her spirit was laid to rest. He lumbered forwards and kicked out in a last act of strength at something on the floor. Grace saw something skidding towards the door as Bishop fell forwards into the smoke, still clutching the burning spirit of Sophia. A great funnel of flame twisted into the air as the spirit succumbed, setting the silk of the chandelier alight as the key slid under the door and knocked against Grace's foot.

Grace felt for the key in the darkness. The smoke was thick in every breath, and she gasped to get clean air into her lungs. Shuffling through the smoke, she felt the metal object and raised her foot over it like a protective rugby player to stop it sliding further. Grace groped beneath and spluttered as she fumbled to insert it into the lock. From within, Rose stumbled to her feet and staggered over to the centre of the room.

'Rose!' cried Grace, coughing to clear the drought in her throat.

Rose turned and called back. Whether it was from the finding of Bishop or the strenuous effort of her fragile recovery, she collapsed below the swinging chandelier.

The vision of the flaming chandelier came back, and Grace saw the end and the solving of the riddle. The distant salon and the question in her first joining came sharply back with the acrid taste of certain death.

What was it I last saw?

'The future' came the voice of Lady Foster.

Whose?

Grace felt for the keyhole in desperation as Rose disappeared within the rising smoke and encroaching flame. Her fingers searching for any void within which to force the key.

The fire behind her was now fierce, and she felt the heat prickle the back of her bare neck. Why had she come here? Why not the position in the almshouse, or even the situation in Chelsea?

The crackle of burning wallpaper and splitting wood added to the urgency. Grace found the hole and rattled the key in as a panel from the adjacent wall swung open, dragging the smoke through it and temporarily clearing the space around the lock. Grace felt the rush of air drawn out like a flue and peered through as she turned the key in the lock. The undiscovered passage was small, but it led to the outer wall, and Grace could see the distant lamps of vehicles and people rushing to the burning hall. She cried out, but they were too distant to hear her. The fire was behind and before her, and her fear ground her to the spot. The silk-papered walls within the tower were alight, and the silken threads snapped and caught fire, sending their bells tinkling and tumbling. Only the small area on the ground where Rose lay, gasping for breath, remained safe.

She could not make it into the room and back to escape this way; she knew her strength, and the fire within would claim her. She would have to drag the child up the staircase and would just as likely end up dead halfway to the tower room. A backdraft of cool and precious fresh air funnelled down the tiny passage and Grace wavered, fearing for her life.

The sign in the alleyway came back to her as her head and lungs cleared.

She will die without you.

Grace turned both handles of the tower wing doors and swung them open.

The heat assaulted her in a wave, and she threw her arms up, feeling her skin blistering under the developing inferno.

'I hold to my promise!' she called, striding through the pools of dark smoke.

'Rose!'

She stumbled around the burning mass of the heroic manservant and dragged the barely conscious girl out of the smoke. Rose glanced up with red eyes and then beyond to the sound of the chandelier chain snapping under the weight of its damaged links. The silk wrapping was all but burned away, dripping its sticky gleeds of fire like fireflies upon them. Grace looked up, barely in time to see it snap and tilt. She fought against her instinct to hold on to the child or cover her head as she had done in the salon and dragged Rose backwards as the chandelier came crashing down, setting the floor ablaze.

From the corridor beyond came a dreadful crack and the main staircase to the hall collapsed against the opening, sealing them both in the burning tower.

CHAPTER 26

'Y ou came back!' whispered Rose, dry-throated but clear. 'Is Ma-ma—?'

'Yes,' said Grace, pulling her to her feet and squeezing her tight at the foot of the stairs. 'She can't hurt you now. There's no need to be silent anymore.'

The child peered round at the smoke-covered shape in the centre of the room.

'Bishop?'

Grace shielded her from the dead man and nodded.

'He did it to make sure you were safe.'

Rose burst into tears that dried on her blistered cheeks.

'We have little time, Rose. We need to get higher and try the doors and away from the fire.' She looked up at the smoke-filled ceiling, knowing that suffocation was a distinct possibility.

'Can you walk?'

Rose nodded, shakily pulling the governess to the first step. The spirit's passage had cleared most of the lighter threads, and Grace saw the smouldering finger scratches etched into the wall. 'Keep looking straight ahead and up,

Rose.' Rose ducked beneath and clambered over ropes still attached to the railings, setting off the bells. Grace shivered suddenly in the dreadful heat.

'Look!' cried Rose, pointing to the third-floor landing.

High above, the spirit of Arthur beckoned.

Rose quickened her step as the smoke began to rise behind. The spirit pointed to a panel beyond the third-floor landing. The tiny half-panel opened, and Arthur disappeared inside.

'Up, Rose,' urged Grace. 'Quickly!'

They passed the first-floor door, barricaded to the adjoining wing, and Grace halted, hearing the sounds from the corridor beyond. It was James.

She beat upon the door, as his voice became clearer.

'Grace? Is that you?'

'Yes, I've got Rose, but the whole tower is on fire!'

James beat against the door with something hard and metallic.

'Where's Bishop?'

'He's dead,' she said. 'He took Sophia with him; I can't explain it now, the room's full of smoke.'

'Just hold on,' he said. 'Most of the villagers are here putting out the hall and Billy's bringing back the fire brigade.'

'We can't get out that way,' said Grace. 'The main staircase has collapsed over the entrance.'

'There are men on the way. We can break through these bloody doors.'

'There isn't time,' she said. 'Get Charles and Lady Foster out.'

'They're with the ambulance crew now,' said James, raging against the metal bands and solid oak. 'I can't break in. Get to the next level!'

'What about you? Don't be foolish!'

James was already retreating to the back staircase. 'The

fire's contained within the wing and the main hall; there's only smoke this side. Hurry!'

Her legs burned from the exertion, and the lack of clean air was making her light-headed. She fumbled her way through the threads to the second-floor door, searching for Rose who was making for the smoke-shrouded panel above.

James was already there, hammering on the door.

'I'm here,' said Grace, watching as the thuds from beyond became weaker, and the iron-banded door reverberated less with every impact. James coughed from a few feet away.

'There's more smoke up here; I can't get it open. The keys are locked in the basement. I don't know what to do!'

Grace put her face to the door.

'James, it's all right. You've got to get out; we are making for the roof.'

He mumbled something incoherently in panic.

'James, listen to me,' she said. 'Rose has found a passage that leads up on to the roof. You must go up and meet us there, but you'll have to use the wooden staircase on the outside to reach it.'

James paused in his attempts to open the barricaded door.

'Hurry, there isn't much time,' she said.

'You'd better get out, Grace,' he said. 'Foster was right, I mean Sophia was right; what I mean is—'

'I know, James,' said Grace. 'It's all right, I know. Now go, get to the roof.'

James slammed his fist on the door, and Grace heard his footsteps race away. She glanced down at the sea of smoke swirling up from the first floor, ringing with fire. The smell of paraffin was strong, and Grace wondered how long it would be until the conflagration consumed the drums.

Up above, the smoke trapped by the ceiling began to descend, squeezing them like a billowing deadly vice.

Grace staggered up and over the threads in pursuit of

Rose stumbling forwards on her hands and knees. Smoke now shrouded the panel above, but Rose reached it and turned.

'It goes to the roof!' said Rose. 'But it's really small; I don't think you can fit.'

'Get out, Rose,' cried Grace. 'Don't wait for me; I'll follow you—Dr Croswell and men are coming. Hurry.'

Grace picked her way through the remaining threads as the layers of breathable air squeezed together. She took a deep breath and coughed before sipping in the air gently and plunging into the layer of smoke above, feeling for the panel. Her hand dragged along the wooden squares until it met with a box-like opening. She knelt and opened her stinging eyes, furiously blinking them to wash away the acrid smoke that blurred her vision. Rose was squeezing herself through, pausing to cough in the deadly, claustrophobic chimney.

'I'm ... right ... behind you,' she called, forcing her arms through the passage.

Her shoulders jabbed against the sides of the opening, barring her entry. Grace forced her hands together like a diver, diagonally through the shaft. It was no use. Her shoulders scraped the inside of the chamber, and she knew that her hips would likely snag, making her unable to push with her feet. Her lungs screamed for air as she saw Rose exit onto the roof.

'Call for help,' croaked Grace, using the last of her breath. 'I can't get out this way.'

She retreated down a few steps in search of air, panicking when it did not materialise. The smoke was descending rapidly, and she slipped and rolled down the stairs, snagging herself painfully to a stop, right by the missing section of the railing where Jane had fallen. The air cleared, and she rolled down a few steps to draw painful breaths.

It was all over; there would be no second attempt. Grace had survived the vision of the falling chandelier, and now she would end here, high in the bell staircase tower of Hemingworth Hall.

But not alone.

She brushed her hair from her eyes and gazed down at the ring of fire, boiling around the sea of turbulent smoke.

'*It's not fire you are afraid of...*' came the memory of Lady Foster's words. '*It's failure.*'

She heard the distant bells of the fire-engine approaching over the roar and crackle of the fire, and something else.

'*Gr...ace?*' came a small voice from a few steps below.

She lifted her head to see the unblemished and beautiful face of a boy holding out his hands. Grace inched towards the child, unsure if she was hallucinating or already dead.

'Arthur?' she whispered.

The boy smiled and lifted up her hands to touch his face. It was cool, soft and pale, just as Grace had remembered it, that fateful last night.

'I'm sorry,' said Grace, resting her head against his own and grabbing the spirit tight to her chest. 'Sorry for what I did and being too frightened to save you. It's all my fault.'

The spirit mumbled, repeating more clearly as he glanced up.

'*Forgive, sad Grace. No crying now.*'

He pushed himself gently away and made a sign.

'*Have nice lady, no more loneliness. Happy now.*' He pointed back through the smoke as Grace heard pounding on the distant tower room above. Someone was coming, but they would not find her, the smoke was too dense, and she choked as the two layers of smoke met and the pocket of air vanished. Her eyes blurred with the water drying on her eyes.

A few steps away in the firelit smoke appeared the silhouette of a woman in a bonnet and formal governess gown. The woman beckoned for Arthur to join her, and he retreated to her side with a sad smile. Above, the sounds of entry echoed from the uppermost room as the men began to break through into the tower room. Men called out to her with muffled voices as they pounded against the other side of the tower door with a battering ram.

Grace tried to call out but choked with her final intake of breath.

Losing consciousness, she heard the men breach and call out in desperate and blinding frustration.

The two figures below tugged on the threads, setting the remaining bells ringing, and Grace knew no more.

CHAPTER 27

I t was the firm grip on her left hand and the tickling
sensation in her right that woke her.

'She's coming round,' said a familiar voice.

Everything about her body ached and protested against
the return to life: her bare skin, tight and raw with the effects
of the intense heat, stung with every minor movement and
her lungs stabbed with pain at more than the lightest
inhalation.

'Where am I?' she said, opening her eyes to a white ceiling
fan and the muted sounds of a hospital ward.

'Warwick Infirmary,' said a soothing voice. 'You've had a
lucky escape.'

Grace rotated her head on the soft pillow to see the
joyous face of James. He squeezed her left hand again. 'You're
safe, now.'

'What about—'

The tickling of her right wrist continued, and she turned
to see Rose, teary-eyed and overjoyed, launch into an unwise
embrace around her chest.

Grace winced with the pain as James berated the young

child. Rose returned to her seat and kicked at the bedspread in glee.

'My ribs—'

'From our attempts to resuscitate you,' said James. 'It was touch and go when we dragged you to the roof. I thought—I thought I'd lost you,' he said squeezing her free hand. 'I'm just glad you had the sense to ring the bells; otherwise, the men from the brigade would never have found you.'

Grace shook her head as her last memory returned. 'I didn't—'

'Didn't what?' said James.

She smiled. 'Never mind; I'll tell you some other time. How long have I been asleep?' she asked, spluttering into a wheezing cough.

James called over a nurse and gently raised her into a more upright position using several pillows. Rose poured a glass of water from a nearby jug and offered it to her lips.

'Close to two days,' said James. 'It's Monday evening, and you've been in and out of consciousness since the night before last.'

Grace sipped the clear liquid from the eager seven-year-old nurse as James continued. 'You're going to have to stay put,' he said, 'for a week or so. Your lungs took a battering, but you are going to be all right.'

'What about Lady Foster and Charles?'

'Lady Foster is back in London, undergoing treatment. We've told her there would be no more smoking or drinking if she wanted to carry on plaguing the borough of Mayfair. She's lucky to be alive and didn't take kindly to my professional assertion that she should quit raising the dead unless she wants to join them by the time she reaches fifty. The woman needs something else to live for.'

Grace smiled. 'She's going to be all right?'

James nodded and shrugged. 'Providing she behaves

herself. Her speech is poor, but she refuses to engage with any of the specialists. They can make out her bad language well enough, but I think she needs your help, even if she doesn't say so herself.'

'What about Charles and the hall, is there anything left?'

'The tower is a ruin, and there's smoke damage, but the metal bands to the wings prevented complete devastation. Charles is being discharged tomorrow, being almost as rancorous a patient as Emeline Foster. Mrs Stanton is collecting and sticking by him as a personal nurse as well as every other role in the house. She was here a few hours ago; she feels the need for forgiveness in how she treated you. It was born out of fear, and not just of ghosts, bells or poisons. She feared losing Charles.'

Rose beamed and put down the glass before holding up her hands to make a sign.

'*Is it safe to speak now, forever?*'

Grace nodded. 'She's gone, Rose. I think they've all gone now.'

'I can't sleep without Pa-pa or you nearby,' said Rose.

Grace turned to the doctor with a pleading glance.

'I'll see what I can do about a bed beside you,' said James, meeting the wide-eyed, expectant gaze of the child opposite, 'but only for a few nights till we get the ground-floor rooms sorted and your father is settled in. A stuffy old doctor's house is no place for a noisy child. I can argue the case that it will speed your recovery, providing there is no dancing or over-exertion.'

Rose jumped up and danced around the bed, knocking over a vase of blue asters.

'Are they from you?' said Grace, turning to the blushing face of the doctor.

'Lady Foster suggested them. Did I do right?'

Rose rectified the vase and peered between the flowers,

making an exaggerated pucker of her lips on the back of her tiny hand. Grace stuck out her tongue at the bold and highly amused child as the doctor lowered his lips to kiss his patient's hand.

'Yes,' said Grace. 'They're very worthy.'

The Sigma 10 turned into the infirmary drive as Grace was assisted to the kerb by the attentive doctor.

'Who's driving?' said Grace, shielding her eyes in the low December sun.

'Wait and see,' said James, carrying the bags to the slowing car. A young man got out and took off a formal chauffeur cap, waving it in greeting.

'Billy!' cried Grace, racing to embrace him. He gave her an awkward hug and blushed. 'It's so good to see you, Miss Grace, up and about, I mean.'

'Time enough for talk in the car,' said James, opening the door and assisting her into the back seat. 'I don't want Miss Meadows in the damp air any longer than necessary.'

Billy closed the door behind the doctor and got into the driver's seat. Several large and thick cushions bolstered the back of the seat, enabling him to reach the pedals. Grace exchanged a quick and understanding look with the young chauffeur in the mirror. It was Bishop's seat, and Billy had to fill large shoes and long legs in the service of Charles Ferris.

'Is Ann all right?' she asked, as the car juddered forwards, crunching into an unknown gear.

'She's well, thank you. Going to be made chief housemaid once we get the place sorted. She's already trying to get back some of the old staff—only the good ones, mind you.'

She paused, desperate to ask the question that most

concerned her. 'James, has there been any notion that Bishop died in vain?'

James twisted in his seat and looked long into her eyes.

'None,' he said, settling back into his seat and advising Billy to change to a lower gear to avoid stalling the labouring engine.

After several more miles, Billy drove more competently following advice from the eager backseat passenger. Grace dozed against his shoulder until the car slowed and turned in to the drive. The sun beamed on the house, turning the mellow ironstone and ruddy brick to gold and light. The tower-room window was the only blackened stain on an otherwise idyllic building. The car sped over the crossroads, and Grace saw a small, white-dressed child jumping up and down at the bridge behind the rising figure of Charles Ferris, supported on one arm by the newly promoted Ann and by a sturdy cane in the other. The child turned and bounded back into the courtyard and into the house.

'I arranged a set of aids to enable him to stand. I'm hoping that one day he'll be able to do more than just stand by himself.'

'That's marvellous!' said Grace, feeling a little uncomfortable with the special treatment.

'There's someone else waiting for you, too,' said James, pointing over to the drawing-room window. Grace saw the dark figure of a well-dressed woman retreating into the shadows. Grace gripped the doctor tightly, unsure as to what or who she was seeing.

'She wouldn't take no for an answer, and arrived last night against the express instructions of her doctor,' said James, rolling his eyes. 'Can you *please* talk some sense into her?'

Grace breathed easier as Lady Foster appeared, leaning heavily on the ebony umbrella and wrapped in furs. Rose assisted her down the flight of steps and through the archway.

Billy stalled the car close enough to the bridge to allow the young driver to rush round and allow his passengers to alight into the bright sunshine.

'Welcome home,' said Charles, as Grace curtsied before the entrance to the hall. Lady Foster smiled despite the obvious droop to her mouth and waved Rose away like a starting greyhound after a rabbit. Grace knelt, awaiting the charge from the youngster.

'Oommpphh!' said Grace, reeling from the hug. 'My ribs are happy to see you, that's for certain.'

'Will you come and help put up the Christmas things? We've been waiting for you! Billy's cut down the biggest tree you've ever seen for the drawing room, and the new cook has made dough decorations for us to paint—I've left you the ones shaped like bells.'

Rose tugged on her wrist, desperate to claim the governess for herself.

'You promised me she'd talk,' said Charles, extending a steady hand. 'I doubted you, and for that I am sorry. There's also the matter of saving my life and that of my child, as well as providing me means to pass on an inheritance.'

'I doubted myself,' said Grace, taking the hand warmly and turning to Lady Foster. 'I made a promise to do anything within my power to save her.'

The noblewoman bowed her head and spoke slowly with great difficulty. 'It's ... not ... over,' she slurred sarcastically, turning round to see Rose bouncing up and down, bobbing her tongue out. 'Your ... nightmare has only ... just begun.'

Grace smiled and was ushered into the house. The grand hall welcomed her with the smell of fresh paint and only the faintest of lingering smoke. The far staircase was temporarily rebuilt in makeshift pine. Workers hurried to and fro, some wiring new lines of electric, some repairing the panelling, and a pair of burly men turning round the charred frames of mirrors safe from the ravages of the fire.

'It's like the place is being reborn,' she whispered. Missing panels revealed the extent of the secret passages and priest holes, and several men were fixing sheets of glass across the many openings throughout the house. Grace turned with a look of confusion.

'No more secrets and no more curfews,' said Charles, seated once more in his chair and escorted by the housemaid. He followed her gaze to the closest aperture. 'They are doing the whole house; I never believed there were so many of them.' He looked over at Rose.

'It's also child-proof.'

Rose grabbed her hand, tugging her onwards. 'Come and see your new room,' she said. 'It's next to mine, and they are putting a door in the wall so—'

The excited babble continued as Grace turned to see James smiling, urging her to go.

'Take it steady, you are going to be busy,' he said, putting down the bags.

Grace turned and strode away with the child leading. Rose's chatter echoed throughout the hall and through the open passageways of the busy house, full of the prospect of what could be, and free of the fears of an unfulfilled future.

EPILOGUE

The great Christmas tree glittered in the glow from the newly installed electric lights of the drawing room. It sparkled with hundreds of tarnished silver bells recovered from the ruins of the tower.

'Did I do right?' said Grace, glancing across at Charles Ferris as he wheeled over to the tree to study the specks of light.

'Yes,' he said. 'They belong in the house, and I didn't have the heart to throw them out. Perhaps they'll ring one day if the need arises.'

Grace squeezed his hand and placed the glass of lemonade into his fingers.

'This tastes awful,' he said, 'but I made a promise, and look—'

He held out his arm holding the drink.

'It's as steady as a rock,' said Grace. 'You should be proud of yourself.'

Charles nodded and took a bitter sip of the citrus water. 'I think some of my vision is steadier, too, now that I'm sober most of the time.'

Outside, and distant at first, many voices sang as the villagers made their carolling journey along the drive to the bridge. Rose skidded into the room, followed by Ann, out of breath and struggling to keep up.

'They're here!' Rose cried.

'Well, let them in, foolish girl,' said Charles, leaning on his cane and rising to his feet. Grace pushed back the chair as he turned to the child. 'You are the lady of the house, are you not?'

Rose scrunched her eyebrows at the suggestion before the confirmation of its message sunk in. She bounded out of the room followed by Ann, who was probably wishing in some part that she had not volunteered to mind the young heiress while the governess was officially her father's guest for the evening.

'We always used to have people from the village on Christmas Eve,' he said, straightening his tie. 'I've neglected my duties for so long in that department, but it will all be set right.'

The sound of handbells rang out in the courtyard, resonating more clearly as the temporary doors swung open to allow the well-wishers and merry sounds into and throughout the myriad of rooms and dark passages of Hemingworth Hall. One by one they shuffled in, along with Lady Foster, elegantly dressed in a stunning ermine-trimmed admiral-blue ball gown. She lightly held on to the hand of the handsomely dressed doctor, still using the umbrella as an occasional walking aid. Her face had recovered, but her speech and frustration in retaining short-term memories put her into occasional glooms—moods that Grace would work quickly and skilfully to remedy.

The household staff ceased their labour and looked on, merrily, at the prospect of a Christmas without fear or war. Men were returning to the countryside, and plans were in motion to build a rehabilitation barracks in the grounds, ready to train the men able to work, preparing them with skills to revitalise the estate as well as their lives. Charles had a new passion for life, encouraged by the strong bond and emotional and professional support of his closest friend, James Croswell.

The money flowed in from the sale of silver, and there seemed no lack of supply. Indeed, Billy, armed with the acid from the doctor's medicine bag, had discovered several more rooms containing ornate metalwork proving to be precious metal in origin.

Grace caught the eye of her new-found love, and he took his leave of the noblewoman and squeezed his way through the crowd of singers and ringers to stand by her side.

'You look stunning,' he said, not looking over, as though giving his wedding vows early.

Grace warmed to the compliment. 'Lady Foster is stunning,' she said, teasing him. 'I'll settle for charming.'

'Speaking of Lady Foster,' he said, bending to her ear over the sound of voices and bells. 'She suspects something, and you know how I feel about being left alone with her.'

Grace giggled. 'You're frightened she'll look into your mind and tell me all your secrets?'

James gave a mock look of pain, tinged with some uncertainty.

'Well, she did kind of force out my feelings during the seance, not that I believe in that sort of thing—'

Grace lifted a finger to his lips. 'You can relax. She's not a mind reader. Trust me, most of the reason she's sad hasn't anything to do with the stroke.'

James looked confused.

'She admitted to me she has lost the ability to communicate with—'

'Don't say it,' whispered James. 'I know what you mean. But isn't that a good thing?'

'Not when your reputation and ability to discern the truth in others is no longer there,' replied Grace.

'Well, why can't she be like every other agent and do things in the usual way?'

'It's more than that; it's being wanted by others for who she is. Now that Lady Foster feels she is someone else, she doesn't know who that is anymore.'

'What about you? Are you taking up her offer to return to London with her?'

Grace caught the brief, pained look on the doctor's face. 'Yes, but only for a few weeks while Mrs Stanton sets the place up. It's a temporary arrangement until her new aid is comfortable with the exercises I'm setting, and her temper.'

'You are playing with fire, Miss Meadows,' he said, twitching his nose. 'I don't know whether to look forward to the day after tomorrow, or hope for an outbreak of measles in the village that requires my urgent attention.'

'You are going to be right here, Dr Croswell,' she said, pointing to the giggling Rose perched high on Billy's shoulders. 'I only hope she won't have another stroke when she finds out.'

'Well, I'll bring my bag just in case,' said James, clasping her hand.

Rose and the dolls sulked in the nursery, eager to go out into the misty, frosty morning.

'Later,' said Grace firmly, 'when the cold has lifted a little, and you've finished your drawing for our guest.'

'Can I finish it next to the window?' asked Rose.

'I don't see why not. I'll be back soon; I want to see someone.'

'Who?'

'None of your business; now get creative before I give you some sums to do instead.'

Rose glanced up in terror and grabbed her colouring pencils.

Grace put on her coat and sturdy fur-lined boots, a Christmas present from James, and made her way carefully down the icy steps and over the bridge.

The gravel barely shifted in its frozen state as she strode towards the walled garden gate. Her lungs protested with the exertion and at the bitter cold stinging their fragile new lining, and she slowed, pulling round her scarf to take the chill from the air.

The gardens lay under a heavy frost that dusted the fennel's seed heads and glittered against the threads of arching lengths of spider silk. The curfew bell lay just at the edge of sight; its three baulks of oak suspended the silent bell against its rigid, frozen rope. Crunching over the frozen lawn, she reached the bell, ringed with rime. Grace shivered, closed her eyes and nudged the dangling clapper with a gloved hand. The bell chimed softly, quietly enough not to disturb the hall, but just enough to startle the rooks. The sound of a disturbed pheasant came from beyond the thorn-stalked blackberry bushes and the log pile, and she opened her eyes. A ghostly figure rose from his stoop to stand nearly seven feet tall.

She hurried through the maze of brittle fennel stalks before the man held up a great hand for her to go no further.

Grace lowered her scarf, and her breath obscured the air in front of her. The shade was recognisable, but much less substantial than she had imagined.

'I wasn't sure if you would be here,' she said. 'I wanted you to know how much you did to save everyone—what you did to protect the family, and me.'

The spirit nodded in understanding.

Grace removed her gloves and raised her hand to sign. '*I wanted to ask*—'

'*You wanted to ask if Mrs Ferris was gone, for good?*' he signed, glancing over at the tower. '*And if things with the family could return to how they once were?*'

'Yes,' said Grace. 'Is it true?'

The giant raised his head to the sun, high above the thin fog. A hint of blue promised a brighter afternoon, and she waited anxiously for his reply.

'*The madness has passed,*' he signed. '*Be at peace. She is gone, and may God have mercy on her soul.*'

Grace breathed out a long sigh, clouding the figure who returned to the memory of his duties. He struck out a hand, unable to interact with the split oak and beech, but toiled nonetheless to load the empty cart.

'What about the others?' she said. 'Jane and Arthur.'

He turned to sign. '*The door is closing, and they are departing. Whatever errand has kept them here is done.*'

Grace stamped her feet, trying to remove the cold nipping at her toes through the fur. '*And what of you? Is your errand done?*' she signed.

'*A guardian's work is never done, but go on now, forward and through life. Look to see me no more.*'

He skirted around the path and made his way to the curfew bell; he tugged down on the stiff, silken bell rope, pulling out the bell clapper from its rusted mount.

'*Curfew is ended,*' signed the spirit as the bulbous metal bar thudded into the bare patch of ground. Bishop held up a hand in farewell and faded against a backdrop of briar and bramble.

Grace took off her gloves and rubbed at her red cheeks. The nursery fireplace burned brightly, and she turned to the flames to recover the feeling in her pinched fingers. The warmth from the coal and wood fire still felt like a novelty, and Grace watched as the flames danced against the back-plate, drawn upwards to the crisp December sky. Silently, she dared the fire to frighten her, and it crackled and spat in resinous indignation at the opportunity.

Rose stood at the central bay window, hands outstretched on the glass overlooking the moat lawn.

'Have you finished your drawing?' asked Grace, tidying the pencil-and-paper-strewn table.

Rose nodded but did not turn round.

'Don't put your hands on the glass,' she said, taking out a handkerchief in readiness to wipe the greasy smear. 'Ann will have a fit.'

Rose returned to the table, unusually quiet.

Grace wiped over the handprints to discover they were paired with imprints from the other side. A small pair of child's hands faded as the sun warmed the glass.

'Was it—?'

Rose nodded and held up the colourful drawing.

'The little boy came to say goodbye; they all did.'

Grace held up the latest drawing. Beyond the arched bridge and under the face of a joyous sun, stood a blonde-haired woman in a blue gown and bonnet, staring at a smiling giant carrying a stick boy upon his broad shoulders.

'I think you should keep this one,' said Grace. 'For yourself, I mean.'

Rose smiled. 'I hoped you would say that. Do you think I could give the visitor my drawing of Pa-pa's motorcar instead?'

'I think he'd like that,' said Grace.

James stuck his head around the door.

'He's arrived,' he said. 'Charles has gone to meet him; I didn't know his father used to play cricket with our guest?'

'Apparently so,' said Grace. 'I don't believe in coincidences, and I hope I have done the right thing.'

'You are about to find out,' said James. 'Lady Foster's in the snug, sulking.'

They entered the hall and Grace curtsied as Charles came in with Lady Foster's prospective aid.

'A pleasure to see you again, Miss Meadows,' said the tall gentleman, nervously fidgeting with a ring on his hand. 'Thank you for the opportunity to be of service to you once more.'

Rose rushed in and curtsied to the newly arrived guest.

'You must be Rose,' he said, giving a short, formal bow. 'I understand you like motorcars?'

Rose nodded and followed the gentleman's hand to the open door where Billy and a chauffeur were deep in conversation next to a silver bonnet.

'Can I—?' pleaded Rose, turning to her father.

'If you put on your coat first, and touch nothing,' said Charles, rolling his eyes.

The tall gentleman breathed deeply and nervously. 'Lead on, before my courage fails me.'

Grace clasped his cold, shaking hands. 'I'll be with you and teach you everything you need to know,' she whispered. 'Follow me, and I'll take you to her. Don't worry—there's nothing breakable in the room ...'

He took her arm and stepped across to the small day room, followed by James, pushing the revitalised Charles Ferris.

Lady Foster sat reading a small book in front of a small fire. Her claret silk gown reflected between the dark brocade of a full-length day-coat. By her side stood the ebony umbrella, no longer a walking aid, but an accessory she was rarely without. Her hand gripped the handle, toying with the silver collar.

'Lady Foster,' said Grace. 'You have a guest.'

The noblewoman turned slowly and removed her spectacles. The lines on her forehead vanished as she glanced at the stranger, seeing the aged but otherwise unchanged countenance of a face never forgotten.

'Emeline?' said the old duke. 'I've come to take you home, and address the short-comings of my past by playing a part in your future, if you'll allow me?'

It was a speech long-prepared, and he rushed to her side as she cast aside the umbrella in disbelief and mounting emotion.

Lady Foster tried to form the words, but the shock was too great.

She raised her stronger hand and rubbed at the cheek she had last caressed over thirty-five years earlier, unsure of the sudden and unlooked-for blessing.

The duke quivered, fearful of some sudden rejection. 'I'm so sorry about—'

She smoothed a finger against his lips. For a moment, they knelt before each other, youthful and unchanged, trembling in each other's loving grasp before the medium of Mayfair recovered herself and sat upright, ready to speak. She did not let go of the handsome face now full of joyful tears.

'You're ... l ... late,' she said, losing control and falling into his arms.

In the hall beyond came the urgent cries of an excitable child. 'Pa-pa! Come quickly. There's a real Rolls-Royce outside!'

Charles reversed out of the room in pursuit.

'I don't think I'll need that bag, after all,' said James,

ushering Grace away from the privacy and intimacy of the couple by the fire.

'That went better than expected,' confessed Grace. 'I was dreadfully anxious, almost as much as I used to be about—'

'About what?' asked James, escorting her to the drawing room.

'Nothing,' she lied, gripping him tightly. 'Funny. Lady Foster said that one day she might end up owing me.'

'Then I would hold her to it,' said James. 'What shall we do now?'

'Now I will keep another promise,' she said, dragging him to the card table. 'To teach you how to play poker. The duke doesn't play bridge, and he'll expect a rematch. He's rather good, and I'll need every bit of help I can get.'

GET EXCLUSIVE CONTENT

Thank you for reading *A House of Bells*.

Building a relationship with my readers is the very best thing about writing. I send monthly newsletters with details on new releases, special offers and other news relating to my books.

Sign up to my readers' group at www.jtcroft.com or by scanning the QR code below, and I'll send you further stories in my collection, *Free Spirits,* exclusive to my reader's group– you can't get this anywhere else.

AFTERWORD

I have always been fascinated by bells. It is the sound that breaks the every day, replacing it with a sudden need to understand the sound of its significance at a singular point in time.

Historically, the ringing of bells signals an invitation to come together, for worship or some other social gathering in peacetime. It also served as a warning for the approach of invasion or the need for immediate help with fire. Even today, with super-fast broadband, the sound of a bell conveyed over a wide area by a solitary bell and its ringer, is far quicker.

This story is set in 1918, at a time of great social change in the great households of the landed gentry. Fire was the greatest of all household fears in an age still transitioning from candle and gas, to the electric age, and the curfew bell signalled a time of night when fires should be covered or damped down to keep the house and the occupants safe. The tolling of an unexpected bell, late into the night, would have struck fear and uncertainty into the hearts of many.

This story deals with fear, the managing and overcoming of it, despite the urge to run, to hide, and to get as far away as possible from the danger. I think we can all point to some struggle in our lives where the decision to stand or run has been front and central. Even the most timid of us can summon the courage to triumph over adversity whilst still being afraid. A brave person is not someone who does not feel afraid, but someone who conquers that fear, knowing there is something more important than that most crippling of human emotions.

After all, how can you overcome fear if you don't have it in the first place?

This story also deals with second chances, when that courage fails, and the need for redemption and forgiveness both to ourselves and others. Sometimes I feel that I fall down more times than I have been knocked over, but as the author, James Patterson, paraphrasing, once wrote:

'Failure is not falling down, it's staying down.'

We are the sum of all our experiences, our flaws, and our 'falling downs'. We are also the sum of our 'getting ups' and this belief is a powerful motivator to embrace the future whilst remembering what our past continues to teach us.

J. T. Croft
February 2021

ALSO BY J. T. CROFT

Firelight and Frost

Maiden Point

High Spirits

Midnight's Treasury

"Dead Brilliant"

⭐⭐⭐⭐⭐

"Well written. Fascinating and original"

⭐⭐⭐⭐⭐

"Beautifully dark and bittersweet"

⭐⭐⭐⭐⭐

ABOUT THE AUTHOR

J. T. Croft is the author of Gothic fiction, supernatural mystery and ghostly short stories.
For more information:
www.jtcroft.com

I hope you enjoyed reading this book as much as I loved writing it. If you did, I'd really appreciate you leaving me a quick review on whichever platform you prefer. Reviews are extremely helpful for any author, and even just a line or two can make a big difference. I'm independently published, so I rely on good folks like you spreading the word!

facebook.com/jtcroftauthor

twitter.com/jtcroftauthor

instagram.com/jtcroftauthor